ROKKA:
Braves of the Six Flowers

4

Illustration / MIYAGI

ROKKA:
Braves of the Six Flowers

4

ISHIO YAMAGATA

ILLUSTRATION BY
MIYAGI

YEN
ON

NEW YORK

ROKKA: Braves of the Six Flowers 4

ISHIO YAMAGATA

Translation by Jennifer Ward
Cover art by Miyagi

ROKKA NO YUSHA
© 2013 by Ishio Yamagata, Miyagi
All rights reserved. First published in Japan in 2013 by SHUEISHA, Inc.
English translation rights arranged with SHUEISHA, Inc.
through Tuttle-Mori Agency, Inc., Tokyo.

English translation © 2018 by Yen Press, LLC

Yen On
1290 Avenue of the Americas
New York, NY 10104

Visit us at yenpress.com
facebook.com/yenpress
twitter.com/yenpress
yenpress.tumblr.com
instagram.com/yenpress

First Yen On Edition: April 2018

Yen On is an imprint of Yen Press, LLC.
The Yen On name and logo are trademarks of Yen Press, LLC.

The publisher is not responsible for websites (or their content)
that are not owned by the publisher. .

Library of Congress Cataloging-in-Publication Data
Names: Yamagata, Ishio, author. | Miyagi, illustrator. | Ward, Jennifer (Jennifer J.), translator.
Title: Rokka : braves of the six flowers / Ishio Yamagata ; illustration by Miyagi ;
translation by Jennifer Ward.
Description: First Yen On edition. | New York, NY : Yen On, 2017—
Identifiers: LCCN 2017000469 | ISBN 9780316501415 (v. 1 : pbk.) |
ISBN 9780316556194 (v. 2 : pbk.) | ISBN 9780316556200 (v. 3 : pbk.) |
ISBN 9780316556224 (v. 4 : pbk.)
Subjects: | CYAC: Heroes—Fiction. | Fantasy. | BISAC: FICTION / Fantasy / General.
Classification: LCC PZ7.1.Y35 Ro 2017 | DDC [Fic]—dc23
LC record available at https://lccn.loc.gov/2017000469

ISBN: 978-0-316-55622-4

10 9 8 7 6 5 4 3 2 1

LSC-C

Printed in the United States of America

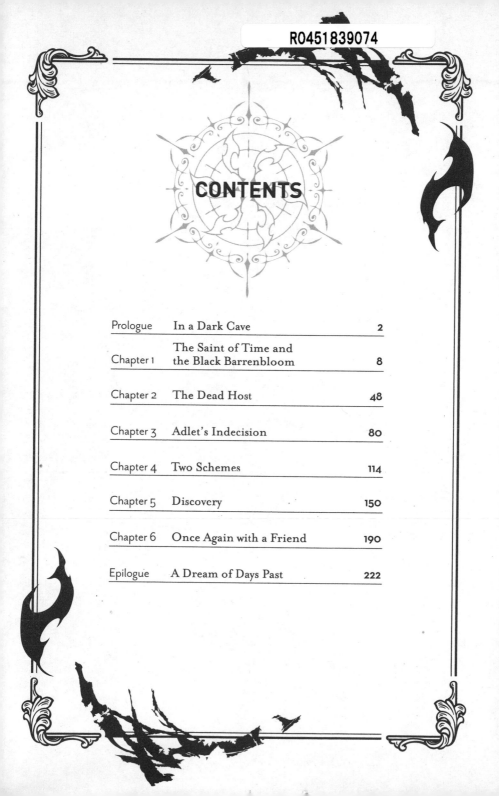

CONTENTS

Adlet

Fremy

Rolonia

Mora

Goldof

Nashetania

Hans

Chamo

◆ THE EVENTS THUS FAR ◆

When the Evil God awakened from the depths of darkness, the Spirit of Fate chose six Braves and bestowed upon them the power to save humanity. The self-proclaimed "strongest man in the world," a boy named Adlet, was chosen as one of these Braves of the Six Flowers and headed out to battle to prevent the resurrection of the Evil God.

But when the Braves gathered to meet at the designated location, they found that, for some reason, there were seven of them. The Braves, realizing that one among them was the enemy, fell prey to suspicion and paranoia. However, with their leader, Adlet, their wits, and the powers of the Saints in their party, they slowly but surely solved these mysteries.

As the fiend commanders Tgurneu and Dozzu scheme to impede the progress of the Six Braves, the story moves deeper into the Howling Vilelands...

Illustration: Miyagi

Prologue

In a
Dark Cave

His arms were immobile. So were his legs. He couldn't speak, and he couldn't raise himself up. Not a single part of his body would move: not his eyelids, eyebrows, mouth, neck, shoulders, chest, stomach, or torso. Lying on the cold earth, mouth hanging open, arms and legs loosely splayed, he stared up at the dark ceiling. Water dripped from the ceiling, hitting the tip of his nose. He didn't scrunch up his face or twitch in reaction.

But he was alive.

He was in the mountainous region occupying the central-northern area of the Howling Vilelands. It was there that the Evil God had once struck the Saint of the Single Flower in the stomach with its tentacle. The blow had winded her, knocking her out. Thus, the land was dubbed the Fainting Mountains.

The north wind gusted from the sea, freezing cold. The Evil God's toxin had colored the whole environs red-black. Within a dense woodland at the foot of one mountain was a massive cave with a gaping mouth. In that cavern lay the man.

Any normal person who saw him there would surely want to quickly avert their eyes. His dessicated skin was deathly pale and had been cruelly peeled off in places to reveal the muscle and fat underneath. His flesh had turned a muddy dark color as it rotted. His unshorn hair was utterly filthy. His crude garments were also frayed so badly they resembled rags.

The back of his neck was what drew the eye. A large insect clung there: a strange thing, big as a dagger, with a gnarled body and wings like a mayfly. Its feelers and legs were plunged deep into the man's body.

The man appeared to be nothing more than an abandoned, half-rotten corpse.

But he was alive.

A small lamp dangled from the ceiling, illuminating the cave. The faint light revealed a bizarre sight.

The floor of the large hollow had been smoothed flat and covered in rows of bodies, all lying faceup like the man. They were a varied lot: men, women, old, young. But all of them were shriveled and rotting, just like him. Also the same was the strange type of bug attached to the backs of their necks. There were far more than one or two hundred bodies here. A huge mass of corpses, far too many to count, were lined up in orderly rows, both lengthwise and crosswise. The man was near the center of the array.

And there, he was alive.

Unable to move, unable to speak, he would seem no different from all the other corpses. Only one thing about him set him apart—he was still capable of thought. As he gazed up at the ceiling, his ears drawn to the dripping water and other sounds, only one thing was on his mind.

He had to save the Braves of the Six Flowers.

He knew that at this very moment, the Braves were in greater danger than they could have known. They were caught in a terrible predicament, one incomparable to the challenges their predecessors had overcome seven hundred years ago, and again three hundred years ago. Most likely, they had not even realized it yet. They probably didn't yet know what unbelievable feat the fiend commander Tgurneu had accomplished. They had no idea what a dreadful weapon it had prepared.

The Braves of the Six Flowers were warriors with the power to save the world. They would be unusually insightful, and some among them would be Saints, gifted with powers that surpassed human knowledge. But this man doubted they would be able to discern the true nature of Tgurneu's secret weapon. What it had prepared was so unbelievable.

The man knew he was the only one who could warn the six Braves of Tgurneu's plot, because he was the only one in the world who knew the fiend's true intentions. If he failed to save the Braves, the world would be destroyed.

His body wouldn't move. Nothing—not his hands, feet, mouth, or fingers. Yet the fate of the world rested on his shoulders.

It wasn't a question of whether he could. Success was the only option. He would save the Braves of the Six Flowers. And no matter how dark this crisis seemed, he would believe in hope.

He would alert the Braves of the Six Flowers to Tgurneu's ultimate weapon and the secret of the Black Barrenbloom.

Chapter 1

The Saint of
Time and
the Black
Barrenbloom

It was late at night on the seventeenth day after the Evil God's awakening. In the Cut-Finger Forest, all eight humans sat in a circle as they listened to Dozzu's story.

"The first fake Crest, the one that Nashetania has now, was originally given to me by Hayuha, Saint of Time," said Dozzu before pausing to scan all their faces. "Before I tell you the clues you need to defeat the seventh, I must tell you about Hayuha. Do you need me to explain in detail about her?"

"*Neow.* Even I know Hayuha's name at least," said Hans. Fremy shook her head, too, to indicate it wasn't necessary. For the others, it went without saying. Of course they knew about her—everyone living on this continent, including children, knew Hayuha.

Hayuha Pressio, Saint of Time, had been a Brave from the second generation and a pivotal actor in the defeat of the Evil God. The details of her character and exploits had been recorded in a book left by another survivor of the battle—Marlie, Saint of Blades. The book stated that Hayuha could manipulate the passage of time for any object she touched. When she touched an ally, they could move several times faster than normal for a brief time. When Hayuha touched an enemy, its speed would be slowed to a fraction of what it was. While none of her abilities could kill, she was still immensely powerful—she could disable any foe simply with physical contact. The common opinion was that the second generation of Braves never would have won without her.

She was also rumored to be an eccentric. The pattern on her robe had looked like a child's scribbles, and she'd worn a large wooden bowl instead of a hat. She had always worn her shoes on the wrong feet, and had just one ripped, shabby glove on her right hand.

Not only was she a very heavy drinker, but she'd had a special love for crude talk and bad puns. She was constantly putting down her allies, and she acted selfishly and capriciously. Marlie, Saint of Blades, had bluntly written that everything about her was disagreeable.

There was also one great mystery surrounding Hayuha. After defeating the Evil God, on the way back to her hometown, she had suddenly vanished. She had been in a village fairly close to the Howling Vilelands when the others lost track of her.

Three exhausted Saints had been in the middle of enjoying the first real meal they'd had in a very long time. Hayuha was dumping booze into her wooden bowl-hat and and pouring it into her mouth like rain. She drank, puked, drank some more, puked some more, and about the time all the booze in town had run dry, she walked out, saying she was going to go relieve herself.

She never returned after that.

Her whereabouts were completely unknown. Some theorized that fiends had captured and killed her, while others said some king had arrested her for fear of her power, and there was even a rumor in circulation that romantic complications involving another Brave had led to her murder.

Some people here and there on the continent occasionally came forward and claimed to have seen someone resembling Hayuha, but none of these claims could be confirmed. But she couldn't have died. After her disappearance, no new Saint had been chosen at the Temple of Time. No replacement would be born as long as the Saint of Time was alive.

The search for Hayuha went on for five years, but it was in vain.

Eventually, a new Saint was chosen at the Temple of Time, and everyone concluded that Hayuha was dead.

"Hayuha couldn't have…" Mora muttered.

Dozzu gave her a small nod. "You're quite right. After she defeated the Evil God, she returned to the Howling Vilelands. She sought to find out what the Braves' enemy really is." Dozzu suddenly broke eye contact, looking down. In the fiend's profile, Adlet could sense the desolation of one who had lost something beloved. "Hayuha came about a month after the Evil God's defeat. She showed up out of nowhere, a large cask of alcohol on her back, to Tgurneu, Cargikk, and me."

Adlet wondered a little about that. He'd thought the three fiends had an antagonistic relationship. But all three had been together?

Anticipating Adlet's question, Dozzu changed the subject. "Before I talk about Hayuha, shall I talk a little about us? Before we met her?"

"I'm interested," said Adlet.

"…Back then, we were friends. All three of us: Tgurneu, Cargikk, and I. At that time, I believed our bond of friendship was eternal."

Five hundred and fifty years ago, a tiny lump of flesh had been born from the Evil God. It was very small, but it had arms, legs, and the instinct to survive. The fleshy thing crawled along the ground, fleeing the Evil God's tentacles. Fortunately, it was able to escape from the reach of those appendages. It was the birth of a new fiend. Aside from certain exceptions like Fremy, all fiends arrived in the world this way.

Bit by bit, the newborn evolved itself, feeding on the small animals that lived in the Howling Vilelands and the fruit from trees. It took ten years for it to attain a form comparable to a thin dog's, and fifty years for it to control lightning. About one hundred years after its birth, it acquired the intellect of a human.

All fiends, even sentient ones, were without will. All every fiend wanted was to revive the Evil God and to kill humans. They only ever thought about slaughtering their foes and obeying higher-ranking fiends.

This fiend would eventually be named Dozzu. But at first, it was just a common brute.

About two hundred years after its birth, Dozzu—though it didn't yet have that name—experienced an inexplicable and unforeseen evolution. Normally, fiends evolved their bodies as they desired. But very rarely, sometimes, fiends would develop in unwanted ways. What Dozzu gained from this evolution was empathy.

The Howling Vilelands was constantly filled with the sounds of wailing fiends. They felt hurt when they couldn't kill humans, frustration about their loss to the Braves of the Six Flowers, and sadness at the cruel imprisonment of their overlord in all things, the Evil God. The name of the Howling Vilelands came from these laments.

Dozzu had been hearing these cries nonstop ever since its birth. Dozzu itself had wailed in a similar way before. But one day, when it heard those familiar cries, Dozzu had sensed a strange pain in its chest. It spent every day for ten years trying to understand what the discomfort was.

It was sadness, and not the sadness of being unable to kill humans or sorrow over the Evil God's defeat. Dozzu was sad that the other fiends were sad.

Fiends never mourned the death of their fellows, nor would they ever sympathize with another's pain. All they could think of was obeying the Evil God's will. Only humans possessed a sense of fellowship.

But Dozzu felt grief at the fiends' pain and came to long for their happiness. This was a fundamentally unbelievable evolution for a fiend to take. They were born only to take the lives of humans.

After that, terrible loneliness tormented Dozzu. No other fiend could understand the pain in its heart. The others scolded it, called it foolish, and cast it out from the group as if it were an incomprehensible foreign object. Dozzu strayed from its former cohort and wandered the Howling Vilelands. Alone, Dozzu roosted on top of a boulder in the Ravine of Spitten Blood. It would gaze out at the continent where the humans lived as it listened to the fiends wailing behind it.

For a long time, Dozzu kept on wishing that someday a time would come when the fiends would no longer weep and the Howling Vilelands would no longer be named for the sound. Dozzu swore that it would defeat the Braves of the Six Flowers, revive the Evil God, and create a world where its race could live with smiles. It was always trying to devise a way to accomplish that.

Unexpectedly, one day, a fiend approached Dozzu. It walked on two legs, had a silver mane, and wore silver armor. Dozzu had seen this creature many times before. It was peculiar, possessed of rare powers but unaffiliated with any pack. Like Dozzu, the fiend stood atop the boulder, gazing out at the human realms. After some time, the newcomer said quietly, "You as well?" Dozzu lifted its head to look at the other fiend. "As am I." It showed Dozzu the fig in its hand. A tiny mouth appeared in the center of the fruit, and Dozzu realized the fig was a fiend, too.

"Me, too," it replied.

Dozzu nodded, and said to the two fiends, "Yes. Me, too."

And that was enough. Their mutual understanding and friendship bound them together. They shared the same desires and the same pain in their hearts. The lion-fiend trained itself day by day in order to protect its kind from the hands of man. The fig-fiend offered its flesh to give strength to weaker comrades. The dog-fiend continuously contemplated how fiends might attain happiness. They became friends and gave each other names. The lion was Cargikk. The fig was Tgurneu. And the dog was named Dozzu.

They were the only three creatures in the world who felt love for fiendkind.

Then, three hundred years ago, the second war with the Braves of the Six Flowers occurred. It ended in disaster. The Evil God was sealed away once more, and many eminent fiends had been lost.

The cause of their defeat was clear. The fiends had had no commander to lead all the forces. They had divided into various small factions of dozens apiece, each fighting and losing to the Braves separately.

Immense power would be necessary to subordinate all the fiends and give them orders. At no point did a fiend appear with real influence, the kind that could lead it in the footsteps of Archfiend Zophrair.

It could be said that Dozzu and its allies, with Cargikk as their leader, had put up the best fight. Dozzu had plotted their moves and done the scouting, Cargikk had contended with the Six Braves head-to-head, while Tgurneu had given their underlings power and advised the other two.

The three of them had explored far afield into the human continent to set a trap in a certain village and lured the Braves of the Six Flowers into it. Far away from the Howling Vilelands, Lowie, Saint of Wind, was careless and paid for it with her life.

In the Cut-Finger Forest, they launched a two-pronged ambush from underground and above the trees, gravely wounding Swordmaster Bodor. When Hayuha and Marlie, Saint of Blades, staged a diversion, the trio saw through the ploy, and they even successfully defended the Weeping Hearth the first time.

But their efforts were in vain. The neverending battle exhausted them, and they couldn't hold back the Braves' second attack on the Weeping Hearth. The Evil God was defeated. .

"Aw, *meow*. So all this blabbin' was just to brag about yer exploits?" Hans cut off Dozzu's dispassionate narration with a shrug. "Sorry, but we ain't got the time fer yer boring story."

"I beg your pardon. I'll soon reach the relevant details, so if I may ask for your patience..." Unruffled by Hans's quip, Dozzu continued its story.

Dozzu's account deeply intrigued Adlet. Even his master, Atreau, had been in the dark about the process of fiends' birth and evolution. Had they time, Adlet would have liked to ask for more detail. It was fascinating to hear about the second Battle of the Six Flowers from the fiends' side, too, and he was also curious about the former friendship shared by the three fiends currently at war—but right now, hearing about Hayuha was a priority.

*   *   *

Dozzu, Cargikk, and Tgurneu wept and wept for a whole month following the Evil God's defeat. Dozzu didn't know how to convey to humans
what a torment the Evil God's death was to their kind. Perhaps it could
be compared to the agony of inescapable death, the misery of losing one's
beloved, or the despair of witnessing the world on the brink of destruction. But Dozzu doubted any of these would come close. Humans were
utterly incapable of understanding the magnitutde of the Evil God's presence in fiends' lives.

The agony of the three was then entrenched even deeper. The ones
they loved were grieving, and yet they could do nothing to help. This reality was torture of a different form.

The three blamed themselves, condemned one another, did harm to
themselves, and from time to time even made plans to die together. At one
point, Dozzu could stand no more of its comrades' wailing and fled from
Cargikk and Tgurneu. It climbed mountains, ran through forests, and
crossed valleys, but no matter where it went, it could still hear the sobbing.

Dozzu smashed its head into a boulder. Bleeding, it rammed the stone
over and over, but that wasn't enough, so it scorched itself with lightning,
too. It continued for a whole day before exhausting itself and passing out.
Lying prostrate on the ground, Dozzu wondered, *Why must they always cry?
Why do they all have to suffer? Why do they have to fight?* Still without answers, it
lost consciousness.

How much time has passed? When Dozzu opened its eyes, it found a
shadow hovering over its body. Someone was standing over it, watching.
Thinking it was Cargikk, Dozzu looked up and was struck dumb.

"Hey there, cute little fiendie," she said, smiling. "Would you be at all
interested in a world where no one, human or fiend, has to cry?"

That was how Dozzu met Hayuha.

"*Meow*, was she pretty?" Hans interrupted the story again.

"Are you incapable of listening in silence?" Mora snapped.

Hans shrunk back. "*Mrow.* I've been nettlin' people since I was a kid." Then he pulled some rags out of his packs and began cutting them into the shape of clothes with a sword. It seemed as if, while he listened, he would sew himself something new to replace his tattered garments.

He just can't sit still, Adlet thought with a sigh.

"...By human measure, Hayuha wouldn't have been considered beautiful. Her features were ordinary—though everything else about her was anything but." Dozzu continued its story.

For a while, Hayuha just smiled, watching Dozzu. It remembered her as the enemy they had fought a month before, but it had no idea what it should do. Why was she there? What did she mean? Why was she smiling? Dozzu was utterly nonplussed.

Eventually, Cargikk came running, Tgurneu in hand. As soon as Tgurneu saw Hayuha, it let out a scream. After a momentary shock, Cargikk jetted poison flames from its body and readied itself for battle.

Hayuha was not in the least perturbed. She smiled, spread her arms, and walked up to them. "Hey there, lion buddy, figgy, good timing. I'm Hayuha, and I'm joining up with you now. So be nice, okay?"

"...What?"

"Hmm, guess I'm getting ahead of myself here. Huh, I wonder where I should start?" Hayuha put a finger to her forehead and considered. "Oh yeah, so I want you guys to help with something. Would you mind listening to what I have to say?"

The next instant, Cargikk's greatsword roared toward Hayuha's face with full force. When it stopped short of her, it wasn't because of Hayuha. In fact, she neither dodged nor blocked it. She just calmly watched the sword hesitating above her head. "Whoa there, lion buddy. Is something wrong?" she asked. By all appearances, it wasn't that she believed they were too weak to possibly kill her. Nothing in her expression indicated such a thought. She had calmly accepted the death that loomed before her.

"Why do you not avoid it, Brave of the Six Flowers?" asked Cargikk.

"Hmm. Well, 'cause it wouldn't bother anyone if I died."

Cargikk raised its sword once more, and Dozzu charged up a lightning strike, too. But Hayuha was so unguarded, they just couldn't seize the moment to attack.

"Well, let's not stand and talk. Why don't we take a seat?" Hayuha lowered the cask of alcohol she carried on her back and sat on the ground. Her manner communicated to the fiends that she quite sincerely wouldn't mind if she died. And because the three believed they could kill her any time, they figured they'd hear her out. If she acted even the slightest bit defensive, they would instantly begin to fight.

"So, like I said before," she continued, "there's something I'd like your help with. I think you're probably the only ones I can ask."

The three fiends didn't so much as nod in response. They would listen to what she had to say, but they had zero intention of assisting her. They were still overwhelmed with rage toward her for her part in defeating the Evil God.

"I've been thinking—I'd like to find out what the Evil God really is," she said, and a thrill of tension raced through the three fiends. "When you get right down to it, what *is* it? How did it end up being born? I'd like to know. And I need your help for that."

The three of them did not reply. Why had the Evil God been born? Dozzu, Cargikk, and Tgurneu had never even considered that subject, nor had any other fiend. The Evil God was simply the Evil God, and they had never questioned its existence.

"I bet you guys don't know the truth, either, huh? That's just my intuition talking. I don't have any basis for saying that."

The three fiends didn't reply. Instead, Cargikk answered her question with another question. "So what would you do after discovering its true nature? Are you unsatisfied with simply sealing it away? Are you saying you would kill it?!"

"Kill the Evil God? What for?" Hayuha tilted her head in puzzlement.

The fiends were taken aback. "To protect humanity…perhaps?" said Cargikk.

"Oh, I get what you mean. Protecting humanity. I never thought of that."

Dozzu was momentarily stunned. Wasn't she one of the Braves of the Six Flowers? Just one month ago, she'd fought with them for that very purpose.

"Well, I'm not gonna kill the Evil God. I think it'd be more fun if it was alive."

"…F-fun?"

"If the Evil God is alive, we can hang out, right? Can't do that if it's dead. It would be so dull."

The three fiends were simply flabbergasted.

"Personally speaking, it's all about the fun. Nothing else matters. It's all just an illusion. I don't get people who get so hung up on love and justice and all that pointless bull. Don't you agree, my fine fiendy friends?" Hayuha pulled the bowl off her head, tilted her cask of alcohol, and began pouring the contents into the bowl. She took one satisfied swig and offered the bowl to Cargikk. "Anyway, you want a bowl? I bet I'd enjoy drinking with fiends, too."

Cargikk looked at the bowl of alcohol for a while. Then it took the drink and guzzled it down all at once, alcohol dripping from the corners of its mouth.

"Aww, what a waste," Hayuha lamented. "Don't spill it. That's the good stuff."

"It's so foul, I could vomit," Cargikk said, shoving the vessel back at Hayuha. Sorrowfully, Hayuha licked up the remaining alcohol. "We live to defend the Evil God. We live to fulfill its desires. Do you think we would take part in any act that would pose it danger?"

"Huh. I guess it's no use after all."

"However," Cargikk added, "knowledge of the Evil God's true nature could lead us to victory in the upcoming battle."

Shocked, Dozzu looked up at Cargikk.

"By cooperating with you, we may learn of means to strengthen the fiends, increase our numbers further, or undo the seal on the Evil God."

"Cargikk!" Dozzu cried. "What are you thinking?!"

"Dozzu, the third war has already begun. And I will do anything if it means the defeat of the Braves of the Six Flowers."

"But she's a human! And one of the Braves! How could we collude with her?!"

"Are you crazy, Cargikk?" Tgurneu was appalled, too.

"If you believe me mad, then abandon me here and leave. I will not stop you," said Cargikk.

"But…"

Hayuha carelessly interrupted the bewildered party of fiends. "You shouldn't argue."

Whose fault do you think this is? thought Dozzu.

"Hayuha," said Cargikk, "we will use you to destroy humanity. If you have no quarrel with that, we shall cooperate."

"Of course I'm thrilled to have you with me, my lion buddy. Can I just call you Cargikk, then?" Smiling, Hayuha served some more alcohol. "Oh! Yeah, I'll answer your question from before. About what I'll do once I find out the truth of the Evil God."

"Tell us."

"If I do find out what it is—or, well, if it's what I think it is, then…" Hayuha knocked back the alcohol all at once. "Then I think I'll make friends with it. I'd like us to have a drink together. Me and the Evil God."

"Friends, you say?"

"Doesn't that sound like a blast? It'd be the best party of all time! It'd be kinda lonely with just me and the Evil God, though. So I'd invite everyone in the world to my party, human and fiend. That sounds the most fun." Hayuha laughed. "Maybe humanity'll get wiped out after that. If that happens…eh, oh well."

Cargikk's shoulders trembled a bit. For a second, Dozzu thought it was angry, but then it burst into raucous laughter. "Hayuha. You're truly not bothered if your kind is destroyed?" Cargikk asked.

Hayuha responded cheerfully. "I mean, I've already saved the world once. Might be interesting to take a shot at destroying it next."

Dozzu utterly failed to comprehend Hayuha's logic, but it understood now that they would be forced to cooperate with her. Cargikk was their leader, so come what may, Dozzu and Tgurneu had to follow.

As Adlet listened to Dozzu's story, he mused, *Hayuha wasn't right in the head.* He'd known from the stories that she was eccentric, but he'd had no idea she was this bad.

"Hayuha did not identify with the human race in the slightest," said Dozzu. "She was indifferent to notions of responsibility, duty, or justice. Personal enjoyment was all she needed. She didn't care about the fate of humanity or even her own life. In her mind, fighting the Evil God as a Brave was nothing more than an amusing pastime."

"..."

"After the Evil God's defeat, she became bored, so she invented a new game to play and gave it a try. I think that was the only reason she came to the Howling Vilelands. She hit upon an outrageous way to entertain herself: a great drinking game with all humans and fiends invited."

The Braves were speechless.

"And so, Hayuha and we joined forces for the next five years." Dozzu finished the first part of its story there and took a brief break.

Before listening to the rest of the tale, the group scouted around nearby since Tgurneu might discover them and launch an attack here. But there was no sign of any fiends, so they went back to their camp and sat down around Dozzu.

"But how did you investigate the Evil God?" asked Mora.

Adlet had wondered about that, too. Humanity had been trying to unearth those answers for the past millennium. He doubted it would be an easy task even with the fiends' cooperation. Plus, judging from Dozzu's story, the fiends were in the dark, too.

"It was possible for her," said Dozzu. "She was the only person in all of history who could have done it."

"What powers did she use?" asked Mora.

"She could manipulate the flow of time to see the events of the past with her own eyes."

Mora was shocked, and Chamo and Rolonia, too.

"Is that so ameowzin'?" asked Hans. "Sounds to me like that'd be a cinch for a Saint of Time." He'd pulled out a needle and thread as Dozzu spoke and was skillfully sewing away.

"Of all the many Saints' powers, command of time is known to be the most challenging to use," explained Mora. "Most past Saints of Time could muster only enough power to slow an object's decay. Hayuha's ability to use the power of time in battle made it clear her mastery of it was exceptional. But to see the past..."

Chamo said, "It's like she's the cream of the cream of the crop. Even I might be a tiny bit surprised."

"Well, comin' from you, that must mean she was as ameowzin' as they come," commented Hans.

Dozzu continued its story. "However, there were restrictions to her ability to view the past. In order to look back, she had to go to the location where the event had occurred, inscribe hieroglyphs there to strengthen her powers of time, and then activate her ability. So the three of us gathered information from fiends that had survived since olden times and guided Hayuha to places where we might find clues. Then we ensured that other fiends would stay away. Hayuha would use her ability to discover what had occurred there in the past, and thus we investigated the Evil God. We traversed the Howling Vilelands, uncovering the events of the past. Occasionally, we would even borrow the powers of a transforming fiend to change shape and visit the human realms together with Hayuha. Finally, we found our answer."

"Which is?" Adlet asked.

But right when Dozzu was about to reply, a tiny blade sprouted out of the ground before Dozzu.

"!" They all looked at Nashetania. She was still in Goldof's arms, watching Dozzu. She silently shook her head.

"You're right, Nashetania." Dozzu returned its attention to the Braves. "My apologies, but I still cannot tell you about the Evil God. Eventually, when the time comes, we will reveal it to you."

"I thought you were gonna tell us everything," said Adlet.

"What I promised was to share our clues regarding the seventh. I never said I'd tell you everything." Adlet and Dozzu glared at each other.

"Talkin' it up until it gets good and then leavin' us on a cliffhanger, huh? Ya hear the minstrels at the bars use that one, *meow.*" But Hans's quip didn't bother Dozzu.

"Why won't you talk?"

"In order to defeat you all, we cannot disclose to you everything that we know," reasoned Dozzu.

"...I see."

Dozzu had said that it and Nashetania planned to replace the Evil God, but they had yet to reveal their means of doing so. If Dozzu divulged the true nature of the Evil God, that information would most likely also reveal how it could be supplanted.

But what the hell does "when the time comes" mean? thought Adlet. Did that mean that they wouldn't talk until everything was over?

"Chamo's pretty curious about the Evil God, though. If you don't tell us, Chamo's gonna kill you both." Chamo's foxtail swayed as a vein bulged on her forehead. Not long ago, she'd been near death. She was listening calmly for the time being, but she was not in a good mood.

"I believe it would be better if you refrained. If you kill us, you will never find out what we have to say."

"You're right. So...torture." Chamo was right about to gleefully stuff her foxtail down her throat when Rolonia leaped on her from behind.

"Wait, please, Chamo!"

"Let me go, moo-head!" The two of them began grappling with each other. Adlet and Mora sighed as Nashetania watched, giggling.

"Well, it's a shame, but it doesn't look like we can make them talk," said Adlet.

"I apologize. There is our situation to consider as well. If we were to tell you everything, then you would have no more use for us and thus no reason to let us live. We cannot tell you everything, for the sake of our survival."

Right now, the most important intelligence Dozzu held was the clues that could lead them to the seventh. It was best for now to drop the question of the Evil God's secrets.

"Ugh, torture is too much trouble! Chamo's just gonna kill you!"

"Please, calm down!" Rolonia cried as Chamo tried to peel her off. Mora punched the younger Saint in the head.

Once Chamo had reluctantly settled down, Fremy asked, "So how are the story of Hayuha and this clue regarding the seventh connected?"

"Yes, let me get to that," replied Dozzu. "Even once we had uncovered the Evil God's past, we continued our investigation in search of further knowledge. We researched the Saint of the Single Flower."

"So what did you discover?"

"I cannot answer that," Dozzu said curtly. "However, our search didn't go on very long. Just a month after we began seeking the truth behind the Saint of the Single Flower, Hayuha died suddenly, and our investigation of the past died with her."

"How did she die?" asked Adlet.

"I suppose it should be assumed that someone killed her."

That's a weird way to put it, thought Adlet. If she'd been murdered, then why didn't Dozzu come out and say so? "What do you mean?"

"Given the circumstances, it couldn't have been anything else. But at the time, no one could have managed it—not the three of us, and certainly not any other fiends or humans."

"*Hrmeow-meow.* So it wasn't you guys that killed her?" Hans asked, smiling. In the course of the conversation, he'd finished sewing himself a new jacket.

"No. But I can't prove that." The cause of Hayuha's death wasn't important. Dozzu continued. "After that, we started quarrelling. I began dreaming of a world ruled by a new god, one where humans and fiends could live in harmony. Cargikk was fiercely opposed to this and confronted me. Even now that he knew the true nature of the Evil God, Cargikk was no less loyal to it. Tgurneu did his best to mediate between Cargikk and myself, but after a hundred years our alliance broke down, and I ended up leaving the Howling Vilelands and taking my meager forces with me."

"Pretty fragile friendship, then," said Fremy.

Dozzu raised its hackles slightly and glared at her. It seemed about to retort, but then quickly looked away and suppressed its anger as it continued. "However, Tgurneu had deceived both Cargikk and myself. He had been investigating the Saint of the Single Flower while keeping it secret from us."

"Tgurneu, huh?"

"Hayuha had left behind a hieroform for learning about the past. I had thought it was lost with her death. But Tgurneu had surreptitiously acquired it and began investigating the Saint of the Single Flower—not long after Hayuha's demise, most likely. I'm quite ashamed to say this, but it wasn't until two hundred years after she died that I figured it out."

Adlet considered. "So in other words, Tgurneu sniffed out some secret about the Saint of the Single Flower, killed Hayuha to silence her, and then hid everything from you and Cargikk. Is that it?"

"…I can't say that for certain."

"Sounds like the only possible answer, circumstantially," Adlet said.

Dozzu began to ponder, eyes still downcast. "No, Tgurneu could never have killed Hayuha then…" The fiend was lost in thought for a while, until it seemed to realize that there was no point in worrying and resumed the conversation. "Let's leave Hayuha's story for now. It's time to get to the real issue at hand. I'll tell you what clues I have regarding the seventh."

Finally, thought Adlet.

"As I just said, Tgurneu was researching the Saint of the Single Flower in secret. What's more, he was also studying the very power of Saints. Tgurneu and his fiends abducted humans from all over and brought them to the Howling Vilelands—acolytes from All Heavens Temple or the regional temples, theologians who studied the power of Saints—occasionally even Saints themselves."

They had already been aware of this. Tgurneu had created Fremy, Saint of Gunpowder, clear evidence that Tgurneu possessed a wealth of knowledge regarding the Spirits' power and their chosen ones.

"His goal was, of course, to kill the Braves of the Six Flowers. To create the ultimate weapon for such a purpose."

"I heard the reason Tgurneu was learning so much about the Saints was to create me," said Fremy.

Dozzu shook its head. "No. I doubt you were anything more than a by-product of his research—a cover project to distract from his true goal."

Fremy's expression betrayed her mixed feelings.

"I've also considered that perhaps you were Tgurneu's secret weapon. But although you're powerful in combat, you're still just a single Saint. And besides, if you *were* the trump card, he wouldn't have made you fight Chamo. Certainly wouldn't have let you go."

"...True." Fremy looked away.

"My comrades infiltrated Tgurneu's forces to attempt to discover what his secret weapon was. They made contact with core members of his faction, sometimes tailing them, listening closely for any intelligence. But Tgurneu is so adept at keeping secrets, I could only manage to learn bits and pieces of what was really going on. Cargikk was also trying to investigate the plot, but I believe he failed to get any results."

"So what did you get?" asked Adlet.

"The first thing we figured out is that Tgurneu's secret weapon is a hieroform. It's not a human Saint or a fiend with the power of a Spirit, meaning it has to be a hieroform. A fiend from the inner circle of Tgurneu's faction told us this explicitly."

Hieroform was a general term that referred to a tool that a Saint had imbued with a Spirit's power. The Braves' Crests of the Six Flowers were also a type of hieroform.

"The second thing we learned was its name. This we found out by intercepting some of Tgurneu's correspondence. He called this hieroform the Black Barrenbloom."

A *barrenbloom* was a flower that died without bearing fruit. Adlet muttered the words quietly under his breath. Somehow, this felt terribly foreboding.

"The third bit of intel I have is my own conjecture. Most likely, this hieroform that he calls the Black Barrenbloom holds the power of the Spirit of Fate, the very same as the Saint of the Single Flower. Tgurneu researched the Saint of the Single Flower quite deeply and concealed his findings for hundreds of years, so this is the obvious conclusion.

"The fourth thing I have to tell you is... Adlet. Could you bring out a map?"

Adlet pulled a map out of his iron box and spread it before Dozzu. This diagram had been drawn based on information passed down from the Saint of the Single Flower and Braves of past generations. Adlet had also added some details himself about the locations their party had passed through.

"Right here." Dozzu placed a plump foreleg on the map, right in the central-northern region of the Howling Vilelands, known as the Fainting Mountains. Its front paw pointed to a place a little north of the mountains' center. "Right here is where Tgurneu built a temple for the worship of the Spirit of Fate."

All the Braves, except for Goldof, fixed their eyes on the spot Dozzu indicated. In the past, the Saint of the Single Flower had constructed temples all over the world for the worship of the Spirit of Fate. The tournament Adlet had interrupted had been held in one of them.

"A Temple of Fate can only be constructed by the Saint of the Single Flower. If someone else were to attempt it, they would fail to summon the Spirit," said Mora.

"But Tgurneu has, in fact, successfully constructed one," refuted Dozzu. "And in this temple, he created the Black Barrenbloom. A comrade risked life and limb to gain this information, and I'm certain it's true."

"The Black Barrenbloom... So you're saying that this is the seventh's fake Crest?" asked Adlet.

"I believe it's extremely likely. Furthermore, even if it's not, I believe it would be worthwhile to visit this place—since that would mean Tgurneu's ultimate weapon, the Black Barrenbloom, is something other than the seventh.

"And one last thing. Even now, it seems that Tgurneu has deployed fiends around here, and what's more, they're the most elite of his specialists. Even now that you're here in the Howling Vilelands, Tgurneu has yet to deploy them." Dozzu removed its paw from the map, but even then, Adlet remained fixated on that point.

"These are all the clues I have regarding the seventh. I leave it to you whether to trust this information and act on it or not," Dozzu said, backing away and drawing close to where Nashetania lay in Goldof's embrace. Smiling, the princess lifted her hand to gently stroke Dozzu's cheek.

"What will we do, Adlet?" Mora asked.

Still staring at the map, Adlet continued to think. The place Dozzu had indicated as the Temple of Fate wasn't too far away. They could make it there in a day, if there were no interruptions. It would be a detour on their way to the Weeping Hearth, but it wouldn't waste that much time. The question was if it was really worth going there—and if they could be sure it wasn't a trap.

"I wish we had more information." Adlet looked at Dozzu again. "You said that your followers had infiltrated Tgurneu's faction. You didn't learn anything else?"

"To be frank, I don't have much to go on at all." Dozzu considered for a bit, and then spoke again. "Well, then I can tell you this: the majority of Tgurneu's troops still don't know who the seventh is."

Adlet was shocked. That was a pretty crucial detail, wasn't it?

"Like Fremy, my comrades who infiltrated Tgurneu's forces didn't know a thing about the plan to send you an impostor Brave. I'm sure this was also the case for the majority of his subordinates. The fiends were informed about the seventh only after your group approached the Howling Vilelands—specifically, ten days after the Evil God's awakening." Adlet thought back. The tenth day would have been just before their fight in the Phantasmal Barrier.

"On the afternoon of the tenth day," Dozzu continued, "messengers ran all over the Howling Vilelands, letting my fiends know about the seventh. They were told that Tgurneu had infiltrated the Braves of the Six Flowers with an impostor—one who would bring them victory, according to him."

"..."

"The messenger also told my fiends that they didn't need to know who the seventh was. They were told, *Think of every Brave as an enemy, and fight with intent to kill. Even if a Brave approaches you claiming to be the seventh, don't hesitate to kill them.*"

"What would Tgurneu do if a fiend killed the seventh, then?" asked Adlet.

"One of my spies went to Tgurneu to find out just that. Of course, the other fiends in his camp had received the same orders. Tgurneu simply smiled and replied that countermeasures were in place, and the seventh would not die."

"I wonder what those countermeasures are," Fremy muttered.

"...I couldn't hazard a guess myself." Dozzu shook its head.

During all their fights so far, Adlet had kept his eye on the fiends' behavior, trying to see if they ever held back or did anything unnatural. He'd been trying to figure out who the seventh was based on how their enemies fought them. But now, he finally understood the reason that avenue had turned up nothing.

"Tgurneu has been quite thorough, hasn't it?" said Fremy. "It seems it doesn't want the seventh to be found out, no matter what that takes."

"But what could these 'countermeasures' be? How is the seventh protecting themselves from the fiends?" asked Mora.

Rolonia tilted her head. "Hmm...could it be smell or something? Like a perfume that stops fiends from attacking them?"

"If so, I'd be able to tell," said Fremy. "It would make the fiends act strangely, too."

"Oh yeah," Hans interjected, ignoring his allies' conversation. "Are yer buddies still over in Tgurneu's camp?"

Dozzu shook its head. "No. They were all killed protecting Nashetania. When she fled, they were forced to leave Tgurneu's command."

"So what day did they leave?" asked Hans.

"The evening of the twelfth day."

Hans seemed to be in thought. "By the way, while we was fightin' the princess, what were you doin'?"

"I was in the Howling Vilelands, working with my comrades to ensure that Tgurneu and Cargikk would not interfere with our plans. Why? Does that concern you?"

"*Hrmeow.* Not really," Hans replied, and he stopped asking questions. Something was evidently on his mind, but Adlet couldn't quite pin down what it was.

Then Goldof broke his silence and suddenly spoke. "Didn't... anything happen...when Her Highness...was captured?"

Adlet was startled—he'd assumed Goldof wasn't going to participate in the conversation. But it wasn't that Goldof was deliberately keeping silent—rather that he simply hadn't spoken yet.

"Huh? Oh yes," said Dozzu. Even it and Nashetania were a little perplexed to hear Goldof talk. "There was just one thing. After specialist number twenty-six swallowed Nashetania, I tried tricking Tgurneu into revealing something and asked if he would seize the opportunity to have the seventh make their move and kill the Braves of the Six Flowers."

"And?"

"Tgurneu replied quite contemptuously, 'What are you talking about? The attack's already been carried out.'"

"..."

"I thought that the seventh had already killed one or two of your party, so when I found out that all of you were still alive, I was frankly a little shocked."

Adlet put his hand to his chin and considered. *The attack's already been carried out.* That wasn't a remark he could ignore. There was a chance Dozzu was just lying. But if the deed had already been done, that would mean that the Braves were in serious danger right now. Nothing was more dangerous than failing to even notice an incoming strike.

"Those are all the clues that I can offer you," said Dozzu.

So that's the end of this discussion, Adlet thought.

But Fremy asked one more question. "There's an important thing you haven't mentioned: How did you get the first fake Crest, the one Nashetania has?"

She was right—Dozzu hadn't mentioned that yet. There had been so many things to consider, such as Hayuha and the Black Barrenbloom, that it had slipped Adlet's mind. This information could serve as a clue to as to how Tgurneu had gotten its fake Crest.

"Yes, I can tell you that. The story isn't all that complicated. As you know, Hayuha had the power to control the flow of time of each object she touched. She used this power on her own Crest. By nature, the Crest of the Six Flowers disappears on its own within six months of the Evil God's defeat, but Hayuha extended the time it lasted to something practically infinite. She used this skill immediately after being chosen as a Brave of the Six Flowers, so her Crest wouldn't disappear or lose any petals."

Dozzu had said that Hayuha had spent five years in the Howling Vilelands. *So that was how she could do it. She used her power,* thought Adlet, convinced.

"Shortly before Hayuha's death, she left the Howling Vilelands for a time. I was traveling with her, and that was when she transferred the Crest of the Six Flowers to me. I kept this a secret from Tgurneu and Cargikk. Some time later, I passed it on to Nashetania. That's all."

"Huh? You can hand over the Crest of the Six Flowers?" Chamo was surprised.

"What, Chamo—you didn't know?" said Mora. "If the bearer of the Crest determines that another should have it, they can surrender it immediately. Though it's never actually been done."

Adlet had known that, too. On his way to the Howling Vilelands, one of the Braves of the first generation, Bowmaster Barnah, had competed with the chief of a savage tribe with his Crest as his wager. At the time, his witness, Pruka, Saint of Fire, had said just the same thing.

"But is it possible to transfer the Crest to a fiend?" Mora asked Dozzu.

"It was," said Dozzu. "We had no problem at all. It was simply that nobody had considered it. Besides..."

"There's a fiend right here with a Crest," finished Fremy.

"*Hrmeow*. So why'd Hayuha give the Crest to just you?" Hans asked.

Dozzu paused, searching for the words. "In order to realize my dream, the replacement of the Evil God, I needed the Crest of the Six Flowers no matter what. I could never tell what Hayuha was thinking, but I believe we shared an aspiration for coexistence between humans and fiends. Or perhaps it was just another of her characteristic whims."

"*Meow*, so why'd ya need it?"

Dozzu fell silent, and Hans shrugged.

"Guess that means ya can't say, then."

Dozzu nodded.

But how could you replace the Evil God and make humanity and fiendkind co-exist? And why did Dozzu need the Crest of the Six Flowers for that? Adlet's doubts only grew deeper, but he figured that for the time being, he wouldn't be able to get the answers out of the fiend commander.

"So Tgurneu's fake Crest was made the same way?" asked Fremy.

"I believe that's unlikely," said Dozzu. "Merlania and Marlie were the Braves who survived along with Hayuha—and it's been confirmed that their Crests vanished uneventfully."

"And the other three?"

"Lowie, Saint of Wind, was killed by Cargikk before even arriving in the Howling Vilelands. I was told that one of us decapitated Swordmaster Bodor in a single strike, and that Manyacam, Saint of Salt, acted as a decoy to protect the others and took out a great number of fiends in a suicide blast. I highly doubt that any of them would have had the time to pass on their Crests to anyone."

"And the first generation of Braves?"

"You're suggesting another Saint of Time could manage what Hayuha did?" Dozzu asked. Fremy shook her head.

"Then how did Tgurneu make the fake Crest?" asked Chamo.

"Unfortunately, I don't know."

"You're pretty useless. Should we kill it after all?" Chamo chirped. Rolonia leaped onto her again, but it seemed Chamo wasn't serious this time.

"Should we assume the fake Crest was created at Tgurneu's Temple of Fate, then? What do you think, Mora?" Adlet asked, looking toward her. She would know more about Saints' powers than any of them.

"Frankly speaking, I cannot even hazard a guess," Mora replied. "There are too many unknowns regarding the Saint of the Single Flower—the Saint of Fate. We cannot be sure that the laws that apply to other Saints would also apply to her."

She was quite right. The mysteries surrounding the Saint of the Single Flower were as numerous and deep as those of the Evil God. She had appeared like a bolt from the blue, just as the Evil God was about to destroy the world. Before her, there had been nothing resembling a Saint anywhere. All of the other Saints had emerged after the defeat of the Evil God, when the Saint of the Single Flower had instructed the people in how one might gain the power of a Spirit. How did she become a Saint? And how did she know how? Where was the Temple of Fate where she became a Saint? History didn't say.

What's more, there were no tales of her death passed down to the present day. She had constructed Temples of Fate for the purpose of choosing the Braves of the Six Flowers, chosen various Saints, and shared information with the people regarding the Six Braves. When all she had to do was done, she disappeared quietly. No body and no grave. Even the Saint of the Single Flower's real name was unknown. Just like the Evil God, she had appeared in the world without warning, and then, once she had saved the world, she vanished in a flash. It was even doubtful if she were really human.

"When ya think ameowt it, it's a real funny story. We don't even know who the Saint of the Single Flower really is. But we go along and do what she says anyway, and here we are now fightin'."

"...You've got a point," said Adlet.

"I ain't in the habit of accepting kills from a client without even hearin' their name, ya neow?"

Did he mean that as a joke, or was he seriously complaining about this? Adlet couldn't tell.

Adlet's eyes happened to shift to the Crest on his right hand, the symbol that gave its bearer the power to save the world. Without that, he wouldn't even be able to wound the immortal and invincible Evil God. It was said that the power of fate imbued in these markings negated the Evil God's fate of immortality. What's more, without it, Adlet wouldn't even be able to breathe in the Howling Vilelands. The Crest of the Six Flowers was essential to saving the world. But maybe they didn't know the first thing about it.

Unease surged in Adlet's heart. Just who was the Saint of the Single Flower? "Mora, if we were to go to the Temple of Fate, would you be able to tell what was done there?"

"If there remains a hieroglyphic barrier or an altar used for making hieroforms, that would give me some understanding of what had been created there," said Mora. "However, as I said before, the Saint of Fate is shrouded in mystery. I couldn't promise that I would discern everything."

"*Meow*, then why wouldn't we just ask the folks at the temple?" inquired Hans.

That was where Dozzu cut in. "I've been informed that there were once many humans at the temple: acolytes and scholars, and others knowledgeable about Saintly abilities. They'd most certainly know."

"I highly doubt Tgurneu would let them live," said Fremy. Dozzu nodded. Tgurneu would be trying to erase every one of its own secrets. If there was even the smallest chance of a leak, Tgurncu would be forced to eliminate them.

"But even so, if we don't go, we'll learn nothing," concluded Mora, her expression somber. Silence fell among the group. They were all considering their next move carefully.

"Our number one question is: Is Dozzu telling the truth?" said Adlet.

Though she'd been silent for a while now, Chamo piped up. "Chamo's totally against this. Dozzu just isn't trustworthy. We've heard everything, so we should just kill it."

"Chamo," Mora replied, "to be honest, I'm unbearably curious to know the truth behind the Evil God. If we must kill Dozzu, it should be after learning the truth."

"So let's torture it, c'mooon! Chamo'll rip up all its bones and organs." She waved her foxtail.

But Fremy shook her head at Chamo. "We know for certain that Dozzu and Tgurneu are at war. I think Dozzu's offer of cooperation is sincere. I doubt everything it's told us so far has been true, but I also don't think it's all lies."

"Huh? You believe this stupid dog, Fremy?" Chamo's eyebrows furrowed into a grumpy scowl.

"I think so, too… Maybe it isn't lying," said Rolonia, examining all of their reactions as she spoke.

"*Meow*, if we find out it's been pullin' one over on us, we just hafta kill it then. Though I know why Chamo wants to get rid of it. So why don't we just hold off for a bit?"

"…If you say so, catboy." Chamo reluctantly put her foxtail away.

Out of the blue, Goldof commented, "I think…it's a trap." All of them, including Dozzu, stared at him. "It's possible…that Her Highness…

and Dozzu…are working with Tgurneu…in a plot to kill us. Dozzu and Tgurneu are at war. But they…might prioritize…killing us…and work together."

"…I'm surprised you'd say that, Goldof. Aren't you on their side?" asked Adlet. He'd thought that Goldof was a member of Dozzu's camp now.

"I will…protect Her Highness. But…I won't support…her and Dozzu's…ambitions. I will protect…both her…and the world." Looking into Goldof's eyes, Adlet understood that the other boy was serious. In Goldof's arms, Nashetania's gaze was fixed on him. Adlet couldn't read her expression.

"I thought you would say that, Goldof. That's why we didn't have you join us," said Dozzu.

"I see."

"If you weren't such a stubborn man, our plans would have been different, though." Dozzu sighed.

"So you'll protect the princess, even though she's our enemy? Good grief. What are you thinking?" Mora grumbled.

Adlet sympathized, and the others surely felt the same. But still, he didn't find a speck of doubt or hesitation in Goldof's eyes. "Goldof, from what I can tell during the last fight, Tgurneu fully intended to kill Nashetania. I just can't believe that they're working together now."

"The possibility…is low. But…the risk is still there."

"You're right," Adlet agreed, "we can't let our guard down. But I also can't ignore the chance that Dozzu is telling the truth."

"…I understand." Goldof relented, and Nashetania breathed a sigh of relief.

"Problem number two, then," Adlet said. "Assuming what Dozzu says is true, is there really anything to learn here that can benefit us?" On the map, he indicated the spot in the center of the Fainting Mountains where the Temple of Fate lay.

"Would Tgurneu leave behind any evidence or possible sources of informeowtion?" said Hans. "If it was me, I'd be sure to destroy everything."

"That's not necessarily so," surmised Mora. "Some hieroform effects would terminate should the corresponding hieroformic barrier or altar be destroyed. The more powerful the hieroform, the more often this is the case."

"*Meow*, Saints are complicated. I don't get that stuff." Hans scratched his head.

"Well," Adlet said, "Tgurneu has fiends stationed there protecting the place, right? At the very least, there's something there it doesn't want us to see."

"That might just be a ploy to try to lure us in and snuff us out, ya neow? If the evidence is gone and all that's left is a trap, we'll be wastin' our time."

He was right—that was also quite possible.

That was when Rolonia spoke up. "Um…Dozzu. Do you know specifically where the Temple of Fate is?"

"No. I just know that it's in this vicinity."

Staring at the map, Rolonia continued. "I think we'll have a hard time searching for the Temple of Fate. It looks like this mountainous area is pretty big."

The entire group fell silent. *Your concerns are totally misplaced, Rolonia,* thought Adlet.

"Rolonia, I'm the Saint of Mountains."

"Oh! Of course. Pardon me. I'm sorry." Finally having figured it out, Rolonia bowed to everyone.

Mora possessed a power of clairvoyance that she could only use when on a mountain. She could observe everything that took place on that mountain. With her on their team, they shouldn't have a hard time finding the temple.

"But first of all," said Mora, "what exactly is the Black Barrenbloom? Does it refer to the false Crest of the seventh?"

"The fake Crest isn't black, though," countered Adlet.

"We can't assume it's black, just based off the name," said Fremy. "It seems like it could be the fake Crest, but it could possibly be something else."

"I'd actually be meowr worried if it ain't the Crest. That'd mean Tgurneu has some other card up its sleeve besides the seventh."

Dozzu and Nashetania were staring at Adlet as he continued the discussion. Neither said anything, but they seemed eager for him to hurry up and reach a conclusion. *But the decision's really already been made*, thought Adlet. "I've made up my mind. We're headed to the Fainting Mountains. We'll go to the Temple of Fate and find out what this Black Barrenbloom really is." He usually came to a decision after hearing everyone's opinions, but this time he was going to choose for them.

"...It'll be dangerous," said Goldof.

"You're ignoring Chamo?" Chamo griped, too. Rolonia and Mora also still seemed hesitant about the idea.

But even so, Adlet was not going back on this. "You're right. It'll be dangerous. But I'm the strongest man in the world, and I believe we have to take advantage of this opportunity."

"How come?" asked Chamo.

"I think everything about our fight so far has been pretty much what Tgurneu anticipated. We've just been reacting to its plots: the incident with Mora, the stuff with Goldof, everything. But this time, it's different. Tgurneu won't have predicted that we'd join forces with Dozzu, or that Dozzu knows about that Temple of Fate. This is our chance to stop tap dancing in the palm of its hand. This might be our only chance."

Chamo was silent.

"I agree," said Fremy. "We need to know about the Black Barrenbloom."

"*Hrmeow*. This is unusual. I thought you'd generally be thinkin' to avoid danger."

"Normally, I would be. But this time, I think we have to take that risk."

"How come?"

"A hunch," noted Fremy, though Chamo's expression said she

couldn't believe that. "For quite some time now, I've had this suffocating feeling, like an invisible hand around my throat. I'm afraid if I don't wrench it away, it'll kill me—but I don't know what that hand really is. I have this feeling that if we don't figure out the truth behind the Black Barrenbloom, then it's over. It's not a rational thing."

To be honest, Adlet had been feeling the same way. The name of the Black Barrenbloom had sent shivers down his spine. The moment that feeling had struck him, he'd felt compelled to find that thing, no matter what.

"Are we decided, then?" asked Dozzu. "You'll come with us to the Fainting Mountains, and there we'll investigate the Black Barrenbloom."

"Yeah. We're doing it," concluded Adlet. The others seemed to have mixed feelings, but they weren't objecting.

"Understood," said Dozzu. "Then we'll commit everything we have to this, too. Let's find out what the Black Barrenbloom really is and unmask the seventh together. Nashetania, you're all right with this?"

She nodded.

"But we're going to take some precautions, in case you betray us," said Fremy. She approached Goldof and Nashetania and put her hands on the princess's legs.

"What...are you doing?" demanded Goldof.

"I'm going to plant bombs on her legs. If your party betrays us, I'll blow them up."

Tension shot through the whole group. Dozzu's hackles raised, while Goldof clenched his spear. "You think...I'll allow that?"

"I'm the one making concessions. Normally, I'd put it around her filthy neck."

Goldof and Fremy glared at each other, while Dozzu's body sparked. Chamo smirked, touching her foxtail to her mouth. Adlet interrupted the volatile situation. "Just until we defeat either Tgurneu or Cargikk. I promise we'll remove the bombs once we've killed one of them."

"You're too soft, Adlet," said Fremy. She was right; they had to be prepared. But if they set any more strict conditions, the two parties might just start a deathmatch right there. He had to maintain this alliance with Dozzu and Nashetania.

"I suppose I have no choice," Nashetania rasped, spitting bubbles of blood from her mouth. She made Goldof lower his hand from his spear and flung out her legs in front of Fremy.

"You're being unexpectedly gracious about this," said Fremy. She put her hands on Nashetania's knees and focused her mind. In a few moments, a claylike substance appeared in her hands and adhered to the other girl. "Don't worry. They won't be set off by fire or shock. The only thing that can ignite them is my signal."

"If you…break your promise…I'll kill you," Goldof said to Fremy. "If she hasn't betrayed you…and you explode them anyway…I'll kill you. If Tgurneu or Cargikk are eliminated…and you still don't remove them… I'll kill you. I don't care if you're an impostor or a real Brave…I'll kill you…either way."

"Oh, will you? Do as you please," Fremy answered curtly.

"So we have our goal," said Adlet. "Now we decide exactly how we're gonna pull it off." He spread out his map, and all eyes gathered on it. "There's no sign of any enemies around here. It looks to me like Tgurneu is planning to pull all its forces back and station them beyond Cargikk's Canyon. The question is, where is it waiting for us?"

Dozzu placed a front paw at the center of his map, indicating a place called the Plain of Cropped Ears that covered the expanse just south of the central Howling Vilelands. The plain was dotted with forests and rocky areas suitable for hiding, as well as two Buds of Eternity, their safe zones. "If Tgurneu believes we'll head straight for the Weeping Hearth, he should be waiting here. He would lay his main forces here and form a net around it. And if he predicts we'll visit the Temple of Fate, he'll probably be waiting for us here." The second location that Dozzu pointed out was near the Fainting Mountains, in the northern-central area of the Howling Vilelands.

"If Tgurneu blocks our way, we'll be forced to fight," said Adlet. "We'd have to hurt it bad enough to incapacitate it for a while, at least."

"It will be a relentless battle," said Dozzu.

"That just means the strongest man in the world gets his time to shine."

"...Okay." The dog-fiend was baffled.

I've gotta convince this thing soon that I am *the strongest man in the world*, thought Adlet. "If Tgurneu's on the plains, that'll make things a little easier for us. We have to figure out what the Black Barrenbloom is before it comes to the Temple of Fate with its main forces. We'll be fighting against the clock."

"This spot will be our other problem." Next, Dozzu pointed to a location on the eastern side of the Fainting Mountains. "The Fainting Mountains are steep, and I'm sure your group will take some time to cross them. To arrive at the Temple of Fate safely and quickly, you'll have no choice but to pass through the forest from the eastern side, here, and proceed through the mountain valley. Tgurneu may lay a trap or have powerful fiends stationed here."

"Whatever it is, we just have to force them back," Adlet said firmly. He judged that it was better to meet the enemy head-on there rather than come up with some scheme to avoid fighting.

"Then let's hammer out the details of the plan on the way to the Temple of Fate," Fremy cut in. "There's no point in further discussion now."

"You're right," said Dozzu.

"Let's take a break here for now," suggested Adlet. "We'll get going after we've rested up. We'll alternate who's on watch, two on at a time. First watch will be me and Fremy, and Mora and Rolonia are up after that. The rest of you, just get some sleep."

The group followed Adlet's orders, lying down for the night. Dozzu was apparently exhausted, resting its head on its front legs, about to fall asleep when Fremy spoke.

"There's one last thing I want to ask, though." Dozzu opened its eyes, and she continued. "What did Tgurneu say about my joining the Braves of the Six Flowers?"

Dozzu gave Fremy a hard look, and then shook its head. "He didn't say anything."

"Oh? Good."

Why's that good? Adlet was confused, unsure what she meant.

"Then just one more thing…the dog I had. Would you know what happened to it?"

Dozzu tilted its head. "My apologies. I don't know a thing about that."

"Of course…you wouldn't, would you? You can sleep now," said Fremy.

Dozzu nodded and closed its eyes. The others were already asleep.

Time passed. The group's rest went uninterrupted with no sign of any fiends nearby. In the stillness, Adlet asked Fremy a question. He was curious about what she'd said before. "…Hey, Fremy. What was good about that?"

"What are you talking about?" she asked.

"Why was it good that Tgurneu didn't say anything about you?"

Fremy considered a moment and then replied, "If the fiends still thought of me as their ally, they would have commented on it. That they didn't say anything means they think nothing of my betrayal, and that they see me only as the enemy." Fremy's cold eyes were fixed westward. "So I won't hesitate when I kill them."

Adlet swallowed his next question: *If the fiends had still recognized you as their ally, what would you have done then?* He could tell the conflict about killing her former brethren was still raging in her heart. The same with fighting Tgurneu, who had been practically a parent to her. But her cold expression revealed neither distress nor hesitation. What did she really feel when she was so dispassionately following Adlet's orders and coolly battling the fiends? Perhaps she'd been deeply wounded because of him. Suddenly, he wanted to wrap his arms around her, but his hands wouldn't move. He just wasn't confident he could embrace her without hurting her. He couldn't think of any words to offer her right now. "I hope that dog is okay." The harmless remark was what he settled on.

"It's old—since I've had it since I was a baby. If it was abandoned..." Fremy went quiet. "No, it'll be okay. It's a smart dog, and it was still in good health. I'm sure it can survive without an owner."

"I love dogs, too," said Adlet. "Once we've beaten the Evil God, you should let me see him."

"...All right. Sure." He didn't know why, but she'd hesitated to reply. She looked away, her alert eyes on the quiet forest. "First, we have to deal with the Black Barrenbloom. We'll find out what it is and destroy it."

"I doubt this fight will be straightforward," Adlet replied. Still, it would be worth a shot. Until now, all Tgurneu's plans had been entirely shrouded in mystery. This was the first time they'd encountered a clue that could lead them to uncovering the full story. From here on out, it was time for the Braves to be on the offensive. It was Tgurneu's turn to be afraid of them. They'd make it regret leaving Dozzu alive. Adlet would teach it a lesson about what a big mistake it was to carelessly let the strongest man in the world get a hold of this information.

"Hayuha... The true nature of the Evil God... The true nature of the Saint of the Single Flower... The mysteries we're after might be deeper than we think," Fremy murmured, sounding composed, like she always did.

Meanwhile, Dozzu was drowsily nodding off as it pondered. So far, things were going well. It had succeeded in gaining the cooperation of the Braves of the Six Flowers and also managed to steer them toward the Temple of Fate. It had believed the former was possible, but the latter had not been a guaranteed success.

Dozzu had never before been able to approach the Temple of Fate. There should be something at that temple that was absolutely key to victory. If their battle in the Phantasmal Barrier had been a success, then Dozzu's contract with Tgurneu would have compelled the fig-fiend to bow to the dog-fiend, and Dozzu could have acquired that key easily. But now, there was nothing for it but to cooperate with the Braves of the Six Flowers and visit the Temple of Fate. It seemed Adlet intended to use them, and Dozzu was fine with that—though Dozzu also intended to take full advantage of the Six Braves itself.

Dozzu was after something else, too: it had to find out Tgurneu's real goal. Though Dozzu could guess at what that goal was, it still had to find out how Tgurneu intended to realize it. The answers to that question were also likely in that Temple of Fate.

There was much to do. It would be a long, ongoing battle on a tightrope—but even so, Dozzu would never give up.

Time passed, and dawn broke. It was morning on the eighteenth day since the Evil God's awakening.

"...So no more clues, huh?" Tgurneu muttered. The fiend had discarded the yeti body that it had been using until the day before. It was currently in the form of a wolf with tentacles growing from its shoulders. The fig that was Tgurneu's main body was inside the wolf's mouth.

Tgurneu stood on the plains at the center the Howling Vilelands. The area was called the Plain of Cropped Ears because a fiend had once attacked the Saint of the Single Flower here, hitting her in the ear. Tgurneu had laid its forces in wait for the Braves of the Six Flowers around the Bud of Eternity in the center of the plain.

By Tgurneu's side was a bird-fiend. It was called "specialist number two," and its duty was to work as Tgurneu's aide, messenger, and scout. Due to the nature of its role, it was in a position to know all of its commander's plans.

"Perhaps the Braves are resting," said Tgurneu. "Or could they be in the middle of a discussion? They're not so stupid as to fight Dozzu's lot, are they?" Tgurneu's minions were scattered about the Plain of Cropped Ears, on the prowl for the Braves of the Six Flowers. There were still no reports of their discovery. But Tgurneu didn't sound worried.

"They might have anticipated that we would be stationed here, and plan to pass through the Fainting Mountains instead."

"I think they'd have a rough time going through there, though."

"Or pérhaps they've gleaned some information ön the Temple of Fate through Dozzu."

"I highly doubt that's the case," Tgurneu replied, wriggling its tentacles.

Specialist number two considered. If the Braves of the Six Flowers were going straight for the Weeping Hearth, then this battle was over. The power of the Black Barrenbloom would kill all of them before they reached their destination. Tgurneu would have to think up a way to hold back Cargikk's forces, though, since it would be troublesome if a rival managed to kill three of the Six Braves first.

If Dozzu did know about the Temple of Fate, it would prolong the battle a bit, but it really wouldn't pose any problem. Even if Dozzu's group did reach the Temple of Fate, they had no way to discover the true nature of the Black Barrenbloom. Either way, there was hardly a problem.

An eagle-fiend flew toward them from the west, a member of the lower ranks with no name or number. "A report for you, Commander Tgurneu."

"Proper greetings first!" Tgurneu's harsh tone made the eagle-fiend cower.

How undisciplined, thought specialist number two.

"Good mörning, Commander Tgurneu. I pray this day will be most fortuitous for you."

"Good. Your report?"

"Cargïkk's forces still have yet to act. He's only sënt just a few scouts out near the Plain of Cropped Ears."

"I see. You may go."

Flapping its wings, the eagle-fiend returned to its post. It seemed the activities of Cargikk's forces would pose no problems, either. They were acting entirely based off false rumors Tgurneu had disseminated and would be unable to leave the Weeping Hearth.

Everything was going well. Tgurneu had failed to kill a single Brave of the Six Flowers so far, but that was no great concern. Tgurneu waved its tentacles, lost in thought.

"What is it, Commander Tgürneu?" asked specialist number two.

"I'm just thinking of starting a little game. But whatever shall I do? I can't think of how I might play."

"What might your plän be, Commander?"

"You know, I'm thinking I'll invite the Braves of the Six Flowers to the Temple of Fate. What do you think? Could be fun, right?" Drooling, Tgurneu smiled.

I see. That does indeed sound promising, thought specialist number two.

"Let's put up a sign. It'll say, *Come right this way, O great Braves of the Six Flowers! The Temple of Fate is right over here!*" Tgurneu said, still smiling.

Chapter 2

The
Dead Host

It was eighteen days after the Evil God's awakening and seven days since Adlet's party had first set foot in the Howling Vilelands. It was a lot sunnier than it had been the day before, not a single cloud in the sky. The celestial light shone brightly over the red-black stained earth of the Howling Vilelands. It was past noon, and the group was making its way along a steep mountain path in the central-northern region of the Howling Vilelands.

"Will you show me the map, Adlet?" Dozzu asked, turning around from its position in front to speak. Adlet placed the map on the ground, and the dog indicated a spot with a foreleg. "Tgurneu has built a lookout post at the summit of this mountain. That means he will be keeping watch over all of the territory near the foot. Destroying the lookout would be easy, but I believe it would be safer to circumvent it for now and pass through this valley to the south."

"Roger. Everyone, southwest. Let's go," Adlet said, prompting his allies, and the group started off down the mountain path again.

They'd headed out immediately after a brief nap at their old camp. Goldof, Nashetania, and Chamo were all injured—not that the others weren't unscathed—but the group chose to hurry on ahead anyway. Any lingering would risk a surprise attack from Tgurneu. Besides, Adlet wanted to reach this Temple of Fate that Dozzu had informed them of as quickly as possible.

"The enemy," Dozzu said softly. They could see a fiend in the shadow of a boulder. It hadn't noticed them yet.

Instantly, too fast for the eye to see, Fremy couched her gun. Right as her weapon appeared, Mora gently put her hand on its tip. Fremy fired, the bullet burst the fiend's head open, and the thunderous gunshot that should have accompanied it could only be heard nearby. Mora had applied her power of mountain echo to Fremy's shot, canceling the noise. The pair used this method to eliminate all the fiends on watch.

Their path was uneventful. In the less than half a day since their departure, they'd come quite close to the Fainting Mountains. They'd even managed to cross Cargikk's Canyon—which had been an unresolved problem for them—quite easily with Dozzu's guidance. The commander had recited an incantation in front of a stake hidden in the canyon wall. The ravine was shrouded in cold air, and a path opened. Dozzu told them that the Saint of Ice, three generations previously, had been a comrade.

Even once they were over the ravine, it was Dozzu's further direction that allowed them to safely evade enemies as they made their way forward. Dozzu understood the layout of Tgurneu's forces and accurately predicted which avenues the fiends were likely to block off.

"In the valleys, we may be discovered from above. We also cannot use Mora's clairvoyant eye. I believe we should handle any fiends with Fremy's shooting and Chamo's slave-fiends." Dozzu was briskly giving out orders, and there was nothing left for Adlet to do.

"Dozzu's being a better leader than you," said Fremy coldly.

Adlet smiled and replied, "I'm impressed. It's not bad—though not as good as the strongest man in the world."

Dozzu, walking in the lead, turned back to look at them in bafflement. "I've been meaning to ask this for a while now... When you say you're the strongest man in the world, that's...a joke, right?"

"What're you talking about? Of course I'm serious."

"...Um...well...then... I don't quite know what to say."

"That's just how he is," said Fremy. "Don't worry about it."

Dozzu tilted its head, seemingly at a loss.

The eight humans and one fiend proceeded, all in a line. Goldof, who was the most severely wounded, was in the center of the formation, under the protection of the group. He lay on top of a slug slave-fiend from Chamo's stomach, his eyes closed. Adlet had ordered him to focus on healing up for the time being.

Chamo was walking with Rolonia's support, but she was acting energetic enough that it was hard to tell she'd been on death's door just the day before. Adlet probably wouldn't have to worry about her.

As for Nashetania, he was even less worried about her.

"I see," she said. "So the king of Gwenvaella came. I was wondering who had reactivated the Phantasmal Barrier. Now it finally makes sense." She was walking at the tail end of the line. Hans walked in front of her, getting her up to speed on their battles so far.

In the few hours since their fight, her wounds had healed up. Her left arm was still gone, but her crushed throat was already back to normal. It looked as though she'd recovered all her strength, too. Had a regular human lost an arm, they would have been off-balance and had difficulty walking right. But Nashetania had no such trouble. She'd explained that she'd fused with various fiends to make their powers her own. Once again, Adlet was reminded just what a superhuman creature she had become.

On their way to the Temple, they stopped by one of Dozzu's hideouts. Nashetania discarded her ragged clothes for new armor and a new sword. This armor was different from her previous set, mainly black and dark brown in color. To Adlet, it made her silhouette seem somehow more provocative than her previous armor had. The scars on her body and her missing left arm gave her a newfound air of degenerate sensuality.

"*Meow*, oh yeah! And listen to this, Princess. This lady killed me once." Hans pointed at Mora, right in front of him.

"Killed? Not nearly killed?" Nashetania tilted her head, her eyes puzzled.

"Hans... I-I'd really rather you not..." Mora began.

"I figgered she had to be plottin' somethin'," Hans said, "but I never thought she'd kill me."

"Hold on now. That's not something to be spoken of so casually."

"It's not like we have to keep it a secret." Adlet's tone was cold.

"I'd like to hear more," said Nashetania. "What happened?"

"Mora acts all stuck-up, but she's actually a pretty meowtrageous woman," said Hans. "It all started back at the Bud of Eternity." He began a humorous rendition of the incident four days ago.

Nashetania listened, one hand over her mouth. "I can't believe it. I never thought Lady Mora would do such a thing. I thought of her a trustworthy person," she commented, quite hypocritically.

"...Hey, Addy, do you think this is all right?" Rolonia had come away from Chamo to approach Adlet. She spoke quietly, so none of the others would hear. "I kind of feel like...everyone is too relaxed. I think we have to be more cautious."

"Don't worry about it. It's not a problem," he replied. He was watching the others even more attentively than before. If there were significant secrets hidden in the Temple of Fate, the seventh would probably challenge the Braves now. This peaceful atmosphere was ultimately superficial.

The other thing Adlet was watching out for was to never leave Dozzu and Nashetania alone together. If he could prevent the two of them from plotting, he should be able to limit their activities considerably.

Hans might have looked like he was having a fun little chat, but he was actually using his conversation with Nashetania to sound out her reactions. He was trying to pick up on what she might be scheming. Fremy, Mora, and Chamo would be on high alert, too.

"Listen, Rolonia," said Adlet. "Act friendly with Dozzu and Nashetania."

"All right. But why?"

"It'll make it easier to take them by surprise." Rolonia was a little surprised to hear him say that. But on the battlefield, betrayals and trickery should be taken for granted. "Hey, Dozzu," Adlet called out to the fiend walking at the front of the line. "What's your take on our situation? Who do you figure is the seventh?"

"Judging from what Hans has told me," said Dozzu, "I believe I can assume it is not Mora. By the same token, the chances are also low that it's Hans, Chamo, or Goldof."

"And your logic?" prompted Adlet.

"Tgurneu is trying to protect the seventh. That's why he hasn't even told the fiends under his command which of you is the impostor. I can't be certain how he's managing to do so, but I doubt he was lying about how he has a secret plan to protect them."

"Makes sense."

"Meanwhile, the seventh must also be trying to conceal their identity. They would contribute to victories, defeat enemies, and protect their allies. One might even save an ally's life, but that doesn't imply they're not a traitor. Thus only one thing can be used as evidence: Anyone that Tgurneu has made a serious attempt to kill is not the seventh, and anyone Tgurneu has left to their fate, even at the risk of their death, is also an unlikely candidate."

Dozzu continued.

"Without you, Adlet, Mora most certainly would have died. I'm quite convinced she's not the seventh. Hans was nearly killed, and your group also came close to killing Goldof. As far as I can tell, Tgurneu fully intended to take Chamo's life. For the aforementioned reasons, this makes it less likely that any of these three is the imposter."

That was more or less Adlet's reasoning.

"Remaining are Fremy, Rolonia, and you, Adlet." Dozzu watched Adlet with sharp eyes.

The boy was also aware of this. The others had been treating him like he couldn't be the seventh because Nashetania had nearly killed him. Now that they knew that Nashetania and Tgurneu's seventh were on opposite sides, he had nothing else to prove he was genuine.

"I beg your pardon, Adlet, but..." Dozzu began, "I think perhaps you should cede the role of leader to Mora. Presently, you're a likely candidate for seventh. I feel rather uneasy about leaving the leadership of the Braves to you."

"Maybe you're right," Adlet acquiesced. Of course, he didn't believe he was the seventh. But the reality was that from where the others stood, he was a candidate. For now, he didn't sense any misgivings from them, but he wasn't sure if he should continue acting as the leader.

"Now that you mention it, yeah. Adlet's kinda suspicious," Chamo interjected.

Mora said, "I trust him. Besides, Dozzu's our enemy. I'm not so certain I want to agree to any of its propositions."

"I just can't see Addy as the enemy, either," Rolonia agreed.

"But, like, Chamo'd be kinda worried about having Auntie as our leader, too. She's an idiot," the youngest Saint offered bluntly.

Mora couldn't argue with that. "Frankly speaking...I don't have the confidence to take up the role of leader, considering my string of failures."

"Chamo'd rather have catboy. It doesn't seem like he's the enemy. And he protected Chamo."

The group all looked toward Hans, who stood at the tail end of the line. Now done with his talk with Nashetania, Hans shrugged and said, "*Hrmeow*. Leadin' just ain't in my nature. I'll leave it to Adlet."

"Wouldn't that be dangerous?" asked Dozzu.

"It wouldn't change neowthin'. I always suspected him anyway. Like I said before, if one of us is the seventh, the most dangerous choice would be Adlet. My take is that he might not believe he's the seventh himself, or he could be leadin' us into danger without even kneowin' it. So I'll just keep on doin' what I've always been doin'."

"...I see."

"If I happen to disagree with Adlet, I'll say so," Hans continued. "If that happens, go with my decision. Meow about that?"

"In other words," Fremy explained, "a parliamentary system, with Hans and Adlet as leaders. I think that's fairly rational."

"Chamo'd rather have catboy give orders, though." Chamo seemed to disapprove.

"If you're fine with that, then so am I," said Adlet. None of the others voiced any opposition.

Though this meant that Adlet would continue acting as leader, they probably wouldn't give him the same kind of wholehearted trust they had before. *I just hope that won't cause a disaster,* he thought.

As they made their way closer to their goal, the number of watchers in the sky gradually increased. "As I expected, the Fainting Mountains region is under watch," Dozzu muttered as it scanned the area.

"Yeah, but Tgurneu isn't around. Which means it's expecting us to cross the Plain of Cropped Ears, and it's concentrated its main forces there," Adlet replied. If Tgurneu had predicted that the Braves would go to the temple, there would be more forces here than just a few guards. The fiends would have completely surrounded them long ago. It seemed they'd overcome the first hurdle to reaching the Temple of Fate: running into Tgurneu.

As one would expect, the group's chatter decreased. Staying attentive to their surroundings while also monitoring one another was mentally exhausting. "So? See anything odd?" Adlet asked the group. All of them—aside from Goldof, who was lying on top of the slug-fiend—shook their heads. As far as they could tell, the seventh had yet to act.

After they crossed a hill, the forest that covered the base of the Fainting Mountains came into view. That was when Dozzu said to Adlet, "It will be dangerous up ahead. All of you, please wait for a little while. I'll go scout the area."

"You're planning to scout alone?" asked Adlet.

"I'm small, so I can hide easily. It's more effective than the whole party going." Dozzu had a point. But Adlet couldn't let a fiend and potential traitor head out solo.

"I'll go too, *meow,*" Hans volunteered.

Adlet nodded. "Go, then. And watch out. We'll be healing Goldof's wounds in the meantime."

"Y'all eat some food, too. We don't neow when we'll be able to get our next meal. I'll eat on the way, so don't ya worry about me." Fierce battles would be waiting for them in the Fainting Mountains. It was a good idea to make sure they were ready.

"Is there anywhere nearby we can hide?" Adlet addressed the party.

They all looked around. Fremy, perched up on a tree, spotted something and pointed to it. "We should be able to hide over there."

"All right," said Dozzu, "then let's meet up there in thirty minutes. Please watch out for traps." Dozzu and Hans disappeared into the forest while the rest of them headed off toward Fremy's discovery.

The place she had found was an old wooden hut. It was not a fiend's den but clearly a former human dwelling. Crude as a horse's stable, it had only two rooms. It seemed a rough place to live, with cracks all over the walls and ceiling. They'd seen many similar huts in their journey so far. They'd checked them out but never encountered any living humans. Surveying the shabby hut, Adlet could easily imagine how the humans of the Howling Vilelands were treated—like slaves, or cattle.

"Adlet, hurry up! What if you're seen?" Fremy called out to him. The boy, who'd been staring at the hut, got flustered and went inside.

"Lady Mora, could you please handle Goldof?" asked Nashetania.

Mora nodded. "Mm-hmm. Leave him to me."

"Rolonia, you treat Chamo," said Fremy. "She seems to be doing well, so I doubt there's much to worry about, though."

"R-right away!" Rolonia chirped.

Mora and Rolonia began treating their two casualties while Adlet and Fremy examined the hut's floor and walls for traps. The interior of the building was a ruin. There was oatmeal on the stove, entirely dried up. The few household items to be had were lying broken and scattered about, and the pile of straw used for a bed was rotten.

And then Adlet saw it. His eyes locked on to one corner of the hut.

"..."

There was a little fragment of pottery on the ground there. Anyone else would have probably taken it to be nothing but debris. But Adlet knew what it was.

He gently picked up the ceramic fragment. It was a piece of a flute that had been handed down in Adlet's home village. It was a plain instrument kneaded from clay, molded into shape and fired, then painted with a simple pattern. The dye was made from a flower that bloomed on the banks of the lake.

In Adlet's village, when the harvest season had passed and they were done preparing the earth for the planting the following year, they would hold a small festival. They would get together and drink murky beer, the women would play flutes, and the men would sing with them. Nothing more than that.

"I don't see any traps," said Fremy. "I'll go keep watch outside."

"Thank you," said Mora. "Stay alert until Hans and Dozzu come back."

Their conversation sounded so far away. Adlet just kept staring at the clay in his hand. In his mind, vivid memories played across his mind: the song the men sang together, the cooling winds, the smell of the beer and the modest foods that each of the families had brought. The sights that never changed, year after year, rose in his mind's eye.

He could even tell from the pattern on the flute that it had belonged to the old lady who lived next to the village elder. She was a mean-spirited person and often unpleasant to Adlet's sister. But he also remembered that when she was in a good mood, she would hand out fried bread snacks to the village children. Adlet's heart leaped to his throat, and he reflexively clutched his chest.

"What's wrong, Addy?"

"Don't worry about it. It's nothing."

Mora's voice had pulled him from his reverie. He threw the flute shard on the ground, and it shattered into even smaller pieces. He averted his eyes, avoiding looking straight at it.

In the center of the hut, Goldof was getting to his feet. He swung his spear around loosely, then bent and stretched his legs.

"Better already?" asked Adlet.

"I can't say...I feel perfect. But...I can fight."

When Adlet and Hans had been badly hurt, even with treatment from Mora and Rolonia it had taken them over a day to heal. Goldof's recovery was unusually fast, even considering his rest on the slug's back.

"I envy your youth," Mora commented.

Goldof peered into Adlet's face and muttered, "You seem...unsettled. Did something...happen?"

The others were looking at him with concern, too. Adlet was surprised by himself. So he looked so upset that even Goldof was pointing it out? "It's nothing major."

"Oh dear," Nashetania teased. "If you hide things, you'll make everyone suspicious, Adlet."

"Um... There was something on the floor from my village, a long time ago. I was just a little startled. Don't worry about it."

That was enough for them to figure it out. At the Bud of Eternity, while they had been waiting for Mora's and Hans's wounds to heal, Adlet had told them all about what had happened in his home village. Nashetania, the only one who didn't know, seemed curious.

"I'll go help keep watch," Adlet said, and he left the hut to take up position outside, opposite of Fremy. He pulled his travel rations from one of the pouches at his waist, chewed them up, and washed them down with water all in one go. The food got stuck in his throat, and he coughed a few times. He knew that he'd been shaken unbelievably hard, though all that had happened was he'd found a piece of a flute.

Adlet had done his best to forget his home for a long time. Homesickness didn't make you stronger. The only things that did were anger and determination. Reminiscing about those halcyon days just made it harder to fight. Thinking about the people of his village would make even winnable battles impossible. That was why Adlet hadn't spared much thought to his home village all this time. He'd believed his memories of the past were gone. Now, he realized that he hadn't forgotten—he'd just been trying to forget.

Don't think about the people from home. There's no point. What's important right now is to protect my allies, beat the seventh, and take down Tgurneu. Then I'll find out what that Black Barrenbloom hieroform is.

But the dam in his heart had already burst open, and the memories rose once again in his mind.

Adlet's older sister, Schetra, had been a wise and astute woman. His best friend, Rainer, had been brave and big-hearted besides. Back then, all Adlet ever did was hang on to them from behind.

Rainer and Adlet had practiced swordsmanship, just the two of them, to protect the village from the Evil God. Though Schetra seemed anxious about it, she warmly watched over them.

Once, Adlet had hit Rainer by mistake, clocking him above the eye with his wooden stick. Upset, Adlet had started to cry, but Rainer just ignored that and calmly called for Schetra. Entirely unruffled, Schetra treated the wound. Rainer was left with a big scar, but he didn't seem to mind. He called it his proof of bravery and smiled.

Sometimes, Rainer talked about how he would become a Brave of the Six Flowers. Back then, Adlet had never imagined that the Brave among them wouldn't be Rainer, but himself.

Shortly before Tgurneu invaded the village, Adlet was practicing singing at home with Rainer watching. Adlet sang his heart out, trying to keep in tune with Schetra's flute.

Singing wasn't that hard. The entire village would sing together, so they performed simple melodies that anyone could manage. But Adlet was terrible at it. With Rainer beside him, singing with him, he could somehow stay on pitch. But whenever Rainer stopped and Adlet was left on his own, he'd immediately mess it all up. So much that even Schetra's playing would go off-key. His singing was so bad, Rainer started laughing. Schetra started making silly noises with her flute to tease him and, face bright red, Adlet yelled at the both of them.

"Hey, let me touch your throat," said Rainer, grabbing the other boy's neck. He lifted and lowered Adlet's voice box along with the song. "Come on, try singing now. Maybe you can sing it right if I do this."

Adlet tried making some sounds. When Rainer lifted his larynx, a high noise came out. When he pushed it down, the pitch was low. But this wasn't going to make him sing properly. "Stop! You don't have to do that! I can do it!" Adlet cried.

"Oh my, Adlet. That's a lot better than before," Schetra said, smiling.

Back then, that had been like a life crisis to him.

Now, Schetra and Rainer were both gone. Tgurneu had tricked the people of his village and taken them all to the Howling Vilelands. When Schetra had opposed it, the villagers had killed her. Rainer and Adlet had been hiding in earthenware pots. She had told them to run, and immediately afterward, she'd been stabbed in the chest with a knife.

Adlet couldn't do anything but cry, so Rainer ran and pulled him by the arm. When Adlet was about to be captured, Rainer had bitten their pursuer's arm to save him and was stabbed in the back with a scythe. With the time Rainer had bought for him, Adlet had escaped alone.

"Whatcha doin'?" Hans's voice pulled Adlet back to reality. Hans and Dozzu were standing in front of him, and Adlet hadn't even noticed their approach. "Were ya keepin' watch? Or were ya asleep on yer feet? Huh?" Hans scolded him for his inattention. "Pull yerself together. It's gonna get harder from here on meowt."

The two scouts went toward the hut. Looking over its shoulder, Dozzu said, "We have a problem. Let's all discuss this together."

That was when Adlet noticed that Hans held a strange insect in his hand. It had a gnarled body, thin wings, and long, wirelike feelers.

"The enemy has blocked our path," said Dozzu. "Unfortunately, I believe it would be quite difficult to defeat them." The fiend's expression was severe.

Adlet asked, "What did you find?"

"Specialist number nine is protecting the forest that leads to the Temple of Fate. Or rather, the Dead Host under its command are."

"...'Dead Host'?"

But before Adlet could get a detailed explanation, Dozzu and Hans went into the hut.

The Fainting Mountains were a line of cliffs that towered up so sharply they looked vertical. On their eastern side was a gently sloping valley, and beyond it, a forest that wasn't very big—you could travel through it in less than two hours on foot. It had no particular name.

"...Aghhhhhh..."

About a thousand dead bodies wandered that forest—or rather, bodies that very clearly should be dead.

They were parched to an ashen gray, their skin filigreed with cracks over rotting flesh. No one in this state could possibly still be alive. But these thousand bodies were walking on their own two feet. They turned their heads left and right as if scanning for something, their cloudy eyeballs swiveling about as they wandered.

Something rustled in the forest. Instantly, the corpses let out piercing shrieks and surged far faster than any regular human could to the source of the sound, grabbing at it with hands outstretched. The culprit was a deer. The bodies captured the animal, crushing its bones and ripping off its flesh with their fists, and shortly, all that was left was a mass of meat. Having finished their work, the corpses returned to ambling around the forest. There was no sign of individuality or consciousness in their actions. It was as if something else was in control, ordering them to kill everything that moved, everything that lived.

"Ahhhhh..." one of the bodies moaned.

Every one of the thousand corpses, without exception, had a certain unique feature: a large insect clinging to its neck. Upon closer inspection, one could see the antennae and long, thin legs penetrating the back of the corpses' heads and spines. The bugs were the main bodies; these were what controlled the corpses. They manipulated their hosts by sending signals to the regions of the brain and spinal cord that governed movement. Tgurneu had named this group of subjugated living corpses the "Dead Host."

In the center of the forest, under a particularly massive and noticeable tree, was a fiend. Shaped like an insect, it was a little bigger than a large human. Dozens of thin legs supported its knobby, brown body, and an armful of ghastly lumps was attached to the center of its stomach. This fiend was called specialist number nine. It was the creator and controller of the Dead Host, extolled as the most powerful member of Tgurneu's forces.

"The Dead Host?" Adlet repeated, without thinking. The allies sat together in the hut. Dozzu had told them that this "Dead Host" was obstructing the road to the Fainting Mountains. Adlet had never heard of them before. No such fiend had come up during Atreau's lessons. "Explain to me. What kind of fiend is this?"

"It's not a fiend," said Dozzu. "They're humans. Though I'm not sure you could still really call them human." It described the Dead Host to the others, how humans were used to make weapons, and how parasites birthed by specialist number nine would take over their bodies.

Listening to Dozzu's explanation, Adlet restrained his nausea. Mora put her hand over her mouth, while Rolonia blanched. Even Chamo and Goldof were frowning uncomfortably.

"It was uncanny," said Hans. "All these folks about five hundred times dirtier than me was wanderin' around the forest. Even I turned a li'l scaredy-cat." He was smiling—probably not from amusement. Cold sweat beaded on his forehead.

But come to think of it, Fremy had talked about this at the Bud of Eternity. She'd mentioned that one of Tgurneu's fiends could take over and manipulate human bodies. But she hadn't given much detail, so Adlet had never imagined the thing's abilities were this cruel.

"Based on what we saw," Hans continued, "every single part of the forest is full of the Dead Host. We ain't gettin' through that, not unless we got some hieroform that can make us invisible."

Chamo said, "It sure sounds super nasty, but is it really a big problem? They're just normal humans, right? Chamo's pets can kill about a thousand people."

But Hans shook his head. "I tried killin' a few, and I don't think it'll be that easy. I think they're stronger than meowst fiends. They got muscle like Goldof, and they're pretty fast, too."

"Huh?" said Chamo.

"The Dead Host can push their human strength to its limits," Dozzu explained. "People like Hans and Goldof have reached those limits through unusual effort and talent, but what gives the corpses their strength is the power of the parasites attached to them."

"Even all of us at once would have a hard time killin' 'em if we fought 'em head-on," said Hans. "We'd probably tire ourselves meowt first."

"Huh. I guess that's kind of a problem, then." Chamo pondered the issue. Even her seemingly immortal slave-fiends couldn't keep fighting forever.

"Dozzu," said Mora, "must we pass through the forest to reach the Temple of Fate?"

"Any other way would be difficult. Attempting to pass through another area of the Fainting Mountains region would be perilous, even for a fiend. If we search, we might be able to find a way in, but we don't have that kind of time."

"So to investigate the Black Barrenbloom at the Temple of Fate…" Mora trailed off.

"We must defeat the Dead Host and advance straight ahead into the central region of the mountains. If we search for another path, we'll surely be surrounded by Tgurneu's main forces in the process," said Dozzu.

Mora sighed.

"Fortunately," the fiend continued, "it looks as if specialist number nine is the only one guarding this forest. The others are either elsewhere on the mountain or defending the Temple of Fate."

"How…do we kill…the Dead Host?" Goldof asked.

But Adlet cut into their conversation first. "Wait, Dozzu. Are the humans they used to make the Dead Host still alive?"

Dozzu shook its head. "Their hearts are beating, but you couldn't describe them as *alive*…not anymore. The parasites have commandeered their brains entirely, and their conscious minds are presumably entirely gone."

"What do you mean, 'presumably'?" asked Adlet.

"That's all I can say. I've never become one of the Dead Host myself, and I've never heard one of those corpses speak."

Hans added, "*Mya-meow.* After the fight earlier, I tried dissectin' one. Those wirey feelers and legs was jammed in their brains and neck bones. There's neow way they could be alive, not like that."

"Hans, why the hell do you have to act like you're enjoying this?" Adlet demanded, not pleased.

Hans gave Adlet a blank look. "I'm always like this. Why're ya suddenly all grumpy?"

"Oh, never mind." Hans was right. He *was* always like that. But his nonchalance was wearing on Adlet's nerves.

"So what should we do?" asked Rolonia.

"About what?" said Dozzu.

"To save the people of the Dead Host!" Rolonia yelled, and a strange silence fell between them.

Hans, Chamo, and Nashetania all wore looks that said, *What are you talking about?* Mora, Dozzu, and Goldof seemed uncomfortable, and Fremy's eyes were downcast, as if she was at a loss.

"Unfortunately," began Dozzu, "there's no way to save them. Or there may be a way, but I don't know it."

"Th-that can't…!" Rolonia stood up. "Then…what do we have to do to find a way? Can we find out once we reach the Temple of Fate?"

"Hardly. Rolonia, the Dead Host have no connection at all with the Temple of Fate."

"Then we'll have to ask Tgurneu or some other fiend—"

Dozzu shook its head, cutting her off.

Mora grabbed Rolonia by the edges of her armor and forced her to sit. "Sit down, Rolonia. We must consider our course of action now."

"But that's what I was—"

Mora ignored her and addressed Dozzu. "How might we defeat the Dead Host, Dozzu?"

"All of the corpses will be disabled if we can defeat specialist number nine, the one in charge. The parasites themselves don't have individual minds. Specialist number nine controls them by producing a unique sound wave."

"And once we defeat specialist number nine, what will happen to the Dead Host?"

"I should expect they'd all die soon after, in less than fifteen minutes."

"Just as I thought," Mora murmured. Rolonia tried to speak again, but Mora gestured for her to remain silent.

"Have my…? Have the people of my home village been turned into part of the Dead Host, too?" Adlet asked.

Dozzu replied with some trepidation. "I don't know anything about your home village. However, according to my comrades' reports…all of the humans in the Howling Vilelands have joined the Dead Host."

Adlet felt like he'd been punched in the head. He closed his eyes.

"Keep yourself together, Adlet," said Mora.

"Are they all…dead, then? All of them?"

Dozzu nodded sadly.

"Auhhhhh…"

Meanwhile, one particular member of the Dead Host was wandering about the forest. Its mouth was an open, faintly moaning hollow. Head swinging back and forth, it staggered along. The body belonged to a man nearing twenty. He was tall, with long, disheveled red hair. He was covered in old scars that suggested horrible past abuse.

Just like the others of the Dead Host, this body was wandering through the forest searching for living things. If he found anything alive in the forest, aside from his fellows, he would immediately kill it.

But there was one thing about this corpse that differentiated it from the others: it was alive.

How long do I have to wander around this forest? he wondered.

He couldn't move his own body; he was entirely controlled by the parasite attached to the back of his neck. His head was turned and his body forced to walk and fight as the parasite commanded. He couldn't move a single muscle of his own free will. No matter how much he prayed, his arms, legs, fingers, mouth, and even his eyeballs would not obey his commands. The parasite owned him entirely.

All he could do was listen, watch, and think.

I feel like I'm going crazy, he thought. He'd been compelled to walk around the forest like this for days now. His entire body had reached the extremes of exhaustion; he couldn't even feel his legs anymore. But still the parasite on his neck continued to mercilessly exploit his body.

Don't sleep. Don't pass out. Keep it together, he prayed over and over in his mind. He couldn't let himself lose consciousness. There was something he had to do. He had a duty to fulfill, even if it cost his life. *I will...meet the Braves of the Six Flowers,* he repeated over and over in his head, his consciousness dim. *I'll meet them and tell them...about the Black Barrenbloom.*

He knew the truth about the Black Barrenbloom, the most horrific hieroform ever created by Tgurneu's hand, and he also knew that he was the only one who could tell the Braves about it. *At this rate, they'll all die. The power of the Black Barrenbloom will kill every last one of them. Don't pass out. If you don't tell them about the Black Barrenbloom, the world is over.*

The parasite drove him to keep walking. All he could do now was pray to stay aware and nothing more. *Hurry up and come, Braves! I have to tell you about the Black Barrenbloom!*

His name was Rainer Milan, born in a small village named Hasna in Warlow, the Land of White Lakes.

He was Adlet Mayer's childhood friend.

*   *   *

When Rainer was small, Tgurneu had come to his village, deceived the people there, and moved them all to the Howling Vilelands. The only ones to oppose this plan had been Rainer and his first crush, Schetra, who had lived in the house next door. The villagers killed Schetra, and Rainer took Schetra's little brother, Adlet, by the hand and fled. But the villagers caught up with them. Rainer helped Adlet escape but was very badly wounded in the process.

The next time Rainer opened his eyes, he was already on the way to the Howling Vilelands. The one who had treated Rainer's life-threatening wounds had been Tgurneu.

Tgurneu petted the injured boy's head and told him kindly that soon the human realms would be annihilated, and they would have a new world ruled by the Evil God. But it didn't want to kill all humans. Tgurneu had said that it would gladly welcome anyone who wanted to live together with fiends and serve the Evil God. Just like the other humans, Rainer believed it—for a time. But upon reflection, he just couldn't understand how he could have fallen for such a transparent lie.

They implanted Rainer's body with a parasite that nullified the Evil God's toxin and then took him to a village for humans within the Howling Vilelands. The villagers quickly found out that Tgurneu had deceived them. There were only three kinds of humans in the Howling Vilelands: slaves, cattle, and guinea pigs.

The women able to give birth were the cattle, forced to bear children. The babies would quickly die of the toxin and then be fed to the fiends. The men were made slaves. They grew crops to feed the human population, and the fiends forced them to construct fences and forts for the counterattack against the Braves of the Six Flowers. Occasionally, their captors would collect a few of the cattle and the slaves, and they would never be seen again. Most of them were able-bodied and in good health, so rumor had it they were experimental subjects for creating weapons. The elderly, who were of no use at all, the fiends simply ate.

The village where the humans lived was hell.

They all said, *Why didn't we understand that Tgurneu tricked us?* In hindsight, it was clear enough that it was all lies, wasn't it? And if it was a lie that the fiends would welcome humans, then their story about humanity being doomed to destruction had to be a lie, too.

Tgurneu had told them that the Saint of the Single Flower's powers would soon vanish, the seal upon the Evil God would be removed entirely, and that once that happened, the Braves of the Six Flowers would no longer be able to kill it. But the fiends were still champing at the bit to defeat the six heroes and preparing for their battle, so that was clearly a lie.

In this environment of inescapable despair, they all eventually stopped thinking about it. All except for Rainer.

Ever since Rainer was little, he'd wanted to be one of the Braves of the Six Flowers. He'd fallen in love with the stories the visiting minstrels told. He'd admired Heroic King Folmar from the first generation. He'd cried for Pruka, Saint of Fire, who had put her life on the line to save her allies. He'd raged at the cowardly trap the fiends had set for Lowie, Saint of Wind and second generation Brave; the exploits of Hayuha, Saint of Time, had set his heart aflutter. Young Rainer had made up his mind that he, too, would become a Brave and save the world.

No one understood his dream. His parents would hit him upside the head and admonish him not to say such stupid things. His only friend, Adlet, never rejected the idea, but didn't believe in it, either. Schetra was exasperated with him, calling him hopeless. But Rainer never abandoned his resolve. He knew he had no talent for the sword, but that didn't shake his focus. Even after Tgurneu tricked him and cast him into the hell of the Howling Vilelands, he was still determined.

As the fiends whipped him, as he labored as their slave, Rainer was always waiting for his chance. He was going to get out—and he would tell the world about the captives in the Howling Vilelands, and then eventually, he'd gain the power to save them and come back. For a long, long time, he waited for his chance.

Then suddenly, one year ago, that chance came.

*   *   *

Repulsively enough, there was one human who cooperated with the fiends of his own free will. He received ever so slightly better food than the other humans, along with the right to take women as he pleased and whip the others. That was all it took for him to cooperate with Tgurneu, and sometimes, he would abuse the humans even worse than the fiends did. This man was given the duty of selecting people from the village to be experimental subjects and taking them to the location Tgurneu indicated. Only he, among all the humans, had a map of the Howling Vilelands.

One night, Rainer sneaked into the man's house. Since Rainer was allowed nothing that could be used as a weapon, he carried a string he'd braided from hair. He approached the man quietly from behind and strangled him with the string, right when the man was in the middle of tormenting a woman Tgurneu had given him. Rainer stole the man's map and swore the woman to secrecy about his escape. With some meager rations in hand, he left the village.

From the map, Rainer determined he was on the plains located in the center of the Howling Vilelands. He would cut across the Plain of Cropped Ears and enter the Cut-Finger Forest. Once out of the forest, he'd be in the Ravine of Spitten Blood, and if he could make it through, he'd be out of the Howling Vilelands and back in the human realms.

Without any sleep or rest, Rainer headed eastward. He couldn't stop, even at night. If he did, his pursuers were bound to find him quickly. He certainly couldn't use any lights—that would be suicide. He walked the plains in the dark, tapping the ground with a wooden stick. Many times, he stumbled and fell. His feet were sliced up on the sharp rocks and oozed blood. But Rainer didn't stop.

On the dawn of the second day of his escape, he heard someone calling out to him from somewhere out on the plains. He held his breath and hunkered down.

"Someone's there...right? Could you...come over here?"

At first, he thought it was the fiends looking for him. He couldn't let his guard down, even though he could tell the voice was human—that didn't change his position as a fugitive.

"Did you escape? You did...right? Come over here...I need your help." It sounded like an old woman. Cautiously, Rainer walked over. In the middle of the plains was a tiny hut packed with bodies. An old woman lay among them. "If you're human...then listen to me. It's not me...I need you to help. It's...the world." Careful not to make a sound, Rainer approached her.

"Could you believe the word of an old woman you've never met before?" she asked.

"...Depends on what you have to say."

"Would you believe me if I told you this strange old woman is trying to save the world?" Though hesitant, Rainer nodded. "My name is... well, that doesn't matter. I escaped from the Fainting Mountains. I fled all by myself from the Temple of Fate that Tgurneu built. Please, tell someone..."

"Tell them what?"

"About the Black Barrenbloom."

The old woman told him that her name was Nio Glassta. Once, she had been an acolyte who served at the Temple of Illusion and aspired to Sainthood.

She had been an exceptional student, diligently learning hieroglyphs and the means of controlling Saint's powers, and she had worked hard for the temple. Fate had not blessed her, and she was not chosen as the Saint of Illusion. Instead, she was entrusted with the management of the lands the temple owned, and she helped with temple administration. She never married or had children, but one could say she'd had a good life. While not as prosperous as nobles or great merchants, she had a fairly comfortable lifestyle. Nio had believed her life would remain uneventfully ordinary to the end—until, in her mid-fifties, Torleau, Saint of Medicine, told her that she'd contracted an incurable illness.

Nio wallowed in fear of her death. She'd led a prosperous life, so that should be enough, right? Death comes to all; there's no helping that. But the classic consolations didn't do a thing for her. She was simply terrified of death. Not because she had something to protect or because she had a goal in life. She was just irrationally terrified of mortality.

She prayed. She'd give anything in exchange, she'd make any sacrifice, if she could just live one day, one second longer. Given time, she most likely would have come to accept her death, as is humans' wont when their time comes. But before that could happen, Tgurneu paid her a visit.

In the middle of the night, the kindly smiling fiend had come to stand beside Nio's bed, where she slept alone. And then, without even giving her the time to be surprised, it greeted her with a smile. "Good evening. I apologize for coming at such a late hour." Then it continued. "The powers of fiends could help you survive this. If you're capable enough, you might even attain eternal life. Will you come with me?"

Nio accepted Tgurneu's proposal without question. Her fear of following a fiend was nothing at all compared to the terror of her impending death.

Nio Glassta left the temple. Under Tgurneu's direction, she carefully erased all traces of her departure. The Saint of Illusion and the acolytes must surely have believed that she had a peaceful death off in some village somewhere.

Tgurneu had Nio implanted with a parasite that would nullify the Evil God's toxins, and she journeyed to the Howling Vilelands, whereupon she was guided to the Temple of Fate in a place known as the Fainting Mountains. She followed after Tgurneu through the massive shrine before descending the stairs down, down, down to the underground.

"I want you to create a hieroform for me," said Tgurneu. "You must doubt that such a thing is possible, since you're not a Saint. But I know that even one who is not a Saint can create a hieroform—if she steals a Saint's powers." The fiend smiled. "The Saints are foolish. They've been studying the Spirits' powers over the course of thousands of years and never figured it out? It's laughable."

A technique to steal a Saint's power? How could a fiend know something that even the Elder of All Heavens Temple didn't? Nio was skeptical, but still, lengthening her own life was more important to her.

"Once you use up all of a Saint's powers, they more or less become an empty husk. It's quite the task to wring all their powers from them, too. But I believe that with your help, I can create the hieroform I seek." Deep underground, Tgurneu opened a heavy iron door. In the center of a vast room was a simple stone chair. A mummy sat on it.

It was a pitiful-looking corpse, just skin stretched over bones, restrained to the chair by chains upon chains, bound so heavily the body underneath could hardly be seen. Over the chains, the body was dressed in a simple, fresh robe. On its completely bald head was a decoration made of real flowers. The mummy's head was drooping, its eyes and mouth closed. But Nio got the feeling it might move at any time. It emitted such an overwhelmingly intimidating aura, far more powerful than what she sensed in Tgurneu beside her, or even Leura, Saint of Sun, said to be the strongest alive. Nio's knees began quivering.

"Allow me to introduce you. This is the Saint of the Single Flower, the one you all worship. She's still alive—though she's essentially a hollow shell now. After decades of searching, I finally managed to invite her in."

"The Saint of the Single Flower..." Nio murmured. "But I thought... she'd left no body..."

"Of course she left no body. She's not dead," Tgurneu said, laughing. "She made a genuinely foolish decision. If she'd meekly accepted her fate of death, I'd never have managed to use her like this. Well, it's thanks to that that I can achieve my goal, though."

Nio didn't understand what Tgurneu was talking about, but she could appreciate one thing: She was now involved in momentous events that would influence the fate of the world. But she could no longer turn back.

"Now then, you're going to steal the power of the Saint of the Single Flower for me. I've gathered about twenty other researchers, too. Whichever of you demonstrates the most exceptional ability, I will warmly welcome as a fiend." From behind, Tgurneu gently stroked Nio's cheek. "How about it? We fiends can live over a thousand years. We will never die, as long as the Evil God exists. Come on, don't you want to be free of the fear of death?"

Nio was trapped by both the utter certainty that Tgurneu would kill her if she refused and the temptation of its offer.

One of Tgurneu's subordinates gave her a fiend's power to cure her sickness. For the next ten years, she immersed herself in the research as ordered. If she failed to devote herself to it entirely, she would have died. Caught between guilt and the fear of death, she created the Black Barrenbloom.

The old woman didn't tell Rainer everything. All she told him, in hushed tones, was that she'd been foolish, that she'd met the Saint of the Single Flower, and that she'd been driven to create a hieroform.

"But then I saw one of the fiends looking at me and drooling. That's how I knew we were just food to them."

She said that by something near a miracle, she had managed to escape from the Temple of Fate. She had secretly stolen from the Saint of the Single Flower some of the power to reject the fate of death and then killed herself. The fiends had then carried her to this storehouse for bodies, and she had succeeded in reviving herself with her stolen ability.

Rainer didn't get what all of this meant. What was the power of the Spirit of Fate? What did it mean to steal the power of a Saint?

But the old woman continued her story. "Tgurneu and the other fiends probably think I'm long dead. None of them will have figured out that I'm talking to you right now." She went on, but to Rainer's eyes, it looked as though she was already dying. "I finished the Black Barrenbloom. I was a fool." She clenched her teeth. "Tgurneu is the worst kind of liar. If I'd known this would happen... If I'd only known!" Tears rose in her eyes. "No...perhaps...I would have done all of this anyway."

"Tell me, what is this...Black Barrenbloom?"

The old woman clung to him. "Yes, I'll tell you. That's what I survived this for. There's no hope for me now. I can't go anywhere, not with

these legs. Take this information and run to the continent. See the King of
Gwenvaella, or if not him, then go to All Heavens Temple. Tell this to the
Braves of the Six Flowers."

"I understand. So tell me."

"They made us create the unthinkable. Even I had no idea just how
terrible it was."

"Just tell me! What is the Black Barrenbloom?!"

"Listen closely." The old woman quietly began explaining, and
Rainer learned the true nature of the Black Barrenbloom. By the time she
finished, his face was pale. He had to tell people, no matter what. If he
didn't, the world would be destroyed.

When the old woman had told him all she could, she gently held
her finger out to him. "I'll give you divine protection, the power I stole
from the Saint of the Single Flower. It's not much, but with this power,
you can repel your fate to die." He could just faintly see something like a
tiny flower petal on the old woman's fingertip. She touched it to Rainer,
and then the petal was gone. "Don't rely on this. It's just the dregs of the
power I stole from the Saint of the Single Flower, and she had only dregs
to begin with. I doubt it'll be any use to you at all."

Once the old woman was done telling him everything, she lay down.
Her death was drawing near. "That fecal slime...Tgurneu. You dungpile!
You said you'd let me live..." Finally, she breathed her last. Rainer was
sure she'd told him all this not to protect the world, but most likely as
revenge on Tgurneu for deceiving her.

Rainer made certain that no traces of his visit remained within the
hut and then quietly left. Now he had one more reason to survive—not for
his own sake, but for the sake of the world.

After that, Rainer kept walking. But once he reached the end of the plains,
he came to a ravine so massive it defied imagination. There was no end in
sight in either direction, and the bottom was seething hot with no way to
cross. And no matter how much he walked and walked, he couldn't find a
bridge.

He despaired. This ravine wasn't on the map. He hadn't known that his chart was a hundred years old. A century ago, Cargikk's Canyon was only half done, and not yet drawn on it. There was no way someone like Rainer could cross a ravine created to block the Braves of the Six Flowers.

As Rainer was searching for a bridge, a fiend on watch discovered him. Helpless, he was captured, and they carried him to a cave near the Fainting Mountains. There, they planted a parasite on the back of his neck. Now one of the Dead Host, he was abandoned on the cave floor.

"Auhhhh..."

A year had passed since then.

Rainer figured that the reason he was still conscious was because of the old woman's gift to him, the power of the Saint of the Single Flower that would allegedly stave off his death, just a little. Without it, he probably would have ended up a mere walking corpse like all the rest. But even the borrowed power wouldn't free his body. He was only just barely surviving, and the parasite still controlled his body entirely.

All that happened as he lay in that cave was the passage of time. Rainer endured and endured the endless inactivity. For the first few days, he thought he'd go crazy. Many times, he prayed for them to kill him. He wished he'd never even met that old woman if it meant he would end up feeling like this. He'd rather let go and cease thinking at all.

But Rainer endured the torture. Only one thing carried him through it: He'd risked his life to save a friend, and that friend was still alive in the human realms. Rainer lived for Adlet.

Adlet was a hopeless case. He was smart, in his own way, but he had no backbone, he was physically weak, and he was a horrible coward. He had to be still alive out there, living in fear of the Evil God's revival. Rainer was the only one who could protect him. Yes, he was a Brave who would protect Adlet. He didn't have a Crest of the Six Flowers, but he was still a Brave.

The Heroic King Folmar had overcome even greater trials than this.

Hayuha, Saint of Time, had stood up to more formidable enemies. *I'll over-come this, too,* he repeated to himself silently, over and over.

Are the Braves of the Six Flowers already here in the Howling Vilelands? Rainer wondered as he was driven to walk around the forest. Judging from the situation, he should assume that the battle between the fiends and the Braves of the Six Flowers had already begun. The Dead Host had been released into this forest three days earlier. It had to be to fight the Braves. He couldn't think of any other reason the fiends would deploy them.

He wondered where the human heroes were. Were they heading for this forest? Or would they bypass it and journey down some other path? Or maybe…the power of the Black Barrenbloom had killed them all already. *Please, Braves of the Six Flowers, be alive,* he prayed in his heart.

But even if they were alive, how could he tell them about the Black Barrenbloom? The parasite controlled his body. He couldn't run to them. Even if he could get near them, he couldn't communicate.

Only one option remained: The Braves of the Six Flowers had to save him and remove the parasite from him so he could speak. There was no other way.

Rainer didn't know anything about the nature of this parasite, and he didn't know if removal was possible, either. But the Braves of the Six Flowers would possess unusual abilities, and they would also have Saints among them with powers that surpassed human knowledge. Rainer believed that with their powers, it would be possible for them to remove the parasite and rescue him. But what could he do to make such a feat possible for them?

The Braves of the Six Flowers didn't know he was alive. They didn't know he had information on the Black Barrenbloom, either. And the Dead Host was a weapon made to kill the Six Braves. The Dead Host might have all been human once, but the Braves would surely disregard that and slaughter them all anyway. Of course, that included Rainer.

And even if they didn't want to kill the Dead Host, would the Braves save them? They might consider it, but they also might not have the resources.

The chosen six were in the middle of a mortal struggle. They might give up on saving the Dead Host and just wipe them out, or they could dash right past them and avoid the fight. If they did, Rainer wouldn't be able to tell them about the Black Barrenbloom. Then what should he do?

He had one choice: communicate to the Six Braves that he was still alive, that there was a hieroform called the Black Barrenbloom, and that he knew about it. But was it possible? His body wouldn't move, and he couldn't talk, either. Could he do it?

Still, he wouldn't give up. Even without autonomous movement, even as a living corpse, he believed hope must surely remain.

Please, Braves of the Six Flowers . . . he called out to them in his mind. *Saint of the Single Flower, Spirit of Fate: hear my wish. My life doesn't matter. Once I've told them about the Black Barrenbloom, it won't matter if I die. Just let me meet the Braves.*

In the hut a little ways removed from the Dead Host wandering the forest, the Braves of the Six Flowers were all silent. Adlet was staring at the ground, lips trembling. What Dozzu had just said repeated over and over in his mind.

Every single one of the people from his village had been forced into the Dead Host.

"Addy, are you okay?" Rolonia drew near him, examining his expression.

It's okay, I'm the strongest man in the world, Adlet tried to say with a grin. But his mouth wouldn't move, and he couldn't even summon a smile.

Chapter 3

Adlet's
Indecision

Memories of Adlet's home whirled around in his mind: the old woman who always shared her sweets with him; the old man who lived at the edge of town and always scolded Adlet and Rainer for getting up to mischief; the village elder who had taught Adlet how to make cheese. Everything he remembered bubbled to the surface.

He thought he'd fully processed that they were already dead. He believed he'd given up on ever seeing them again. But now he was so shocked, he couldn't stop trembling. Honestly, in his heart of hearts, he'd still been holding on to hope. He'd just been trying to avoid examining his real emotions.

"Addy...snap out of it..."

Don't worry. I'm the strongest man in the world, he tried to say in reply. But the words just wouldn't form.

"What's wrong? Are some people you know among the Dead Host?" Nashetania asked with concern, unaware of the situation.

"Dozzu...is there really no way...to save the people made into the Dead Host?" Adlet asked.

Dozzu seemed confused, but it replied, "I don't know of any way it could be done, at the very least, and it doesn't seem likely."

Is that really true? Adlet wondered. He hadn't seen these living corpses personally, and he still didn't know anything about the Dead Host. He found himself wondering if there was some way to save them, maybe, if they could do anything with Mora's or Rolonia's powers.

"If we defeat specialist number nine...will all the Dead Host die?" He'd already asked that question once, but he had to make sure. Dozzu nodded.

"...Meowbe this is a harsh thing to say, but we don't have time for grievin'," said Hans. "We're fightin' against the clock. We've gotta kill specialist number nine right now and head to the Temple of Fate."

"H-how can you say that, Hans?!" Rolonia huffed, standing up. "W-we have to think about how we can save the Dead Host! Investigating the Black Barrenbloom is important, too, but h-h-human lives are... i-i-important, too!" Rolonia raised her voice, stammering and unused to asserting her opinions.

"Quit yer yellin', Rolonia. The fiends'll find us," Hans stated coldly. Silence fell in the hut once more.

Hesitantly, Fremy said, "It's difficult to say this, Rolonia, but...you're the only one entertaining that idea."

"...Huh?"

Adlet understood. Hans, Chamo, Dozzu, and Nashetania saw the Dead Host purely as enemies. Mora and Goldof felt some trepidation about killing those who had once been human, but didn't feel obligated to save them, either. Fremy had said nothing, so Adlet didn't know about her. But he doubted she was considering saving them like Rolonia was.

"You can't... But...but...they're humans!"

"Rolonia, they're not humans anymore. Just walking corpses," stated Dozzu.

"But you just said their hearts were beating—" Rolonia surveyed the group and finally realized that nobody was on her side. Then she looked at Adlet, as if begging for help. "Addy...um...what do you think?"

Adlet couldn't reply. *Let's save the Dead Host* came halfway out his throat. But he couldn't say it. Hans was right. They were fighting against time. They had to solve the riddle of the Black Barrenbloom before Tgurneu arrived at the Temple of Fate. They couldn't afford to waste time.

The Braves of the Six Flowers fought to defend the whole world. He couldn't give anyone special treatment, not even people from his home village. That would only be his personal bias. A leader had to be impartial. He couldn't disgrace himself by giving in to emotion and leading his allies into danger like Mora and Goldof had.

But still...

"I'm sorry. Let me think about it." He fled, standing up to walk into the inner room of the hut. On his way out, his eyes met with Fremy's. She was clearly worried. "Hey, Fremy... Did you know...what happened to the people from my village?"

"When Tgurneu cast me out, some humans were still alive. I suspected they might have been killed, but I was afraid you might lose hope, so I couldn't bring myself to tell you."

"...Oh." Adlet went into the other room and sat down in a corner. Alone, he mulled it all over.

The answer was obvious. The most important thing was to learn about the Black Barrenbloom at the Temple of Fate. They had to kill specialist number nine and the Dead Host and make a beeline for the temple. But was there no other way? Couldn't they save the Dead Host and find out about the Black Barrenbloom, too?

They couldn't simply avoid the Dead Host and go straight to the Temple of Fate. That would just mean they'd fight the human captives there. It would make searching through the temple to find the truth impossible. Could they find out about the Black Barrenbloom some other way? No, that was impossible, too. This was their only clue.

Ignoring both the Black Barrenbloom and the Temple of Fate and just heading off to defeat the Evil God wasn't an option, either. Adlet knew—instinctively, not rationally—that the Temple of Fate was their watershed moment. The answer was clear: They had to kill the Dead Host.

So why was he wasting time dithering here? *Aren't you the strongest man in the world?*

"...Damn it." Adlet lifted his head. He noticed something written in a corner of the room. He went up to the note to read it.

This is the end for me. Forgive me, Schetra. Forgive me, Schetra. You were right. We were foolish. Forgive us, Schetra. Forgive me for killing you. The writing was familiar to him. It was the hand of the village elder, the one who had taught Adlet to make cheese.

"You idiot...what use are regrets now? Why did you have to..." He held his head in his hands. So the villagers had regretted their misdeeds after all. They'd been racked with guilt for killing his sister and Rainer. "Give me back my sister...give back Rainer...you stupid bastards..."

Adlet had missed the people of his home village, but he'd also loathed them, unable to forgive them for what they'd done. But now that he knew they'd repented for their sins, he just couldn't hold on to his hatred.

"You stupid bastards..."

Once Adlet was out of the room, the rest of the Braves went silent.

This is worrying, thought Mora. This issue with his hometown had no easy resolution. No one could relieve his pain or support him. This wound in his soul would never heal.

"Hey neow, don't worry about him. That guy always gets back on his feet." Hans smiled.

Mora sighed. *I hope you're right.*

"This ain't no strategy meetin' without him. Let's take a break."

"But you're also our leader," countered Mora.

"I said I'd leave it up to Adlet. I'll keep watch meowtside." Hans left the hut.

Mora felt sorry for Adlet, but now was not the time to be worrying about the Dead Host. If Tgurneu discovered the Braves so close to the Temple of Fate, it would send its whole army to the Fainting Mountains. Once that happened, the Six Braves would have to fight a hybrid force of Dead Host and fiends. They had to take out all of the Dead Host here and now, whatever the cost. Everything about the situation said that was their sole option. They had to give up on saving them.

"Um, guys…what happened to Adlet?" Nashetania asked the group.

"You don't need to know," Fremy replied.

"That's mean. Don't leave me out." Nashetania pouted.

"Was that supposed to be funny?"

"Not at all! I'm concerned about him, too," the former seventh complained, sounding a little angry. It was baffling how she could so brazenly make such a claim when just four days earlier she'd been trying to kill him.

"Tgurneu took away the people of his home village," said Fremy. "He wants to save them, but the situation won't allow it. That's what I've gathered."

"Oh…this must be difficult for him, then, but there's nothing we can do about it." Nashetania looked down sadly. "Shall we leave that aside and think about what comes next? Specialist number nine is a powerful enemy. We need to come up with a plan we know can kill it—and do so quickly."

"How can you talk about this, Nashetania?!" Rolonia seemed angry, which was unusual for her. She'd become terribly emotional after learning about the Dead Host.

"I-I'm sorry. Did I say something to offend you…?" Nashetania was flummoxed. She didn't appear to understand why Rolonia was so mad.

Mora thought she was being a little insensitive. Adlet was grieving over the loss of the people of his home village and racking his brains trying to find a way to save them. Talking about the Dead Host with him in earshot would only hurt him more. Hans had tried to be considerate of his feelings by interrupting the discussion, too.

"I'm sorry, Rolonia. I didn't mean to make you angry," Nashetania said, flustered. Rolonia, having lost a target for her frustration, went quiet.

They waited for a while, but Adlet still didn't emerge from the other room.

"Um…Fremy. Don't you know anything about that specialized weapon number nine?" Rolonia asked her.

"I'm sorry," Fremy replied. "I know it controls humans to make them its weapons, but I don't what its powers are specifically."

Mora interrupted their conversation. "Rolonia, you studied under Atreau Spiker, the fiend specialist. Did you learn nothing about it from him?"

"No. Even Master Atreau doesn't know everything." Next, Rolonia turned to Dozzu. "Dozzu, is there really no way to save the people of the Dead Host?"

Quietly, Nashetania said, "Rolonia, I think you should stop talking about that."

"Why?"

"Because it's impossible."

"We don't know that for sure! If we just look, we might find a way."

"The chances are too low. Besides, the attempt would only cause more problems for us. Searching for a way would only get us all killed."

"What you're saying is…n-not right. I mean, peoples' lives are on the line…" Rolonia said.

But Nashetania just shook her head. "Isn't victory more important? Aren't your lives more important? Are you sure you have your priorities in order, Rolonia?"

"You're talking about human lives… You can't ask which is more… important…" Rolonia's lips trembled, and then her voice rose. "And please think of Addy's feelings, too. I want to help him! These people matter so much to him! They're his fellow villagers, the people he grew up with! How could we not help him save them?!"

"*Hrmeow.* Be quiet, Rolonia," Hans scolded her from outside the hut.

Nashetania's expression changed then. She regarded Rolonia with an icy look, the kind she'd never revealed back when she'd been pretending to be one of the Braves. "I, and Dozzu, and all of you—we're fighting for the world. Not for Adlet."

"But—that's just heartless!" Rolonia protested. "Can't you understand how he must feel, being forced to fight the people he loves?!"

Nashetania gazed up at the ceiling for a bit, reflecting. "It's sad. It's awfully, awfully tragic. But nothing can be done."

Rolonia glared at her, arms trembling. Alarmed, Mora stood up. Rolonia was angry. Mora had known her for a long time, but she'd never seen her like this.

"We're weak," continued Nashetania, "and we cannot save everyone. If the Dead Host is beyond help, then we simply must be rational about this."

"Nashetania...don't you...want to create a world where...e-everyone, human and fiend, can be happy? Don't you ever feel like...h-h-helping people?"

Her tone cruel and cold, Nashetania replied, "No. Not right now. I won't hesitate to make any sacrifice needed to realize my ambition—no matter who gets hurt, and no matter who dies."

Rolonia clenched one hand into a fist. Mora grabbed her arm from behind, and Rolonia whirled around with a yell, raising her other hand. "Let me go!"

A loud slap landed on Mora's cheek. Even she was speechless.

"Ah... s-s-sor..." Rolonia began trembling like a leaf.

Rubbing her cheek, Mora said kindly, "Calm down. I'm not upset that you hit me."

"Rolonia," said Nashetania, "I *am* your enemy. But right now, the only thing on my mind is assisting you Braves. I'm saying this for your sake and for Adlet's."

Hans's voice filtered in from outside the hut. "What're y'all doin'? Princess, you come meowt here for a bit. Rolonia, you calm down, too."

Nashetania sighed and left the hut. Wordlessly, Mora watched her go.

Mora fundamentally agreed with Nashetania—but she could also sense the depths of the darkness in Nashetania's heart that underpinned her logic. Hans was a callous man, too, but he was kind enough to divine Rolonia's and Adlet's feelings and make allowances for them. Nashetania, however, lacked even that much.

Nashetania had admonished them not to let their feelings jerk them around. But she had used Goldof's emotions for the sake of her own survival, hadn't she? Not only was she ruthless, she was terribly selfish. *She's still an inexcusable enemy to the Braves*, thought Mora. *What is Goldof thinking?* How could he swear loyalty to and risk his life to protect a person like her? Mora couldn't comprehend his state of mind.

"Hey, Rolonia. Mind if Chamo gives you a piece of her mind?" Chamo said to Rolonia, who was standing there, downcast. "Not to take the princess's side or anything, but you don't get how bad this is, do you?"

Rolonia was silent.

"We don't know when we might die. And if we do, it's the end for the world. Don't you get that? Chamo does feel bad for those Dead Host people. But we've got bigger fish to fry."

Rolonia didn't reply. Outside, Hans and Nashetania were engaged in a discussion about something, but they couldn't hear what exactly from inside the hut. Adlet still did not emerge from the other room.

Meanwhile, Rainer was in the forest, inclining his ears to the sounds around him, waiting for the Braves of the Six Flowers. What would they do? Would they come to mow down the Dead Host, or would they ignore them and head straight to the Weeping Hearth?

He wouldn't let that happen. He'd make sure the Braves noticed him. He'd convey to them that he was still alive with information he had to pass on to them. But depending on what the Six Braves did, the trap could run its course before he could do anything.

If there was even a single person among the Braves of the Six Flowers who would try to save the Dead Host, then there was hope. He could communicate to them that he was here. But if no one tried to free them—then most likely, it would all be over.

Adlet sat hugging his knees. He could hear the dispute in the other room. Rolonia didn't get it. Nashetania wasn't the one hurting him—Rolonia was the one doing that.

He just couldn't think of anything. He couldn't draw up a plan to save the Dead Host and also learn about the Black Barrenbloom. No matter how he racked his brains, nothing came to mind. At this point, he was just struggling to bring himself to the cold, hard decision that he couldn't save his people. He wanted to tell himself that there was no helping this, and Rolonia was ruining his efforts—though, of course, she surely didn't mean to hurt him.

"They...killed Schetra... They killed Rainer...," Adlet muttered. They'd killed his sister and his friend. He tried to suppress his desire to deliver them from their plight by reminding himself, *This is retribution for their sins.* But a voice deep in his heart was telling him, *They were just deceived by Tgurneu. Tgurneu was the instigator. It wasn't their fault.*

And then he thought, *Isn't Adlet Mayer the strongest man in the world?* Wasn't he at the top because of his ability to protect his allies, defeat his enemies, and also manage to save the people of his village? Did a man who didn't even rise to that challenge really deserve the title of strongest in the world?

"Tgurneu..." The commander's face rose in his mind—the lizard face the fiend had worn when they'd first met. Tgurneu had anticipated that Adlet would suffer like this, hadn't it? It had been expecting the Six Braves to waste time trying to save the people of the Dead Host. Adlet could imagine that sneering visage. He could practically see Tgurneu's contempt for Adlet and his failure to muster the ruthlessness needed for victory.

"...That's right." Adlet stood up and returned to the room where the others waited. Every face turned to him at once. "You guys done fighting?" Adlet asked.

Mora replied, "Were you listening, Adlet?"

"Well, I could hear."

Rolonia was crouched down in the corner of the room, watching his face closely.

"So what shall we do, then, Adlet?" asked Dozzu.

"We're gonna defeat specialist number nine and head to the Temple of Fate. We won't save the Dead Host," Adlet declared firmly. "Hans, Nashetania, come back in. We're resuming our strategy meeting," he said, and the pair returned the hut.

The allies sat in a circle with the map in the center. Rolonia was the only one watching Adlet, silently saying, *I can't believe you.* "No...Addy..."

"Rolonia," Adlet rebuked, his tone harsher than usual, "give up on the Dead Host. There's nothing we can do. Right now our only goal is to go to the Temple of Fate and find out what the Black Barrenbloom is."

"But—"

"Don't give me that." Rolonia bit her lip. Adlet continued. "You're too kind. Normally, that would be fine, but right now, your sympathy is getting in the way. Just do what you're told!"

"But—!" Rolonia yelled.

She really is kind, Adlet thought, watching her. She truly felt compassion for the Dead Host from the bottom of her heart and longed to rescue them.

"I..." She looked down. She was no longer the timid, cowardly Rolonia, the one who could do nothing but follow everyone else. She was brimming with anger and determination.

I've never seen that look in her eyes, Adlet thought, surprised. Very quickly, he realized he understood shockingly little about her.

"I'll try to find a way to save the people of the Dead Host," she said, "even if I have to do it by myself."

"Rolonia—"

"I won't ask for help from any of you. I won't cause trouble for you or anyone else. And I swear, I *swear* I won't die. So let me help them."

"...No." Adlet shut her down with one word. "Listen to me. Don't cause any more trouble for the rest of us," he said, sitting down beside the others. With a glance of distress at Adlet, Rolonia plopped down a ways away.

I was too harsh, thought Adlet. He'd snapped at her because he couldn't shake off his own reservations. He was ashamed for taking it out on

Rolonia. She hadn't done anything wrong. But now, they had to focus on making it to the Temple of Fate.

"Sorry to make you guys wait. Let's hammer out our strategy. Well, you just leave it to me—the strongest man in the world," Adlet said, and smiled. But even he could tell that it wasn't his usual easygoing smile. His face felt stiff.

"Hmm. So they're not coming after all," Tgurneu muttered. It stood on the Plain of Cropped Ears, in the body of a tentacled wolf. If the Six Braves' plan was to cross the plains, Tgurneu's forces should have found them a while ago. "Maybe they went to the Temple of Fate after all. Or did they simply avoid the plains? Well, whichever it is, I suppose I should leave a watch here and move my main forces."

Beside Tgurneu, specialist number two replied, "Then I will send the message to the main forces to move north."

"They don't need to move quite yet. Just get them ready." Specialist number two nodded and then flapped into the sky.

As it flew, specialist number two considered the matter. Dozzu must have known about the Temple of Fate after all. That was quite a feat, considering Tgurneu's army had been strictly controlling the flow of information and had annihilated essentially Dozzu's entire faction.

Still, the information about the Black Barrenbloom couldn't possibly have gotten out. Even if the Braves of the Six Flowers made it to the Temple of Fate, nothing was there for them to learn. Tgurneu had killed every human who knew about the Black Barrenbloom, along with any fiends with the information who were even the slightest bit suspicious. There was an infinitesimal possibility that one of the humans had managed to get ahold of information on the Black Barrenbloom, which was why they had converted all of them to the Dead Host to prevent any leaks.

There was just no way that the Six Braves could have learned the truth. But despite all of these assurances, specialist number two's heart was uneasy. The Black Barrenbloom was the cornerstone of Tgurneu's forces. If the Braves of the Six Flowers were to find out about it, then victory, so close at hand, would be instantly out of their grasp.

Specialist number two remembered number nine, who was guarding the Temple of Fate. "Don't botch this, number nine. You absolutely must not let them make it to the Temple of Fate—just in case of that one-in-a-million chance," it muttered, flying on its way.

They finished their strategy meeting without any further hiccups, and the eight humans and one fiend left the hut. Adlet took the lead as they walked out.

Dozzu and Nashetania hadn't done anything at all suspicious during their discussion. Both of them had actively contributed opinions, and every one of their statements had been rational. No sign that the two of them were plotting anything right now. As usual, Adlet couldn't tell what Goldof was thinking. Even now that Nashetania had joined their group, he was still as taciturn as ever. None of the others did anything strange, either, or made any attempt to hinder the group from reaching the Temple of Fate—aside from Rolonia's initial insistence that they save the Dead Host. Of course, he wasn't going to start suspecting her because of that. That was just who she had always been.

That was when a soft noise came from beyond the thicket. Fremy raised her gun, and Adlet drew his sword.

"I'll go investigate," Nashetania said, and she ran off with Goldof chasing after her.

"It'd be a bad idea to leave those two alone," said Hans. Who knew what those two might start plotting together? He followed after them. The rest of the group decided to stop and wait for their return.

"Rolonia." Adlet addressed her where she stood beside him. "I'm gonna say this again to make it clear. Give up on the Dead Host. They're already gone. There's no way we could ever help them."

Rolonia was silent for a while, and then she quietly said, "...I'm sorry." Adlet looked away.

He understood. If he were really the strongest man in the world, then he'd have trusted himself to both protect his allies and save the Dead Host. It was because he felt Rolonia was blaming him for being too weak to pull it off. Though, of course, he knew full well she didn't feel that way at all.

Goldof knew that Nashetania wasn't actually going out to investigate the sound. It had probably just been a deer. She had something in mind and wanted to get him alone to talk. When the party had left the hut, Goldof had noticed her looking at him.

"I knew you'd come, Goldof. We have no time, so I'll make it short."

Goldof had crossed several thickets to find her waiting for him, as he'd expected. "...What is it, Your Highness?"

If this conversation was about keeping her safe, he would agree to her proposal without hesitation. But if her intention was to bring harm to any of the Six Braves, then he would obviously stop her. He knew Nashetania was willing to deceive him for the sake of her goals. He had to figure out what she was really after.

"Don't act so frightened. It's not the sinister plot you're imagining." Nashetania grinned. "Actually, I'm thinking I'll set a trap for Rolonia."

A shiver ran down Goldof's spine, and Nashetania began to whisper her plan to him.

Once Nashetania, Goldof, and Hans were back with the group, the party continued on.

Trees covered the area to the east of the Fainting Mountains. From the top of a small hill, the group surveyed the adjacent woods and the mountain beyond it.

The terrain was terribly complex. The line of small ridges was forested in parts, and bald in others. On the northern side, a large ravine extended farther northward, while on the south, they could see a low, tree-covered mountain. On his map, Adlet penciled in the terrain visible from here. A path that looked as though it had been cut into the hillside ran through the precipitous Fainting Mountains, probably also blocked by the Dead Host.

For some time now, Adlet had been hearing a noise that sounded like the ill moaning in pain. It was rising from inside the woods, carried on the wind. It was the cries of the Dead Host.

That was when it came—a person shuffled out of the dead forest, swaying right and left, flailing its arms about as if it were swimming. Its head lolled forward and backward; the body didn't resemble a living person at all.

"...Mph," Rolonia whimpered and covered her mouth. Adlet, too, swallowed down his nausea. He'd killed many terrifying-looking fiends, but this foe was repulsive for completely different reasons.

"Let's kill it," Nashetania insisted, and she thrust her slim sword into the ground. Instantly, a blade sprouted at the corpse's feet, reaching up to its throat. But the next moment, the corpse leaped high to avoid it.

"!" Nashetania fired off a second blade right after the first, stabbing the corpse in midair. Goldof rushed up to the body to hide it. "To think it could evade my first strike... We can't underestimate this enemy," she mused, her expression somber.

"Dozzu," said Fremy, "Specialist number nine hasn't noticed yet that one of its corpses was killed, right?"

"No. It won't notice that anything strange has happened unless a corpse yells out to inform it," Dozzu answered her question. If specialist number nine had learned something was wrong, the Dead Host would have immediately converged on them. But the forest edge was still quiet, so Dozzu was probably right.

"All right, then we're carrying out our strategy as planned. You guys are all okay with this?" Adlet said, scanning his allies.

The goal of this battle was to kill specialist number nine, thus rendering the Dead Host helpless—but they didn't have much time. Once the fighting started, a messenger would probably run off to Tgurneu to bring their commander and its main forces to the Fainting Mountains. They didn't know where Tgurneu was, but they had half a day until the fiend arrived, at most. It would take them three hours to reach the Temple of Fate, no matter how fast they ran. If they took that into account, they had three hours tops to defeat specialist number nine.

Specialist number nine had to have a huge number of the Dead Host stationed around it in its defense. The Braves couldn't afford to waste all their time breaking through the fiend's guard to kill it. Once the enemy realized the Six Braves were coming, it was bound to focus on escape. They had to kill specialist number nine instantly beyond its guard of all the Dead Host, and the only way they could do that was to have Fremy snipe it from a distance.

"The tree trunks won't really get in the way. I can hit it," Fremy said, squeezing her gun.

But landing a sure shot on specialist number nine while it was surrounded by dozens of its slaves would be difficult, even for her. Number nine was a little larger than a human, a small target to snipe. And before the attempt, they'd have to get an understanding of its position That was where Mora came in. She could figure out where it was with her clairvoyance.

"I should have no issues using my powers from that low mountain to the south," she said.

The plan was simple. Mora and Fremy would be on standby on the smaller mountain south of the forest. Hans had already confirmed that the area, which was off the path that led to the Temple of Fate, was free of the Dead Host. Adlet's party would lure specialist number nine there, Mora would pin down its location with her abilities, and Fremy would shoot it. The problem was how they would herd their opponent over there.

The key player in this battle was Hans. He would charge into the mass of Dead Host alone and pretend to run away, thus creating a diversion on the far side of the forest from Mora. This plan would both distract number nine and reduce the number of enemies they'd have to deal with. If Hans could lure the Dead Host to the end of the ravine on the north side and then destroy the bridge there, it'd make their fight a lot easier.

The rest of them would charge in once they'd judged that specialist number nine's defenses had thinned. They'd chase it down, blocking every avenue of escape aside from the mountain, steer it to where Fremy and Mora would be lying in wait.

"Will you truly be all right by yourself, Hans? Shouldn't I or Nashetania accompany you?" said Dozzu.

Hans shook his head. "I don't need it. Speed's the name of the game for this diversion. None of y'all can keep up with me at full tilt. It's easier if I'm by meowself." He was right. He was by far the fastest of the group. Adlet or Goldof could probably keep up with him for a short while, but they'd never be able to maintain his speed for half an hour or more.

As for the cornerstone of their strategy, the operation to drive specialist number nine onto the mountain, Adlet had no choice but to play it by ear. If he planned out too many details, he wouldn't be able to adapt to unforeseen circumstances.

Once they had killed specialist number nine, they would continue straight on to the Temple of Fate. They'd all leave the forest, gather temporarily at a meeting point halfway up the mountain, and then make a beeline to their destination. If everything went according to plan, they'd reach the temple that night—though, of course, Adlet didn't expect that everything would go so well.

"I'll be takin' me some bombs, Adlet." Hans popped open Adlet's iron box without asking. He would need bombs not only to blow up the bridge, but also to lure the Dead Host with. He pulled out three bombs and one flash grenade and tucked them all into his jacket. Adlet had extra bombs, so he didn't mind, but the flash grenade he would miss. Still, he couldn't complain.

"If it's bombs you want, I can make as many as you need," Fremy said, but Hans shook his head.

"*Meow.* If yer the seventh, they'd just kill me."

"You're quite cautious for someone who thrives on peril."

"Mew got it. I like playin' it safe with my danger." Hans pulled some thin wire out of the iron box, too, and stuffed half of it into his clothes along with a few strings.

"What's that for?" Adlet asked.

"*Meow-hee.* Gonna make me a little contraption with these to catch the Dead Host's attention." Hans returned Adlet's iron box and then went up to Rolonia. "Don't ya be showin' 'em mercy," he said. He headed toward the forest, the first to leave the group. As he went, he said, "Adlet, watch meowt for the seventh."

Immediately after Hans disappeared into the forest, they heard the shrill screams of the Dead Host. The shrieks spread, and the woodland was suddenly in turmoil. Between the trees, Adlet could see flashes of Hans jumping from trunk to trunk. He had them right where he wanted them with his typical seemingly inhuman maneuvers. But the corpses' jumps were no less powerful as they sprang at the tree trunks, closing in on Hans in the air. Eventually, they all vanished from sight.

"The seventh, huh," Adlet muttered. It would be even harder to be ready for the seventh than to defeat specialist number nine.

Adlet was afraid of Dozzu and Nashetania, too, but he was prepared for their betrayal. He had to be careful of them, but they weren't as dangerous. The problem was the seventh. Getting to the bottom of this Black Barrenbloom would reveal the seventh, too, so the impostor was sure to act now. The faces of his allies rose in his mind as he planned how he might deal with each of them—so he could respond instantly, no matter who the seventh was.

What could he do if Hans were the seventh? Adlet honestly wasn't confident that he could prevent an assassination by him. He was good at sneaking up to his targets and strong enough to kill them in a single blow, so if Hans was the seventh, it'd be hard to keep everyone safe. Even worse, Hans was smart enough to see through any half-baked ploy to stop him. Frankly, it was risky as hell to allow Hans to go solo, but they had no choice if they wanted to reach the Temple of Fate as quickly as possible. Adlet had told Fremy and Mora to be on red alert if Hans approached them. He had also instructed Chamo to deploy her slave-fiends around the area and to inform him immediately if they discovered Hans. That was all Adlet could manage against him.

If Chamo was the seventh—it would be a disaster. Adlet didn't even want to think about it. They didn't have the manpower to fight both the Dead Host and her slave-fiends. If that happened, they'd have no choice but to get the hell out of there. Adlet would use every bomb he had to clear a way through and then slow down the slave-fiends with pain needles to guard their path of escape. Thinking about that potential fight gave him chills. *We could even die*, he thought.

If Fremy was the seventh, then the one in danger would be Mora with her. Adlet had already reminded Mora beforehand to keep on eye on her companion's behavior. He'd also secretly given her a flash grenade. If anything happened, she would use it to signal danger to Adlet's party.

The other threat from Fremy was her gun. She might pretend to target specialist number nine while actually aiming for their allies. When they approached the southern mountain, they'd have to watch out not only for the Dead Host, but also for Fremy.

Fremy could also disable Mora and target the group while they were embroiled in the fight. If that happened, Adlet wouldn't be able to do anything about it. He had no choice but to let Mora handle it if Fremy was the seventh.

And what if Rolonia was the seventh? She might seem less dangerous compared to the others, but conversely, that meant her course of action was eerily uncertain. Adlet just had to remain close to her at all times and keep an eye on her activities.

Adlet thought it was unlikely that Goldof was the seventh, but there was still the risk that he might join in on Dozzu and Nashetania's plot to target the Braves. Adlet had to keep a close watch on the fiend and princess.

The chances that Mora was the seventh were incredibly low, so Adlet hadn't come up with any countermeasures for her.

"Agh," he sighed. The task of suspecting his allies and preparing for the possibility of betrayal was wearing on his nerves. But he had to keep it up nonstop until they could identify the seventh.

In preparation for the worst, Adlet always kept one extra flash grenade and a smoke bomb. The plan was that if he set off both of them in the air at the same time, the operation was canceled, and the whole group was to retreat from the Fainting Mountains. They'd come up with an escape route and rendezvous point for just that occasion.

"Hans is fighting well. I'd expect no less." Mora gazed past the line of trees. The screeches poured incessantly from the forest. The sources were moving northward.

"It sounds like the diversion is working," said Fremy. "We'll head to our standby point, too."

"Don't let them find you on the way," instructed Adlet.

"I'm good at covert operations, don't worry. More importantly, you need to watch out for Dozzu and Nashetania," Fremy said to him quietly, and then she and Mora left for the southern mountain. Once they had safely made it there, Fremy would pop a firecracker that she'd given to Adlet. Then their operation would reach the crucial stage.

"Dozzu, do you know where number nine is?" Nashetania asked as she stared at the trees.

Also observing the forest closely, Dozzu replied, "Unfortunately, I can't tell from here. However, I can estimate the enemy's position somewhat, based on their abilities."

"In other words...?"

"Specialist number nine controls the Dead Host with sound. Their screams also inform number nine as to the situation. This means that all of the Dead Host will be within hearing range, so it's highly likely that specialist number nine is in the center of the forest."

"I see."

The pair coolly analyzed the combat situation. Nothing suggested to Adlet that they were ready to betray the Braves.

"Hey, Rolonia." When Adlet scanned the group, he noticed her sitting beside the corpse Nashetania had stabbed and Goldof had hidden. Her eyes were closed, her hands on the corpse's throat.

"Don't close your eyes. This is enemy territory."

"Oh! S-sorry." Rolonia opened her eyes.

"What were you doing?"

"...I was manipulating the corpse's blood to find out what's happened to its body." Then she put her mouth to the wound on the corpse's stomach, sucking its blood. Tasting an organism's blood to analyze it was her special talent.

"You're not trying to find a way to save it, are you?" Adlet asked her rather sternly.

Flustered, Rolonia shook her head. "N-no! I'm just examining it... um...for fighting." Adlet chose not to press her further.

An instant later, the firecracker in the pouch at Adlet's waist popped. Fremy and Mora had made it to their position safely.

Adlet didn't even have to give the order. At once, all of them raced into the forest.

It had seemed as if all of the Dead Host had disappeared after Hans, but one of them was still there, up in a tree. When it saw Adlet's party, it was ready to scream. "I'll kill it!" Adlet said, and he shot a paralysis needle into its throat while Dozzu fried it with lightning. When another enemy appeared, Goldof charged at it. The corpse managed to block Goldof's first thrust, but the knight drove it back and impaled its stomach.

"What are you doing, Rolonia?!" Adlet yelled.

Rolonia ran to the fallen Dead Host and put her hands on its body, as if she were trying to heal it. She couldn't actually be trying to save the thing, could she?

But evidently she was just checking that the body was indeed dead. She observed it sadly and then followed after the rest of them.

Don't get stupid ideas, Adlet thought, even though not long ago he'd been having those same stupid ideas himself.

*   *   *

From afar, Rainer heard screams. He had been patrolling near the ravine when, instantly, his body shuddered as if jolted with electricity. He was running full speed toward the sound of the screams. He couldn't understand what had happened. Why had one of the Dead Host shrieked so far away, and why was he suddenly running?

Then it hit him. The battle with the Braves of the Six Flowers had begun. He couldn't think of any other reason why the living dead would start screaming and running.

The Six Braves are here! If Rainer still possessed his speech faculties, he would have whooped for joy. Now he knew he'd have his chance to encounter them and tell them the truth.

But immediately, he also realized this was no time for celebration. The fight began now. He had to communicate that he was alive and held information about the Black Barrenbloom, and the only way he could do that was with his right arm. *Please, Braves of the Six Flowers…notice it!*

It was one year ago that Rainer had been turned into a corpse soldier and been laid down in the cave not far from this forest. He'd lost all sense of time, so he was unsure when this was, but at some point he'd hit upon a significant discovery: very rarely, there were times when he could move his left arm of his own free will. Rainer had focused intently on his left arm in an attempt to move it, but no matter how hard he concentrated, his arm wouldn't break free. And upon further reflection, he realized that during every previous success, he'd gone totally limp from exhaustion or nearly given up, believing he'd imagined it. He didn't understand why his arm was sometimes free. At a maximum, he could have control of his arm for about three hundred seconds, and at a minimum, a hundred. He had no control over how long the interval would be. He tried to see if perhaps he could make other parts of his body respond, but no matter how he struggled, nothing aside from his left arm would do so.

Desperately, he had tried to think of a way to communicate that he was there using only a left arm that he could very occasionally move.

He'd picked a little rock off the ground and broke it in two to make a sharp fragment. With the stone shard, he carved words into his right arm. *I'm alive. Tgurneu's weapon. Black Barrenbloom. Know about it.*

He would have liked to engrave his message all over his body, if he could. But occasionally, a gnarled insect-fiend would patrol the cave to check up on the Dead Host, sometimes touching its feelers to the corpses' chests to check for a heartbeat. If the fiend were to notice the message, it would surely kill Rainer. The best he could do was to write the words on his right arm and cover it with his sleeve. He then made a tear in the sleeve so that once the battle began it would rip off on its own.

This is bad. The Braves of the Six Flowers are close, Rainer thought as the parasite forced him to run. His right sleeve was still intact. He'd been thinking that once his left arm could move, he would rip off the sleeve that covered the words on his right arm, and if he had the chance, he would point to his right arm with his left. But the time for his left arm to move hadn't come yet. His message was still hidden.

"*Hrmya-meow!*" Rainer heard an eerie cry coming from above. It was beast-like for a human's, but too human to be a cat's.

Is it a Brave? Rainer wondered, and that was right when he was forced to jump. The leap carried him onto a tree trunk to charge toward the opponent above.

A swordsman with unkempt hair appeared in Rainer's field of vision. He grabbed onto the tree with his feet to dodge Rainer's attack, and then, incredibly, he ran along the trunk and leaped toward Rainer. *He's going to kill me,* Rainer thought.

But the messy-haired warrior passed him by without lopping off his head, moving on to a different tree trunk. "Ya bunch of idiots. I'm meowver here," he said, and then he turned away from Rainer and dashed off. The Dead Host followed, and Rainer had no choice but to run, too.

The disheveled man raced through the forest with frightening speed. As Rainer was forced to follow, he prayed for his left arm to hurry up and move. If it didn't, the Brave would get away before Rainer could warn him about the Black Barrenbloom.

As Rainer involuntarily pursued the swordsman, something suddenly occurred to him: *I wonder why this swordsman is alone? Where did the other Braves go? No way—were they all killed, leaving just him?* But the instant after it crossed his mind, the Dead Host shrieked from far away. Rainer guessed that this man's compatriots were fighting the Dead Host separately.

Suddenly, Rainer experienced a feeling of weakness in his left arm. He knew exactly what was happening: the appendage was now free. Still automatically running, Rainer grabbed the sleeve that covered his right arm and ripped it off. The words etched into his right arm, Rainer's one ray of hope, were now laid bare. He pointed to his right arm with a finger, but the fighter with the unkempt hair was already far away, and his back was turned. He couldn't see what Rainer was doing. Rainer swung his arm wildly, punching the trunk of a tree in an attempt to get the swordsman's attention. He would have screamed, if he could. But all he could move was his left arm, and no matter how much he struggled, he couldn't cry out.

Numbness swallowed his left arm, and it was yanked from his control once more. The scruffy-haired Brave was already out of sight.

"Don't stop! Keep moving forward!" Adlet yelled. The six of them were clustered together, racing through the forest. Goldof was in the lead with Adlet and Nashetania covering his back. Chamo, the most powerful of them, had not yet deployed her slave-fiends. Rolonia and Dozzu were protecting her as they advanced.

After some progress, Adlet stopped. The first thing they had to do was pinpoint the master of the Dead Host, specialist number nine. In such a deep forest, finding a single fiend wouldn't be easy.

They had a clue, though. Specialist number nine safeguarded itself with legions of the Dead Host, so that meant that the fiend would occupy the most easily defensible position. They could predict where that might be: the central area of the forest, near a particularly large tree.

"I'm gonna take a look at how the battle is going. Wait just a minute," Adlet said. He sprang onto a nearby tree, scrambling up it like a monkey. From this vantage point, he surveyed the whole forest.

On the western side, he could see a dense swarm of living dead beyond the edge of the forest. As he'd expected, it would be difficult to break through there without killing specialist number nine. Not that he would even if he could, though.

From the north, Adlet could hear the keening of the Dead Host. Hans had detonated one of his bombs, judging from the black smoke rising over there. Hans must have already taken the fight to the other side of the ravine. Through the gaps between the trees, Adlet could see the enemy forces sprinting north toward the ravine. They were probably just running in the direction of the explosion. Adlet saw one of them attempt to jump over the ravine and fall to the bottom. As he'd expected, these guys were not very intelligent.

He couldn't see anything through the trees to the south, but it was quiet. Nothing suggested that Fremy and Mora had been spotted.

Next, Adlet zeroed in on the area near the great tree in the center of the forest. He found dozens of corpses there in close formation, and among them was specialist number nine. "Okay, found it! Let's go!"

When Adlet clambered back down, they heard a succession of explosions coming from the north, followed by the rumbling of something big collapsing. Hans's diversion had been a success, and he had destroyed the bridge.

"Our goal is that big tree," said Adlet. "Good thing it's easy to find."

That was when they heard a curious, high-pitched note, like the sound of a metal flute. When Adlet looked around, Dozzu noted, "It sounds like specialist number nine has given a command to the Dead Host. They'll do something new now." A chorus of shrieks joined the tone—the Dead Host converging on their location from every direction. "We've been noticed, it seems," said Dozzu.

"We knew this would happen," said Adlet. "Chamo, do your thing."

"Just leave it to Chamo," she replied, shoving her foxtail down her throat to loudly vomit up her slave-fiends.

"Send them out!"

The slave-fiends' job would be to hold back the Dead Host's ranks and keep them confused. The rest pushed on through the forest.

...*Oh shit*, Rainer cursed to himself as he ran. The swordsman was already out of sight. That was his best chance to communicate his presence to the Braves. He'd managed to get close, and his arm had even come free at that moment, too. And considering how rare those opportunities were, the timing had been nothing short of miraculous.

Where did that swordsman go? Rainer and the other living dead searched for the vanished Brave. All around, he could hear dozens of corpses shrieking, but clearly none of them could find him. Rainer heard the sound of an explosion, and then he and a few dozen others gathered around the decimated bridge. But as Rainer had expected, they didn't find who they were looking for. Rainer was astonished at the man's amazing talent for concealment.

...*Well, maybe this is for the best*, he thought. The swordsman had been cutting down the Dead Host without hesitation or consideration to their former humanity. If Rainer had gotten near him, the agile man would surely have killed Rainer without so much as a glance at the message on his right arm. Or even if he had noticed it, he might have ignored it and killed Rainer anyway.

Rainer considered. A little while ago, another fight had broken out somewhere else. The swordsman was not the only Brave in this forest—his allies were here, too. *Even if it won't work out with that guy, the other Braves will find me. There's still hope.*

He had a reason to believe that: his body was not the only one bearing messages. While he was lying in that cave, Rainer had written on a few of the corpses around him, too. Using the brief periods of mobility for his left arm, he had inscribed words into them. He'd been forced to hide his messages, too, to keep the patrolling fiend from noticing them. It had been no simple task.

He'd moved around by pushing himself up with his left arm and then rolling over to the others, where he would reach out to inscribe his plea into their flesh. He had torn their clothes so they'd rip off easily to help the Braves discover the messages. When Rainer felt a faint numbness in his left arm, it meant it was about to be wrested from his control again. When the sensation came, he had to hide the messages under the corpses' clothes and flop back to his original position on his back as though nothing had happened.

The only bodies Rainer had been able to write complete messages on were the two corpses that had lain on either side of him, one at his head, one at his feet.

He'd been able to write enough on the left arm of the corpse to his left. He remembered what he had put: *One is alive. Search and save. Man with words on right arm. Large build. Scar on face. Knows Tgurneu's weapon.* On the corpse to his right he'd written, *Search and save. Man with words on right arm. Tgurneu's weapon.* Even that should be enough to get across the point. He hadn't had time to write enough on the two corpses by his head. He'd only managed, *Man with words on right arm. Knows. Important.* And for the one at his feet, the most he'd been able to handle was *Save him. He knows.* They'd probably need more to understand.

Every time Rainer's arm came free, he spent that time on this task. Just scratching out the letters had been a life-draining battle. A few times when his arm was free, he'd heard fiends walking around, preventing him from acting. Sometimes he would get a rare chance to move, but it was too short for him to write anything, and the numbness would bring his period of freedom to an unfruitful end. Other times, the fiend had come close to discovering his messages, nearly giving him a heart attack. If his writing had been found, he would certainly have been killed on the spot. He was only alive through sheer luck.

That's right. Don't give up, Rainer. The Braves of the Six Flowers are sure to find you.

Rainer didn't know where the corpses bearing his news were now. But there were five of them, so the Braves of the Six Flowers should find at least one. Surely they would search for the corpse with writing on its right arm.

Think! Think of a way to help them find you. Then wait for your arm.

Rainer considered how his arm had come free just now. It had happened right as another battle started someplace a little ways away. That was right when he'd regained control. Rainer also recalled that once, when he had been lying in the cave, he had heard a discussion among the fiends. They had said there was a fiend called specialist number nine that controlled the Dead Host. Judging from that, Rainer could deduce that perhaps the bouts of freedom occurred when something happened to specialist number nine. Maybe when it was attacked or distracted by something it would lose control of the Dead Host, and those were the moments that Rainer could move. There was really no basis for this hypothesis, but he had a hunch he might be right. If he was, he would get another chance. *Believe, Rainer. Believe that it will happen.*

Suddenly, a metallic sound like a whistle rang out through the forest. Rainer's body stopped chasing the disheveled swordsman and started sprinting toward the forest's center. Specialist number nine had sent new orders.

"They üse such stupid, pëtty tricks," a fiend muttered in the forest's center. The creature with a misshapen, insectoid body was specialist number nine. The fiend analyzed the situation based on the calls of the Dead Host that it could hear from various points around the forest.

On specialist number nine's mouth was a flutelike organ that emitted a constant, high-pitched, metallic noise. This was how it gave instructions to the parasites on the back of the Dead Host's necks.

Dead Host on the northern side, come back to the center of the forest! Counter the Braves of the Six Flowers! The corpses in question reacted to the sound and began to move, but the ravine blocked many of them, and number nine could tell from their cries that they couldn't return.

At first, specialist number nine had expected the Six Braves to plow straight through the forest toward the Temple of Fate. But the enemy had veered off to the northern side. Number nine had been confused, not understanding why, and then it had noticed other Braves charging in toward it. The realization that it had been a diversion ploy had momentarily caused mild disturbances in its stream of sound.

But that was no problem. It had already blocked the path to the Temple of Fate, and the walls of Dead Host that defended it were impregnable. It was confident that its forces would not fall, even against all six Braves.

Rainer's conclusion that his arm would move when something happened to number nine was basically on the mark. The specialist emitted an endless stream of high-frequency sound waves. A disruption in this signal also caused mild disturbances in the behavior of the parasites that controlled the Dead Host.

This disturbance didn't cause any difficulties for the regular Dead Host. But the parasite on Rainer's body didn't have a firm grip on the nerves in his left arm, and every time number nine's signal was disrupted, it temporarily lost control. Rainer was lucky. Without this little margin of freedom, he would have died helpless.

Adlet's party was about two hundred meters away from the large tree they were after. The Dead Host attacked them relentlessly from every direction.

"Ngh!" Adlet dodged a corpse's arm—not a fist or an openhanded hit, but a simple attempt to bludgeon him with its limbs. But the corpse's strength was not to be underestimated. When it lost its balance, Adlet swept its feet out from under it, slamming his heel down onto his fallen opponent's throat as hard as he could.

The Dead Host was extremely fast. One moment they'd be staggering along, the next they'd be charging in with fearsome speed. They weren't as quick as Adlet and Goldof, but they were all as fast as first-rate warriors. Chamo had deployed about half of her slave-fiends to stem the tide of the Dead Host, but still couldn't keep them all in check.

"Yah!" Nashetania pierced the throat of an approaching corpse with her sword. But despite being impaled, the body still kept coming.

"Watch out!" Adlet yelled, throwing a paralysis needle at the corpse's throat to stop it in its tracks. Nashetania seized the opportunity to send a blade up from the ground and cleave it clean in two. "Nashe! Stabbing doesn't work on them! Slice them up!"

"Understood!"

He didn't actually want to protect her—but if they lost Nashetania, their alliance with Dozzu would fall apart, and who knew what Goldof might pull if that happened. He had no choice but to keep her safe.

"Dozzu! Rolonia! Are you all right?" Adlet called out to his allies. Rolonia, Dozzu, and Nashetania were the only ones with him. Chamo and Goldof were circling around to the northern side of the great tree. The plan was for Adlet's group to charge at specialist number nine and create an opening for the other two to attack from the north. They would cut off its escape route, forcing it to flee to the south.

About two hundred of the Dead Host had assembled in a dense formation around the great tree. Number nine had to be in the middle. It made no sign of moving. Adlet planned to stay where they were for a few more minutes until Chamo and Goldof were in position.

That was when Adlet saw a corpse charging for Rolonia from above the trees. She hadn't noticed. "Duck, Rolonia!" he yelled, and he threw his cuff-chain at the corpse, catching it around the neck and yanking as hard as he could. Rolonia finally clued in, lashing out at the corpse with her whip. But her attacks were lacking in energy. She was powerful enough to take out every enemy around her if she fought at full strength, but now she was just barely managing to dodge. She wasn't spewing her typical string of insults and rage, either.

"I'll handle Rolonia! Dozzu and Nashetania, you focus on your own opponents!" Adlet yelled. He took up position next to Rolonia, blocking a rushing corpse's attack with his sword. Even when the blade met its arms, the corpse kept swinging downward. Both its hands were severed at the wrist and fell to the ground. "Snap out of it, Rolonia!" Adlet yelled.

An instant later, Rolonia responded in a completely unexpected manner. Her eyes focused on a point, as if she'd noticed something. She grabbed one of the Dead Host and bit into the parasite stuck on the back of its neck, readily slurping up the gushing bodily fluids. From the taste, she analyzed the parasite's biology.

What is she doing? Adlet wondered. Frantically swinging his sword around, he covered her. She was so deeply focused on her analysis that she was blind to her surroundings. Now he had no choice but to protect her himself. Felling enemies with his paralysis needles and sword, Adlet yelled at her, "You big, blundering idiot! What are you doing, Rolonia?!"

The corpse in Rolonia's arms twitched. Immediately, Adlet dashed up to it and stabbed it through the chest with his sword. At this rate, she was going to get herself killed. "Rolonia…"

She wiped her mouth and swung her whip to repel the enemies around her. But she was clearly not focused on the fight.

"Can't you drop it? Enough!" shouted Adlet.

"B-but…"

More enemies were descending upon them. This was no time for discussion.

The four frantically took down the swarm.

Nashetania said, "Let's go. Chamo and Goldof should be ready by now." The hordes of Dead Host were thinning, too. This was the right moment to pull the trigger.

"Yeah. Let's go, guys," Adlet reiterated, and the group started to advance toward the great tree and the Dead Host assembled around it—but Rolonia didn't move. She was peering intently at one of the corpses that Adlet had cut down. "Stop this, Rolonia," he told her. "They're already dead. You can't save them."

Rolonia turned to Adlet and shook her head. "No."

"What?"

"You're wrong, Addy. The Dead Host corpses…are still alive."

"What do you mean?"

"I could tell for sure when I tasted their blood. These people are being controlled, but they're not dead. Plus…plus…" Rolonia pointed to a fallen corpse.

Words were carved into its left arm. *Save him. He knows* was written in horribly awkward script.

"The people turned into the Dead Host aren't dead," asserted Rolonia. "Someone wrote this, begging for help!"

Dumbfounded, Adlet stared at the words.

Chapter 4

Two Schemes

Once Tgurneu received the news that the Braves of the Six Flowers had appeared with Dozzu's faction in the Fainting Mountains, it set off northward as quickly as possible, accompanied by the bulk of its forces. It would most likely be half a day until they reached the Fainting Mountains.

Tgurneu rode on the back of a massive slime mold–fiend, leisurely gazing at the northern sky. Specialist number two soared low over Tgurneu's head, ready for orders.

"Ah-ha-ha! They've saved me some effort, going off to the Temple of Fate all on their own. Now this will get interesting." Tgurneu giggled just like a child. The fiend was frightening and calculating, but sometimes innocent and juvenile. Tgurneu's followers found their leader difficult to understand. "Well, you always have to be cautious. Braves or no Braves, you never know what Dozzu might get up to."

"Still, he shouldn't have many options," said specialist number two.

"I know that. But you can never let your guard down around Dozzu," said Tgurneu. "I wonder how number nine is doing."

"I'm sure just holding them off is all he can manage. I'm leery of expecting too much."

"I disagree. I think he can eliminate at least one of them, if all goes well."

Tgurneu's forces continued on their way.

*   *   *

Meanwhile, Goldof and Chamo were racing toward the northern side of the great tree. The Dead Host was thickest near Adlet's party, so there weren't many here to block their path. Goldof glanced back to make sure Chamo was following. Adlet had reminded him of her poor sense of direction and not to leave her alone. Chamo icily watched Goldof, silently cautioning him that she knew he could stab her in the back at a moment's notice.

"Chamo…I won't…betray the Braves. Even if…Her Highness orders it," said Goldof.

"Uh-huh." Chamo didn't relax her guard. Not much he could do about that. It was inevitable that she'd see him as a traitor.

The two of them stopped where they'd been told to, right at the forest's edge, and peeked through the gaps between the trees at the mass of Dead Host. By all appearances, Adlet's party had the corpses distracted. They weren't watching what Goldof and Chamo were doing. Goldof examined the Dead Host's formation in search of specialist number nine, their target. But the fiend must have been hiding, perhaps cautious of gunfire from Fremy, so it couldn't be seen at all from the outside.

Adlet's party wasn't attacking yet—but it should be about time.

"We don't hafta leave this to Fremy and Auntie. Let's just kill it right now," said Chamo.

"…Yes…that's my intention…too," Goldof replied. He didn't see the Dead Host as a real threat. If they fought now, the Braves would probably be able to win without taking much damage. The real problem was the seventh, who had yet to make a move. The other reason Goldof wanted to kill number nine quickly was to cut off some of the seventh's options.

One other thing was making Goldof uneasy: the plan Nashetania had proposed to him. She'd told him she was going to set a trap for Rolonia, and he couldn't yet decide whether to cooperate or not. He suspected she was trying to trick him. It wasn't too late—shouldn't he tell Adlet everything and put a stop to her plan?

No, I shouldn't. Goldof reconsidered. The plan was dangerous, but they wouldn't accomplish anything by succumbing to fear. This stratagem would be an effective aid to the Braves' victory.

"Adlet? Rolonia? What are you doing?" asked Dozzu. Seeing that Adlet wasn't heading out to attack, it had returned. Rolonia showed Dozzu the message written in scars on the corpse's left arm. Dozzu's eyes widened in shock. "What on earth is this?"

"I'll tell you what it means, Dozzu," explained Rolonia. "Someone among the Dead Host is alive, and they're asking for help."

"Frankly speaking, I find this unbelievable. There's no way one of the Dead Host could be alive in that state, much less write anything..."

Adlet felt the same way. This particular corpse looked very clearly dead. To him, the power of the parasites appeared to be the only thing forcing them into motion.

"And I just made sure of it by tasting the blood of that last one. They were in horrible, horrible shape, but...they were just barely...alive."

"Wait, please, Rolonia," said Dozzu. "We can't bring this operation to a halt now. We've already revealed our position to Tgurneu. If we don't reach the Temple of Fate as soon as possible, we'll end up surrounded, and all of us will die."

"I-I know that. But..." Rolonia protested desperately. "Addy, I think...I really have to... I have to search for a way to save these people! Let's find out about the Black Barrenbloom, and save the Dead Host, too!"

"That's not possible," objected Dozzu.

"P-please, Dozzu. I'll do my very best. I swear I won't cause trouble for you. I'll show you that I can save the people of the Dead Host, too. So please, tell me how I could do it!"

Adlet stared at that message for a long time. Were they really alive? Even after being turned into living dead, even now that they were fighting him, were the people of his village still alive? Suddenly, nausea welled up inside him. Just imagining the living hell of consciousness while a parasite controlled your body as a weapon made him feel sick. Adlet had thought he'd already conquered his indecision, but it came back with a vengeance.

What if there was a way to save the Dead Host? He was about to agree with Rolonia, but suddenly a flash of insight sparked in his mind. "That's not what's going on, Rolonia."

"Huh?"

"It's a trap. Tgurneu's trying to trick us, trying to buy some time by luring us away to save the Dead Host. It wrote this here to confuse us." Adlet didn't have any proof, but he figured that was just the sort of thing Tgurneu was liable to do.

"M-maybe, but...maybe it really is—"

"No. Give up on trying to save them! We can't waste our time! We're going!"

"Addy!" Rolonia yelled at him. Adlet ran off with Dozzu close behind. Nashetania, waiting impatiently, joined them in the charge at their enemy's defenses.

Even if the Dead Host was alive, they were beyond salvation. All the Braves could do was kill them quickly to put them out of their misery.

Why, Addy? How could you kill the Dead Host? Rolonia lamented as she followed after the others.

The corpses were standing in orderly rows, the great tree at their center. Adlet's party charged straight for the middle of the crowd. Their goal was to attack before Chamo and Goldof and disrupt the Dead Host's defensive formation. Of course, Adlet had also told the others that if they could just kill the ringleader then and there, so much the better. But Rolonia still had reservations. Killing it would kill all of the Dead Host, too.

Adlet brandished a bomb while Dozzu readied a lightning strike. Their target was specialist number nine, who was in the center of the enemy camp. But before the pair could attack, the corpses that were not a part of the formation charged them as a group. With so many enemies fighting them off, they couldn't go after the one they really wanted.

"Damn it! They're stubborn!" Adlet cursed. These corpses clearly acted differently from the others they'd fought so far. They were coordinated, attacking in groups of at least three. The earlier mooks had only been given general orders, but now specialist number nine was watching their battle and giving specific orders to the formation around it.

"Nashetania! Back us up!" Adlet yelled.

"I'm sorry! My hands are full here!" she replied.

Adlet, Nashetania, and Dozzu tried to push forward, but Rolonia was the only one at their backs, and all she was doing was blocking the attacks of the enemy wave. She was afraid she might kill them, and it was slowing her down.

The others butchered the Dead Host without batting an eye. Adlet killed them with his sword, Nashetania bisected them with her blades, and Dozzu charred them black with its lightning strikes. As she watched, Rolonia thought, *How can they kill them?*

After tasting that corpse's blood earlier, she had come to understand the Dead Host's physical state. Its heart had been beating, and its brain had been intact. It was racked with thirst and abuse, essentially forced to live by the parasite—but she had discovered that saving them was possible, if you could just remove the parasites.

But despite that, Adlet had ignored all her pleas and decided to annihilate them. Had he always been so ruthless, calmly murdering people who might still be alive, who had simply been forced to fight? Was that the kind of strength needed to win? Did a Brave of the Six Flowers need to be like that? Was she at fault for lacking the capacity?

"Rolonia! Pull it together!" Adlet yelled at her. For a while now, she had done practically nothing but run around. She was burdening everyone again. She could hardly bear it.

"What amazing command it has over them. I didn't think it would be able to keep us away like this," Nashetania said as she summoned blades from the ground. Specialist number nine had hardly moved from its position.

Rolonia heard Adlet murmur softly, as if in reply, "We can deal with that." Then he yelled out, "This is getting us nowhere! We're backing off!" He pulled a smoke bomb out from a pouch at his waist and threw it to the ground, shrouding their surroundings in smoke. The Dead Host all stopped, paralyzed. "This works well on them!" he yelled.

Rolonia was about to withdraw as Adlet had ordered, but within the smoke she could see the others doing something else. Nashetania manifested a blade that thrust up from the ground diagonally, with the flat facing the sky. Under cover of the smoke, Adlet leaped high off the blade and flung a few somethings into the center of specialist number nine's defensive formation.

"!" The fiend emitted a particularly loud, flutelike sound, and when the projectiles landed on the ground, the Dead Host fell upon them all at once. But nothing happened. Rolonia figured it out—Adlet had just thrown rocks or something equally innocuous, and in all the smoke, specialist number nine had mistaken them for bombs.

The enemy formation was in disarray. Immediately, Adlet threw more at them—real bombs, this time—while Dozzu and Nashetania followed up by pushing to the center and hitting with their hardest attacks. Many of the Dead Host protected specialist number nine with their bodies and died instantly. Even though they were enemies, Rolonia was impressed by their flawless coordination.

She was ashamed of herself for vacantly watching the fight from the rear.

She could just barely spot specialist number nine through the gaps in the Dead Host's defenses. It was a large bug-fiend, as big as a human. Dozens of spindly legs supported its knobbly, thin body. In the center of its abdomen was an uncanny lump that seemed to be the ovary that birthed the parasites.

The once-organized movements of the Dead Host had fallen apart, and at the exact same moment, from north in the forest, Goldof commenced his assault with a roar.

They wouldn't have to rely on Fremy to shoot this fiend down; they'd finish it right here. Goldof charged into the ranks so fast he left Chamo's slave-fiends behind.

Noticing his approach, a corpse swung both its arms down at him, shrieking. Goldof chose not to dodge. That would have spelled instant death for any ordinary human, but Goldof took the hit with his helmet, bracing with the powerful muscles of his neck.

"Auuugh!" He slammed shoulder-first into the corpse's stomach, hurling it back into the one behind it and creating an opening that allowed him to advance. One after another, the corpses surrounded him, and he just let their strikes land on his armor as he determinedly flattened the enemies before him.

Then Chamo's slave-fiends flooded into the Dead Host's formation, and the once-flawless defensive structure collapsed all at once. Goldof's eyes were locked on the gnarled figure of specialist number nine.

"…!" Instantly, specialist number nine became agitated and emitted a sound. The Dead Host drew back, surrounding and covering their master. They turned away from Goldof and began fleeing southward.

"Get it, Goldof!" Chamo yelled from behind.

Goldof didn't need to be told—he already planned to. But five of the Dead Host spread their arms to block his path. He tried to break through by stabbing the one in the center, but despite being impaled from chest to spine, the corpse clung to his spear while the others latched onto Goldof's body and refused to let go. "Ngh!" Goldof strained and tried to yank his spear back, but even he was at a disadvantage five-on-one. Now Goldof was the one being lifted up and swung around.

"What're you doing?" asked Chamo. Her water snake slave-fiend came in from behind to crunch the heads of the corpses grappling for Goldof's spear. One of them refused to let go, even in death, but he successfully shook it off.

Meanwhile, specialist number nine and its guard of Dead Host had escaped far away. Adlet and Nashetania chased after the fleeing fiend in an attempt to finish it off, but the guards blocked them, too, and their attacks fell short.

"Chase it!" Adlet yelled, and he dashed off. Nashetania and Dozzu followed, while Rolonia brought up the rear.

*   *   *

From far away, Rainer could hear the clashes, explosions, and thunder. He figured the Braves of the Six Flowers had engaged specialist number nine. That swordsman with the unkempt hair had been acting as a diversion, while their real goal was in the other direction.

Rainer's body was steered toward the center of the forest where the great tree was. *This is good,* he thought. If he had continued pursuing the swordsman, he probably would have been killed before he could do anything, or been abandoned with no chance to meet any of the Braves. If he could encounter them, they might notice the writing on his right arm.

That was when Rainer felt a weakness in his left arm—the signal that he'd be able to move it again. Before, he'd never been able to move his arm twice in one day. His guess had been right: Those periods when his arm was free came when something happened to the controller of the Dead Host.

This could work… This could work! Rainer was exhilarated. If he waved at the Braves of the Six Flowers and pointed to his right arm, one of them had to notice him—at the very least, they wouldn't kill him right off the bat.

Rainer and his fellows were driven into the center of the forest. Running with them, Rainer could hear the shrieks of the Dead Host from the front lines. *It's the Six Braves!* he thought, but an instant later he was greeted by an astonishing sight. Blocking their path were leeches, lizards, slugs, and other strange, fishlike fiends.

This is bad! If the fiends noticed the writing on his right arm, they'd kill him. Rainer tried to hide the words under his sleeve, but then something immediately happened that didn't make sense.

A massive slug spat out acid at Rainer, and he leaped aside involuntarily. His right arm swung up, slamming into the slug. The strike tore off some of its flesh but was otherwise entirely ineffective. What's more, the fiends weren't just attacking Rainer; they were attacking all of the Dead Host.

Why are fiends attacking us?! Still uncomprehending, Rainer was forced to fight them. The fiends also blocked any corpses that tried to go to the great tree. Without a doubt, they were protecting the Braves of the Six Flowers. It couldn't be—did one of the Braves have the power to do this? Was one of the Braves a Saint who could control fiends? Unable to wrap his head around it, Rainer had to continue his battle with the enemies before him.

If these fiends are allies of the Six Braves... With his left arm still under his control, he indicated the message on his right arm. He grabbed his scarred limb, showing the words to the slug. He figured that if this fiend was an ally of the Six Braves, it might notice. But the slug continued its assault, heedless of his efforts, and he had to use the rare freedom of his left arm to protect himself instead.

What the hell is this? What do I do? Without a firm grasp on the situation, Rainer kept fighting.

"Damn it! That thing is fast!" Adlet cursed.

Adlet was chasing after specialist number nine through the steep ups and downs of the forest. The fiend was deploying a steady stream of the Dead Host to hold them off. A considerable gap had formed between the Braves and their target.

"Just like you, Adlet," Nashetania commented as she fought beside him.

"I'd do a better job getting away!"

"...Why are you getting so angry?" She was aghast.

"Dozzu, can I ask something?" Adlet addressed the fiend during the battle. "Is the one we're chasing right now really specialist number nine?"

"Its appearance is consistent with what I've heard of it," replied Dozzu.

"Is there any chance it's actually just a transforming fiend pretending?"

Dozzu considered for a moment before replying. "I doubt it. A transforming fiend can change shape, but not copy abilities. The sounds that control the Dead Host have been coming from that specialist."

"If I were Tgurneu, though, I'd station a bunch of transforming fiends around here and use them as decoys," said Adlet.

"Even if Tgurneu wanted to, I doubt he could. There aren't many transforming fiends out there."

Is that all it is? thought Adlet.

"Incidentally, we've encountered a problem. We're veering off course," said Dozzu, and Adlet realized their quarry was heading southeast. If the chase went on like this, they'd never reach the southern mountain where Fremy and Mora were lying in wait.

No choice but to do this over, thought Adlet. Besides, Goldof, Chamo, and Rolonia had fallen behind. "Quit chasing it. We're going to stop. Dozzu, Nashetania—I'll leave the fighting to you," Adlet said, and they stopped. Adlet let them handle the corpses that had come to them and glanced at the crest on his right hand. The petals were still all there. Hans was safe. Mora and Fremy were alive. The plan was going well.

"I'm gonna go check on the situation."

Adlet climbed a nearby tree. From above, he could observe the goings-on in the forest. Specialist number nine had stopped a little ways away from Adlet, seemingly making its own appraisal of the circumstances. It was still some distance to the mountain where Fremy and Mora waited.

Adlet could hear the endless shrill cries from the central and northern sides of the forest. The Dead Host was fighting with Hans and the slave-fiends Chamo had left stationed there. They wouldn't be a problem for now.

Next, Adlet looked toward the Fainting Mountains. He could see a number of flying fiends in the sky above them. They had to have noticed the Braves' approach long ago, but they didn't seem to be coming any closer. The Fainting Mountains couldn't possibly be completely deserted. Most likely, Tgurneu had given those fiends strict orders not to leave their posts so as to prevent even a single one from setting foot in the Temple of Fate.

Finally, Adlet scanned the area surrounding the forest. Still no sign of any large fiend hordes approaching. But the ones that had been keeping watch on the nearby regions would surely descend on them within a few hours. The central force that Tgurneu commanded could also show up at any time.

"Adlet! Watch out!" Nashetania called out, alerting him to danger. A corpse was scrambling up the tree toward Adlet with frightening speed. The moment his eyes locked on the corpse, it bared its yellow teeth and shrieked.

"Ah—" When Adlet saw its face, he remembered—the good-natured lady who had lived three houses over. She used to come over sometimes to help with household tasks, saying, *It must be so exhausting when there's only two of you living alone together!* She was in front of him now, trying to murder him.

Adlet blocked with his sword and made to decapitate her with his counterattack, but right then, what Rolonia had said—that the Dead Host might still be alive—returned to him. "Guh!" For an instant, his sword hand stopped. The corpse's swing nicked him, but he kicked back reflexively and knocked it to the ground. Dozzu blackened the fallen body with its lightning, and the lady who had once been so kind to him was forever still.

"Haah… Haah… Haah…" Staring at the fallen corpse, Adlet focused on quieting his ragged breathing. *There's nothing I could have done*, he told himself. *If I'd hesitated, it would have killed me.* He attempted to calm his heart.

In his mind, he called out to the dead woman. *Please forgive me. This is so we can win. To protect the world.*

"Are you all right, Adlet?" Dozzu asked.

"I'm not injured. Don't worry," Adlet replied, shimmying along the tree branch to descend to the ground.

"No, that's not what I meant."

"…What are you talking about? I'm the strongest man in the world." Adlet grinned. Even he could tell his face was straining. "No problems right now—it's all going according to plan. Let's attack one more time from the north and east."

That was when Chamo and Goldof caught up to Adlet's group after lagging behind. Just as Adlet thought, *We attack one more time*, he realized Rolonia wasn't there.

"Rolonia...isn't with you?" Goldof said as he scanned the perimeter. They didn't know where she was, either.

"This isn't good. It's dangerous alone," murmured Dozzu.

"Nashetania, come with me," said Adlet. "Chamo, Goldof, Dozzu, you hold down number nine." He took Nashetania and returned the way they had come.

They didn't have time for this. What was Rolonia doing?

Though Rolonia had strayed from the group, it wasn't because she'd decided to go off on her own. She'd been following Adlet, fighting the Dead Host as she went.

But during her skirmishes, Rolonia had been scanning the bodies of the Dead Host for writing. She figured there had to be others with messages carved into them. Someone was alive, and they were writing those messages to ask for help. Adlet had insisted it was a trap, but they didn't know that for sure.

The others gradually got farther away from her, with the majority of the Dead Host behind them. Rolonia couldn't find any bodies bearing messages. *Just searching like this isn't going to work*, she thought.

A corpse jumped down from a tree at her. As she blocked its strike with her whip, she checked around her to make sure there were no other corpses.

"Yahh!" Rolonia cried out and focused her mind hard on her weapon. The thirty-meter-long whip with Rolonia's own blood inside it undulated like a snake and wrapped around the corpse's body. Scanning the area once more, Rolonia confirmed again that no enemies were near and approached her captive.

Earlier, after tasting a parasite's bodily fluids, she had found out that it should be possible to remove the parasite from a Dead Host. If she were to pull it off by force, the parasite's feelers and legs would shred the victim's head and nerves, and the person would die. However, the parasite had very simple anatomy and Rolonia now had a general understanding of it. The thing also had essentially no capacity for independent thought.

Rolonia killed it gradually by pouring her Saint's blood into it. If she could remove it slowly, so as not to damage the person's vitals, it should be possible to save this person. Rolonia immobilized the struggling corpse. She bit her tongue, held the blood in her mouth, and then bit the parasite to slowly pour blood into its body.

I have to hurry—I'm causing trouble for everyone else, she thought as she gradually paralyzed the insect.

Adlet quickly found Rolonia. When he realized what she was doing, he was struck dumb.

"Oh my. This is a problem," Nashetania said, exasperated. Rolonia was attempting to remove the parasite from one of the Dead Host.

"...We're going, Rolonia," insisted Adlet.

Rolonia didn't reply. She was entirely focused on slowly pulling the legs and feelers out of the corpse's body. The expression on her face was completely different from the one she wore when fighting. It struck Adlet that she really should be a healer, not a warrior.

"Rolonia, please stop," said Nashetania.

But Rolonia wasn't listening. Nashetania approached her and tried to pull her away by the arm, but Rolonia stopped her hand. "I'm almost done. Please wait a little longer." She pulled out the feelers and legs, and the instant before the parasite was free, Adlet thought he saw the corpse's lips moving, just barely. With the parasite removed, the body went limp.

"Water...water..." Rolonia muttered, withdrawing a flask from the packs fastened on her belt and pouring some water into her mouth. She dripped the water from her mouth to the mouth of the Dead Host corpse... or rather the man who had once been one of the Dead Host. She also removed one gauntlet, baring her wrist. She bit at an artery, and blood spurted out from the sides of her mouth.

"Rolonia, what are you—?" Nashetania began.

The stream of blood gushed out of her wound toward the corpse.

Wherever Rolonia's blood touched the parched, rotting body, life returned. "This works best for emergency treatment. His eyes should open soon," Rolonia said.

But the man's eyes did not open. Frantic, Rolonia put her hands over his heart and tried to breathe air into his lungs, but to Adlet, watching from the side, the effort appeared entirely pointless.

"It's over now," he said. "Let's go, Rolonia!"

"No, I can't! Wait just a bit longer."

"I thought we decided not to save the Dead Host!"

"This is the one time when I can't do what you say, Addy!"

Adlet grabbed her arm and pulled her to her feet. Rolonia shook him off, glaring at him.

"Come with us!"

Rolonia slung the fallen body over her shoulder and ran after Adlet. Surprisingly, her legs and back were strong, and she didn't seem to struggle carrying a person.

"There's gonna be another fight. Leave that behind," said Adlet.

Rolonia shot back at him, "I told you... This time, I can't follow your orders."

Irritated, Adlet spoke more roughly. "You can't save him. It's just not possible."

"It *is* possible! I removed the parasite. His heart is beating. If I give him enough treatment, I can save him."

Don't be stupid, thought Adlet. "If you give him enough treatment? When are you gonna find the time for that? We have to kill specialist number nine and head to the Temple of Fate, and once we get there, we have to learn about the Black Barrenbloom. When do you plan to heal him?"

"I..." Rolonia faltered. Nashetania silently watched the pair argue.

"You and Mora are the only healers on our team, and we have limited healing supplies, too. There's no way you can save all of the Dead Host."

Rolonia didn't reply.

"Besides, once you've saved him, what happens then? Are you

planning to abandon him in the Howling Vilelands with no way to fight? He'd just be waiting to get killed and eaten by fiends!"

Rolonia listened to him in silence—but her eyes told him that she was steadfastly determined. Without saying a word, she was communicating to him that she would not obey.

Rolonia had always stuck close behind Adlet, fighting timidly and following his orders loyally—so loyally that sometimes he wished she would offer her own opinions a bit more. Adlet could never have imagined she would oppose him so openly. He couldn't believe how impossible it was to reason with her. He just couldn't understand her. Why should she put herself in danger to save the Dead Host? They were total strangers to her. He'd thought she was more afraid of causing trouble for others than anything else. So then why was she suddenly insisting on doing this her way?

"Rolonia…"

Maybe she's hiding something, Adlet thought. For the first time, he began to grow suspicious of her.

Adlet, Nashetania, and Rolonia linked up with the others again. Goldof repeated his charge, trying to break through the enemy's formation, while Chamo's slave-fiends and Dozzu's lightning strikes supported him. But the enemy just wouldn't run southward like they wanted it to.

"We're changing positions," said Adlet. "We'll attack from the northeast to chase it south."

Nashetania nodded. With the man slung over her shoulders, Rolonia followed, too.

Now northeast of the enemy, Adlet started bombing the Dead Host with the explosives Fremy had given him, trying to scatter their formation. They repelled his bombs, and when they failed to do so, they sacrificed themselves to protect specialist number nine.

Nashetania's blades sprang from the ground toward number nine. Now targeted from two directions at once, specialist number nine gave a particularly loud screech, and the Dead Host began to move south en masse.

*   *   *

The six of them were together again and chasing Tgurneu's minion.

Dozzu approached Adlet. "It seems your strategy was the right choice."

"Who the hell do you think you're talking to? I'm the strongest man in the world!" If Fremy had been with them, it would have been difficult for her to shoot her target. Her presence would have made the fiend wary of her fire and tighten its formations further. Who knew how many hours it would've taken to kill it then?

Adlet and Dozzu were staving off the Dead Host's attacks from both sides as they ran, knocking them down with lightning strikes and paralysis needles, when Dozzu said, "One more thing... What is Rolonia hiding?"

That took Adlet by surprise. Dozzu had voiced the very doubts Adlet had been feeling.

Dozzu continued, "I can't understand her reasons for being so obsessed with the Dead Host. Don't you suspect she has a secret?"

"You mean like how Mora betrayed us and Goldof left us?" asked Adlet.

"I'm not saying that."

Adlet and Dozzu covered Goldof as he charged in once more. The young knight was their core fighter in this particular battle. It was his knack for breaching enemy lines that would run down specialist number nine.

"Rolonia was originally just a laundry girl," said Adlet. "She just happened to be chosen as the Saint of Spilled Blood, and then Mora used her. That's all it is. She couldn't be hiding anything."

"Then why?"

Adlet didn't know, either. Even now, Rolonia still had the man slung over her shoulder as she fought.

"Are you satisfied with this state of affairs?" Dozzu asked.

"Of course I'm not. Just stop complaining and let me handle it."

"Understood. Though I feel somewhat uneasy."

Gradually, the number of the Dead Host slowing the Braves' pursuit decreased. Adlet stopped running and left the remaining Dead Host to Chamo's slave-fiends and Nashetania.

Dozzu approached Rolonia, who was at the back of the group. "So you managed to remove the parasite. That's surprising," it said, eyeing the man Rolonia carried.

"He's weak, but doesn't have any major wounds," commented Rolonia. "Now I just have to restore some of his vitality. Dozzu...you said it was...i-impossible, but...it's not."

"No, unfortunately, Rolonia... It's too late." Dozzu shook its head.

Rolonia looked at the man on her back. "...Huh?" She put her hand on the man's neck and leaned over to lower him to the ground. Adlet didn't have to ask—he knew what had happened. "Wh-why? How..."

Softly, Dozzu said, "His mind was already gone. Even if you manage to heal their bodies, their minds won't come back. Rolonia, you're an unusually powerful Saint, but there's still nothing you can do here."

"Is there no way...to restore his mind?"

"At the very least, I don't know of one."

Rolonia couldn't reply. She just hung her head, motionless. Dozzu watched her with undisguised suspicion.

Once they were done finishing off the attacking Dead Host, Chamo and Nashetania gave her similar looks. Nashetania's expression suggested she was considering something.

This isn't good, thought Adlet. Rolonia was becoming a suspect.

"We've got to fight. It's not over yet," Adlet said, prompting them all to dash off.

Quietly, Rolonia murmured, "There should...still be a way. There has to be."

The six of them resumed their attack. The fight was still on.

"Ströng, ströng...so ströng!" exclaimed specialist number nine, under the guard of its Dead Host. It was trembling in delight. Before its eyes, five of the Braves and one fiend were embroiled in a battle with its Dead Host.

The task Tgurneu had assigned to number nine was to delay the Braves of the Six Flowers. Its role was to prevent them from entering the Fainting Mountains until the main forces under Tgurneu's command converged on the scene here. There were other fiends defending the Fainting Mountains, but specialist number nine had been given the most important post.

It didn't know what was hidden in the Fainting Mountains—neither did it know, of course, which of the Braves was Tgurneu's impostor. It believed it had no need to know.

"Damn it! I can't get close!" Goldof yelled.

The Braves' goal was clear: they wanted to defeat number nine to disable its unwilling army. But that army formed a thick wall that prevented them. They couldn't even get near it.

Chamo's slave-fiends were trying to break the formation, and they were gradually pushing their way in, but they didn't reach the leader. Goldof and Dozzu assaulted the fiend again and again, but under number nine's orders, the Dead Host sacrificed their lives to prevent the enemy charge. Number nine could easily block any attack if it discarded five corpses.

This was unquestionably the first time in history that a single fiend had managed to keep all six Braves occupied. Even the Archfiend Zophrair had needed dozens of fiends under its command to manage it. Even when Cargikk, Tgurneu, and Dozzu had combined their powers in the past, the most they'd been able to do was temporarily hold back Hayuha and two others. Number nine was fighting the Braves of the Six Flowers, plus Dozzu and its subordinate.

It was drunk on the power it had amassed. It was glad it had left Cargikk's faction and betrayed them for Tgurneu's side. Tgurneu had given it a power and a new path for self-evolution that had led it to such a formidable level.

"I've got your back, Dozzu! Go!" Adlet yelled. He threw a smoke bomb, obscuring the vision of the Dead Host and their master.

No problem, thought number nine with a smile. The Dead Host picked it up and ran away from Dozzu's attack. Goldof and Dozzu's subordinate lunged in from either side, but number nine had some of its minions sacrifice themselves in its defense.

"It's running away! Adlet! Chase it down!" Chamo cried. Adlet came close, but he was the weakest of the lot, so number nine had never been concerned about attacks from his end.

At this rate, number nine would be victorious simply by continuously running away. It had plenty of corpses to spare. If their numbers were thinned, it just had to call in the many replacements from the central area of the forest.

Specialist number nine analyzed the situation. There were a hundred of the Dead Host guarding the road to the Fainting Mountains. It couldn't reposition those. There were also about two hundred and fifty more cut off from their master on the northern side of the forest. That was a serious setback, but not a fatal one. Of the remaining six hundred and fifty, three hundred were under orders to wander about the forest. If it were to summon the whole army to its location, it could surround Adlet's party—but it decided against that. It couldn't see Hans, Mora, and Fremy, so they might burst into the forest while it was focused on Adlet's group.

As specialist number nine fled the scene, it considered. If this strategy was a success, it would certainly receive the greatest honor: receiving from Tgurneu not a number, but an independent name all its own.

When that honor had once been given to the child of a filthy, ugly human, number nine had trembled with hatred and rage.

Wait, no—with this power, specialist number nine might be able to attain something even greater. It could surpass Tgurneu and Cargikk and become the commander of all fiends. It could become an archfiend, serving the Evil God directly, and choose its own name. Even Dozzu, who had once claimed to be an equal to Tgurneu and Cargikk, didn't stand a chance. That was just how powerful number nine was.

Little by little, something was changing inside the specialist's heart. Slowly, a unique desire and will was born in its soul. Just like Tgurneu, Cargikk, and Dozzu, number nine had in its heart the desire to rule. It had begun to seek out the pleasure of manipulating others to its will.

*   *   *

What the hell is going on?

Meanwhile, Rainer was wandering around in the central region of the forest, on the prowl for moving things. If he found something, he would screech and attack it. His opponents were not the Braves of the Six Flowers. He was fighting dozens of mysterious fiends: lizards, snakes, leeches, and frogs. Massive aquatic fiends were waging war on the Dead Host, but fiends were no match for them. The Dead Host would surround them and take them down, and the mysterious enemies would shift into a strange, mud-like substance. But then, after about half a minute, the mud would return to its original shape. The Dead Host simply fought and killed, fought and killed the things in an endless cycle.

Rainer couldn't communicate his existence to the Six Braves or even encounter them at all. *At this rate…* His high hopes were rapidly falling. Those thunderclaps and explosions that he had surmised were part of the battle with the Braves had already grown distant. There was also no indication that his only hope was approaching the forest's central region. These fiends were brainless. They didn't even notice the words on Rainer's right arm.

Rainer watched as one of the water snake–fiends was revived from mud. A shriek left Rainer's mouth, and all the Dead Host around descended on the enemy in unison. Again, he was compelled to join in.

The weakness pulsed in his left arm—the signal that he could move it again. This would be the third time that day.

If these fiends really are allies of the Six Braves… Frantically, Rainer pulled a sharp rock out of the pocket of his ragged pants, the same one he'd used to write on his arm and those of the other corpses.

Rainer's body charged at the water snake. His right arm grabbed onto it to hold it down, while his now-free left arm reached out to stab the rock into the water snake's flesh. He tried to carve letters into its body—*Save me. I'm alive.* But before he could manage a single letter, the water snake twisted out of his grasp and struck back, its tail skimming Rainer's stomach. It hurt enough to make him want to scream, but the parasite drove Rainer's body forward, heedless of his pain.

It's no good. I can't write on it—I'm going to get killed. Numbness shot through Rainer's left arm, and he panicked and slipped the sharp stone, the only tool he had, back in his pocket. This would never work. But he couldn't think of anything else.

What will happen if...the fight goes on like this? Rainer wondered. He couldn't imagine the chosen heroes would lose. It was surely a matter of time before they defeated specialist number nine. But once the battle was over and the fiend controlling the Dead Host had died, what would happen to Rainer?

If specialist number nine's death restored the humanity of its slaves, that would be fine. And even if they still remained the Dead Host, he could hold out hope the Braves of the Six Flowers might find him. But if specialist number nine's death killed them all...

Rainer didn't have much time left.

Had the Braves noticed yet that one of them was alive and knew about Tgurneu's secret weapon? Had the Braves seen the five corpses with Rainer's messages? *The Braves have to have seen them,* Rainer told himself. *They're sure to find me.*

But what Rainer didn't know was that around the great tree, now suddenly quiet after the departure of number nine and the Braves, lay the bodies of about twenty Dead Host. One of the bodies had been entirely scorched by Dozzu's lightning, contorted in agony as it died. Some letters were faintly discernible on its left wrist.

...ant.

That was one of the bodies that Rainer had written on to tell the Braves of his existence. *Man with words on right arm. Knows. Important.* Dozzu's attack had seared the words into illegibility. One of Rainer's lifelines had just been cut, and no one had even noticed.

Another was wandering on the north side of the ravine, on the forest's edge. It had chased Hans across the ravine, and when the assassin blew up the bridge, the corpse was left with no way back to the forest. The Braves of the Six Flowers were all on the southern side of the valley. None of them would concern themselves with the Dead Host trapped on the northern side. The Six Braves would never see the words written on its left arm: *One is alive. Search and save. Man with words on right arm. Large build. Scar on face. Knows Tgurneu's weapon.*

And just outside the forest, on the road to the Temple of Fate, about a hundred of the Dead Host had assembled in formation. They had been ordered to kill everything that approached. On the arm of one of them were the words, *Man with words on right arm. Knows. Important.* The Six Braves would not head to the temple until specialist number nine was dead. Nobody would read the information on that corpse's left arm.

As the pursuit wore on, all six were relentless in their assault. Whenever specialist number nine judged it was in even the slightest bit of danger, it would flee southward. They had already repeated this same pattern several times over the course of nearly an hour. Behind the group, Rolonia joined the chase as well.

"That damned bug turned tail and ran again!" yelled Adlet.

"Can't you push any farther into its formation, Goldof?" Nashetania called.

During the fight, they couldn't say anything that might hint at their ambush. If specialist number nine realized where Fremy and Mora were, all of this would come to nothing.

Rolonia moaned. "Nngh… What do I do?" she muttered. They could probably win if the fight went on like this. But that would also mean that the Dead Host would die—and she couldn't have that. Rolonia wanted to save them, no matter what. But she was also aware they had no time. They lacked the people and the supplies, and they didn't even know how it could be done. She was helpless in this situation.

Rolonia wanted information. She wanted someone to tell her how to deliver the Dead Host—no matter how faint the hope of success was.

That was when two of the corpses circled around through the forest to attack from the rear. Rolonia, who occupied that position, fought them off with mad lashes of her whip. "I'm sorry!" she cried. She couldn't afford to hold back, and she wasn't nimble enough to disable them rather than kill them. Trembling with guilt, Rolonia flailed her whip. The tip missed during its first strike, but for the second, the middle section struck the corpse right over the heart. The Dead Host expired with a fountain of blood. Another corpse came to grapple with Rolonia, but even pinned to the ground, she manipulated her whip to wring out its blood from its back.

But then a moment later, the corpse's mouth moved, and Rolonia clearly heard it speak. "Please...save...us..."

"Huh?"

"Save us...the cave..."

On the ground, Rolonia stared up at the corpse's face, stunned. She came to her senses with a start and immediately tried to administer emergency treatment. But it had already died at her hand. "No, no..."

"What're you doing, you moo-head?!" Chamo kicked Rolonia's leg where she lay on the ground.

"Chamo, one of the Dead Host people just spoke!"

"Uh-huh? It was just your imagination! You do some fighting, too, moo-head!" Many more of the Dead Host were approaching from behind them, about to attack.

Rolonia flailed her whip wildly, forcing them back. As she did, she listened intently and watched the corpses' mouths. One of them had clearly just talked: *Save us.* The Dead Host were alive after all, and they were trying to tell her something.

That was when she saw a slave-fiend take down one of the Dead Host. The corpse unmistakably fixed its eyes on Rolonia before pointing somewhere in the distance. "Cave..."

Rolonia ran up to the corpse. "What is it? What's over there?"

"Hidden woman...in the cave... Save us..." The corpse fell before it could finish its message. Rolonia looked in the direction it had pointed. It was a little ways south of the road to the Temple of Fate. From this position, she couldn't see what was over there.

"We're taking a break," Adlet gasped. He was a little tired, unsurprisingly. Dozzu, running beside him, stopped the pursuit, and Goldof and Nashetania paused just before they could launch their attack. The tireless slave-fiends continued their assault against the masses of the Dead Host.

They were already close to the low mountain in the south where Fremy and Mora were waiting. About fifteen more minutes of fighting, and they'd chase number nine down. Once they killed this fiend, they'd finally be able to make a beeline for the Temple of Fate. Their goal was to uncover the true nature of the Black Barrenbloom. They couldn't afford to spend time here. *Once we've caught our breath a bit, we'll go back to fighting,* thought Adlet, but just then, someone behind him spoke.

"Didn't any of you hear it? Addy? Anyone?" Rolonia was addressing the group.

What is it this time? he thought.

"What did you hear?" asked Dozzu.

"One of the people in the Dead Host… It talked, and it said to save it…and…it said there's a cave over that way, so we should go there… None of you heard anything?"

Adlet didn't know about this.

Rolonia looked around, but none of the others came forward. "If I go there, I might find out something. Everyone, I'm sorry. I'm…going to go see." Rolonia was about to run off when Adlet halted her.

"Stop it. It's a trap. I told you before, didn't I? Tgurneu is doing this to try to buy itself some time!"

"Rolonia, it would be dangerous…and I doubt there would be any point in going," said Dozzu.

"Do you think these people would make pointless comments right before they died?! Something must be there!" Rolonia snapped back at Dozzu.

"Please, Rolonia. Just stop," Adlet said quietly. He couldn't handle Rolonia's fixation with the Dead Host any longer. "Please. Stop making my doubts worse."

"…Addy." Rolonia gazed at him. Just then, a sword came between the two of them.

"That's enough, Rolonia," Nashetania asserted, cold eyes fixed on her. "Your scheme is entirely transparent." Rolonia's eyes widened.

What the hell, Nashetania? thought Adlet.

"What're you doing, Princess? Aren't we attacking?" asked Chamo.

"Let's wait a little longer before the next round," Nashetania replied. "The enemy doesn't appear to be moving, so that shouldn't pose a problem. More importantly, let's talk about who Rolonia really is."

"What are you getting at, Nashetania?" Adlet tried to grab her wrist, but the princess slipped away from him.

"I'm saying that it's now even more likely that Rolonia is the seventh."

A long silence passed. Adlet softly put a hand on his sword. No matter what Goldof had said, if Nashetania was plotting to deceive them, Adlet would kill her then and there.

"Adlet, you place too much trust in your allies. Dozzu told you already, didn't he? The seventh's attack has already begun. It's really quite simple—so simple, in fact, that any neutral observer could figure it out right away," Nashetania coaxed, as if this was all for his sake. "If your plan is to kill your allies while keeping your own identity hidden, then the most simple and rational way to go about it is to deliberately make mistakes. If you manage to kill a Brave, great. If you fail, you only have to make your excuses and await your next opportunity. Isn't that right?" Nashetania examined Adlet's face. "Has Rolonia been useful to you? Haven't you cleaned up after her mistakes time and time again, Adlet?"

Adlet was about to protest that she was wrong. But the fiends had nearly found Rolonia a number of times during the advance through the Cut-Finger Forest. Still, that was just because she was bad at sneaking. She wasn't trying to be discovered. "Rolonia saved Hans," he said.

"Only to gain your trust."

That's a stretch, thought Adlet. What was her goal in bringing up all of this? "I'm not gonna let you say all this with zero evidence."

"You *can't* think my claims are all completely unfounded." Nashetania approached Rolonia and Goldof grabbed Rolonia's arms. Nashetania reached out to the squirming girl's shoulder and pulled something out from a gap in her armor. It was a small piece of wood. Studying it, Nashetania murmured, "I see. So that's what's going on." Goldof released Rolonia's arms and backed away.

"What is this?" Nashetania presented the small wooden piece to Rolonia.

"...I don't know," said Rolonia. "What is it?"

The moment Adlet saw the wooden piece, he knew what it was: a flute for calling fiends. It could make sounds inaudible to humans but could signal any fiends nearby. Adlet had something similar. However, this flute had many holes in it. It was probably a higher performance instrument than the one Atreau had made.

"It's a flute for summoning fiends," said Nashetania. "Now why would you have something like that?"

"...I-it's not mine. I don't know. I've never seen it before!" Rolonia was panicking.

"You really had your eye on Dozzu during our initial assault. When Dozzu got farther away, you tried to pull something out of your shoulder armor. But then you noticed me looking, and you stopped. I thought something might be up, so I figured I'd check. What do you know, I hit the jackpot."

"I don't know! Stop this, please!"

"Nashetania," said Adlet, "if you don't want to die, then shut up." He was ready to give in to his anger and draw his sword. Nashetania was trying to set Rolonia up. He considered sending the signal to Fremy to detonate the bombs attached to her knees.

"Why do I have to shut up? I'm saying this for *your* sake." Nashetania faced Adlet as he drew his sword. "We've already narrowed down the

possible candidates for the seventh. Along with you and Fremy, Rolonia is a relatively likely suspect. And we're headed toward information on the Black Barrenbloom. It's highly probable the seventh will try to stop us."

"..."

"You're telling me I'm not even allowed to let you know what I've seen? To overlook everything unless I have definite proof?"

Adlet shot back, "You're our enemy. It just looks to me like you're trying to frame Rolonia."

"I have bombs attached to my knees, and I'm surrounded by Braves. Would you consider attempting a setup, in such a predicament?"

"I still can't trust anything you say."

"Maybe," said Chamo. "We can't trust Nashetania, but Chamo's not so sure about what you're saying, either. It's kinda weird to say that you've gotta trust everyone unless there's solid proof they're the seventh."

"That's not what I'm saying. But I—"

"Chamo's been seriously wondering about this stuff. Like, why does that moo-head keep getting in our way?"

"...Well, she's not—"

"We gonna take out Rolonia, Adlet? Or kill the princess?" Chamo touched her foxtail to her mouth, smirking. She still had quite a few slave-fiends left in her stomach.

"Chamo," said Nashetania, "I don't believe we should kill Rolonia right away. The flute may not be hers—since there is a chance the seventh placed it on her, without her realizing."

"Yeah, s'pose so."

"What on earth are you proposing?" demanded Dozzu. "What is this about, Nashetania?" The fiend was rattled. At the very least, its behavior didn't seem like an act to Adlet. Besides, Dozzu and Nashetania wouldn't have had the time to scheme together. This wasn't any scheme of Dozzu's.

"I'm just telling everyone what I saw. I'm not plotting anything, Dozzu." Nashetania turned back to Adlet. "As I said to Chamo, I won't say it's entirely clear that Rolonia is the enemy. But it is possible she's planning to delay us, or perhaps she's laid a trap to kill us in that cave. We cannot let her go."

"But I know what they said!" cried Rolonia. "They said to go to the cave! They said to save them!"

Adlet was shocked. Rolonia was more worried about the Dead Host than about herself. *Why?* he wondered. Was she actually hiding something?

He couldn't believe himself. He'd just been about to trust Nashetania's word over Rolonia's. Unforgivable. But now that the suspicions had been born, they wouldn't go away no matter how much he denied them.

Still, Adlet placed his hand on Rolonia's shoulder and said, "Don't worry. I don't know what Nashetania is plotting, but you've got the strongest man in the world on your side. I'm not gonna let you get killed."

"...Thank you," Rolonia replied. But her attitude revealed it to him. It couldn't be—was she still... "Are you planning on going to that cave?"

Her silence was the same as a yes.

"What are you thinking?!" yelled Adlet. "Do you not get what's going on here?! Nashetania's about to set you up. She's trying to frame you!"

"But I have to go, right now! We might lose the opportunity!"

"Enough about the Dead Host! I told you, that writing and the talking corpses, it's all Tgurneu's plot!" He couldn't understand her. The flute thing wasn't the only cause for suspicion. The other reason was her incomprehensible attempt to try to save the unsaveable Dead Host.

"Obviously, Chamo's not gonna let you go off on your own." Chamo pressed close to Rolonia.

"I agree with Chamo," said Nashetania. "I'm sorry, but we need to prevent Rolonia from doing anything."

"Hey, moo-head. Hand over that whip," Chamo demanded, holding out her hand. Rolonia's eyes filled with fright. Her whip was her only weapon.

"Chamo'll hold on to it until you're cleared of suspicion. That's okay, right? You've been totally useless, anyway."

"B-but this…"

"If you're innocent, Chamo'll give it back. But you still can't hand it over, huh? Why not?" Chamo approached her, waving her foxtail.

Rolonia stepped back. "I can't fight without my whip."

"Exactly. Don't fight. If you can't give it up, then Chamo's got no choice."

Right as Chamo plunged her foxtail down her throat, Adlet sprang into action, using his sword to block the attack of the slave-fiend from her stomach. "Stop it, Chamo!"

"Chamo's not gonna kill her! Just make her kinda so she can't move."

Adlet warded off the slave-fiends she puked up, one after another. He understood that Chamo wasn't trying to kill Rolonia, but still, he couldn't allow this.

"Rolonia…" said Goldof, "hand over…your whip. I don't want this to cause a…falling out in the group."

"I-I can't!"

When Goldof grabbed at her, Adlet kicked him in the side. The slave-fiends took that opportunity to close in on Rolonia. She fought back, unwilling to relinquish her whip.

"You're dumb, Rolonia," said Chamo. "If you'd just done as you were told, you wouldn't get hurt."

"I-I…"

The dispute among the allies continued, all within sight of the enemy. Meanwhile, Nashetania, the one who had incited the uproar, spectated from the side.

"Please, hold on. This isn't good. Specialist number nine is moving." That was when Dozzu, who had been watching the enemy, called out to the others. The long-neglected Dead Host were headed their way. They had apparently discerned that something was wrong, and so they had chosen this time to go on the offensive.

"We've got no choice. We're fighting them!" Adlet stood in the lead, facing the Dead Host.

"Oh, well. Guess dealing with Rolonia comes later," said Chamo, and the slave-fiends attacking Rolonia switched targets to the Dead Host.

The battle became fiercer than ever before, not at all like when they were chasing a fleeing enemy. They had to fend off the Dead Host coming at them while also herding the crowd toward the southern mountain where Fremy and Mora were waiting.

As they fought, Adlet wondered, *What the hell is going on? What should I do? Is Nashetania trying to trick us? Or has she actually figured out that Rolonia could be the seventh and is just telling us?* Either option was viable. He couldn't make a judgment. Did Rolonia just want to save the Dead Host? Or was she actually trying to lure the Braves into a trap? Adlet didn't know about that, either, because he couldn't understand why she would be so obsessed with saving them. Rolonia was kind. She would naturally consider it. But why would she risk her life to do it? Still bewildered, he battled the Dead Host.

Adlet tossed a large bomb while Goldof charged in, breaking the formation. Somehow, they managed to get the enemies to stop attacking and begin their retreat.

That was the moment Nashetania said, "Rolonia is gone!"

Adlet turned around. Rolonia, who had been fighting in the rear, had vanished. *No way. Did she really go off to that cave to try to save the Dead Host?*

"Were you not watching her, Chamo?!" Nashetania yelled.

"No! What were you and Goldof doing?!" Chamo began bickering with her. Goldof seemed unsure of whether he should chase down Rolonia or not.

"Well, this is a mess. Chamo might have to do more than just hurt her," Chamo grumbled. Now the group's suspicions were even stronger.

"What are you doing, Rolonia?" Adlet muttered. He was convinced that the message written on that corpse as well as the talking Dead Host were all part of Tgurneu's trap. At this rate, Rolonia might get herself killed. He had to keep her safe—but how? "Rolonia...are you really...?" He struggled to suppress his growing doubts toward her.

*   *   *

Looks like I caught them, thought specialist number nine. It had gone on the offensive not to try to kill the Six Braves, but to approach them and find out what was going on. Noticing that a discussion had turned into infighting, the fiend had determined that perhaps one of them had fallen into its trap. Having heard their conversation, that suspicion had turned to certainty.

Specialist number nine recalled the past—it had to have been about ten years ago, now. After placing itself under Tgurneu's banner, it had spent a long period of time evolving itself. Using the vast numbers of human test subjects Tgurneu had gathered, it perfected its Dead Host.

But when it had presented the fruits of its efforts to Tgurneu, for some reason the commander's expression turned sour. Number nine had been so confident in its masterpiece, it found the reaction difficult to believe.

"It's just not quite satisfactory," said Tgurneu. "Look, this Dead Host of yours can't talk, can it?" Number nine shook its head. The Dead Host was a weapon for battle. It shouldn't need speech.

"I couldn't call it perfect, then. Make it so they can speak on command. And also..." Tgurneu put one hand to its chin, thinking. "Yes, I'd like just a few of them to be able to move freely."

"What on earth for?" asked number nine.

"Don't ask stupid questions. Just trust me, number nine," Tgurneu said with a smile.

In retrospect, Tgurneu's keen insight astonished number nine. It would never have come up with that idea even if it had racked its brains for a thousand years. Tgurneu had predicted that one of the Braves of the Six Flowers would try to save the Dead Host. It had also said that if number nine could use them effectively, it could lure the Six Braves into a trap and kill them.

At first, number nine had thought this impossible. Humans were foolish creatures, but not so stupid as to want to save the Dead Host. And it couldn't have even imagined that one of them would be so foolish as to go off on their own to make the attempt.

The fiend emitted a special call to the Dead Host in the central area of the forest, ordering them to lure Rolonia Manchetta into the cave and instructing each corpse on what to say to her.

Specialist number nine didn't know if she was a real Brave or the seventh. But Tgurneu surely would never have placed such a foolish girl under its command. *I'll get rid of her quickly*, it concluded.

Meanwhile, Mora was keeping under cover on the slope of the low mountain. With her power of clairvoyance, she observed the whole mountain. There was no sign of the Dead Host or the fiend approaching. The mountain was entirely silent. "Not yet? They're late," Mora murmured.

Fremy replied calmly, "No, they're not. It should take this much time. Just keep calm and wait." Fremy had said that the most important part of a sniping operation was patience. She must have done this many times before, but Mora, who was unaccustomed to it, really couldn't hide her stress.

There were many causes for concern: the seventh, Dozzu and Nashetania, and Tgurneu. And Mora was especially worried about Adlet and Rolonia. Both of them had been terribly troubled over the Dead Host. Mora could only pray that their sympathy wouldn't lead to any erratic behavior.

But despite her worry, Mora couldn't know what was going on with the others from her position. All she could do was keep waiting.

About half an hour before Rolonia left the group, Hans was on the northern end of the forest, standing silently up a tree. The Dead Host were milling about below.

He had strung up wire here and there around the trees. Every time a corpse stepped on one, there was a wooden smack, and every time that sound rang out, the Dead Host would descend into a mad search for the enemy. What Hans had constructed was just a simple clapper device. But the Dead Host didn't have the mental capacity to figure that out, nor did they have the ability to learn that the noise was meaningless.

Hans smirked and soundlessly ran off along the branches of the trees.

Chapter 5

Discovery

They'd killed so many of the Dead Host already, but corpses were still wandering here and there about the forest. Rolonia listened as hard as she could to the sound of their footsteps, seeking out the areas where enemy forces were thinnest so she could run onward.

From far behind her, she heard the shrieks of the Dead Host, followed by the crack of Dozzu's lightning. "They're fighting..." For a second, she felt she had to go back and help out—but a moment later, she decided against that. If she were to go back now, she'd be killed. Nashetania still had her framed. Dozzu, Chamo, and Goldof all doubted her, and now that she'd run off alone like this, they had to be even more suspicious. *Why is this happening?* Rolonia wondered. She couldn't go back. But she didn't know what she should do, either. She couldn't think of any way to prove her innocence.

Just a few hours earlier, back in that hut, she had inspected her equipment. She hadn't had any such flute then. Nashetania must have stuck it in there. But Rolonia also knew she'd been constantly keeping an eye on the princess. If Nashetania had touched her, then Rolonia would have noticed immediately. She couldn't have had a chance to plant that flute on her. So then who was it? Goldof? Dozzu? Or the seventh? No matter how she mulled over it, she couldn't recall anything.

"I'm sorry, Addy." *I've caused trouble for everyone again*, she thought. Her own stupidity was to blame for her falling for Nashetania's trickery. But no amount of frustration or remorse could make her any smarter.

Rolonia recalled the expression on Adlet's face, right before she had left. Even he had been suspicious of her. That was hard to swallow.

But she started running again, weaving between the corpses toward where the cave would be. She could deal with her own problems later. There was something she had to do: she would save the Dead Host.

"It's okay... I can...do this." She was so scared, her teeth wouldn't stop chattering. *What can someone like me even manage, anyway?* she thought. But she was more angry than anything else. To her, everyone involved in this was unforgivable: Tgurneu, for creating the Dead Host, and her allies, for abandoning them.

"!" Had one of them heard Rolonia muttering, or had that just been a coincidence? A corpse had noticed her. Immediately, Rolonia veered off to one side, and she was about to escape when the corpse shrieked, alerting the others.

"Wahh!" Dead Host corpses closed in from either side, swinging at her. She took their strikes with the pauldrons of her armor, but the impact made her stumble forward. She couldn't take hits like Goldof could. She nearly fell over, but she picked herself up again and ran. Before she could get away, another corpse blocked her way. She couldn't get past them without fighting.

She grasped her whip with both hands and swung it. She tried to scream obscenities at the Dead Host, since it was the only way to make herself fight. But the words wouldn't come out. She could battle fiends, but it was humans standing in front of her. She thrashed her whip about, stopping the Dead Host's charge, but she was too slow, and deflecting them was the most she could manage.

"Guh!" Right as she was about to get away, a corpse struck her in the face. Blood spurted from her broken nose. Instantly, she activated her power as the Saint of Spilled Blood, manipulating and coagulating her blood to return her broken nose to its original shape. But the Dead Host didn't even give her the time to recover. They hurled themselves at her one after another.

"I'm sorry!" she yelled, and this time, she struck with all her power behind it. The whip leaped and wove around the trees to take out corpse after corpse. She didn't have the luxury of going easy on them. She'd probably killed a number of them already. Though Rolonia was tortured with guilt, she pushed forward. She didn't have the time to heal them, either. She had to go to the cave and find whatever was there—she didn't know what it was, or if it would really lead her to rescue the Dead Host, but there was meaning in her efforts because she knew what those corpses had told her.

That was when she heard the fallen body speak behind her. "Please... heal me..." was all it said, and then it breathed its last.

"I was right," Rolonia murmured. Some of the Dead Host were still alive. The parasites had infiltrated their nerves and brains, but even so, some of their minds were still alive.

From somewhere else came another voice. One of Rolonia's pursuers was moving its lips. "Don't...kill me..." it said as it lunged for her.

Rolonia rolled away. "Please, hold on! I will save you!" she yelled, and she kept on running.

Rainer wandered about the forest for a long time. He was hearing fewer calls from the Dead Host in the north, and the south had been quiet for a while—but now it seemed that battle had recommenced. *Why aren't the Six Braves coming this way? I'm over here.*

Now there was a lizard-fiend in front of him, and a scream rose from Rainer's throat as his body fought it together with the other members of the Dead Host. The lizard-fiend swung its tail and spat acid at the Dead Host. Its tactics appeared to be pure offense and no defense, as though it wanted nothing more than to take down just one more corpse.

Not again! The mass of Dead Host pinned the lizard-fiend's limbs as Rainer's body stomped on its head over and over. The fiend turned into a lump of mud.

He had lost track of how many of these they had beaten so far. He'd shown them the words on his right arm more than once. But the mysterious fiends never stopped fighting, and the Braves of the Six Flowers hadn't found him, either.

These fiends were a no-go after all. He had to encounter the Braves somehow. But his left arm wasn't moving, and the area where they were fighting was so far away. He desperately racked his brains for a way to get close. But as long as his left arm, his only hope, wouldn't move for him, none of that contemplation was going to be any use at all.

He wondered where the five corpses with the messages on their left arms were. The Braves of the Six Flowers might well have encountered one of them. Had they just not found the words?

...*It couldn't be that...* A terrifying thought came to Rainer, and it chilled him to the core. What if the Braves had already found the messages he had left...and they were ignoring them? That would kill his hope entirely.

Had they decided there was no way to save the Dead Host and given up on them? Or had they decided that Rainer's information wasn't worth the danger? Or maybe they believed the messages were part of Tgurneu's scheme? If so, it was all over.

But the moment that thought struck Rainer, he heard the Dead Host screaming nearby. There shouldn't be any of the mysterious fiends in that direction. Rainer's body reacted to the shrieks and raced away, and other Dead Hosts nearby surged in the same direction. This was different from before. Their numbers were greater now. They had to be headed toward a Brave.

One of them might have come looking for Rainer. His heart swelled with hope. *Have they noticed my messages? No, even if they haven't, it's fine. If they can just read the words on my right arm...*

Eventually, he was able to discern the outline of a warrior. He could faintly see the luster of metal through the trees. The warrior was sprinting for the deepest part of the forest. As Rainer chased her, he noticed that she was a short girl with a whip who was trying to avoid killing the Dead

Host. The messy-haired swordsman Rainer had seen earlier had no compunction about cutting down the enemies in front of him, but this girl was only using her whip to defend herself and avoid fatally wounding any of her targets.

Rainer was certain she was trying to save the Dead Host—or at the very least, she was trying not to kill them. If he showed his message to her, she would notice that Rainer was alive.

I can see there's hope! Come on, arm, move now! Rainer prayed in desperation as he ran. But his left arm wouldn't budge.

That was when he happened to hear a strange-sounding voice, like someone, somewhere, was talking to him. He wanted to look around, but his neck wouldn't move. There couldn't have been any Braves around, though, aside from her, and the Dead Host couldn't speak.

Someone said something again, and this time, Rainer could hear it clearly, too. "Save...me..." It was the Dead Host talking. The corpses with Rainer who were chasing after the armored girl.

Why were they speaking? Rainer was confused. He'd thought that all the rest of them were mindless living corpses. Had he been mistaken?

He could hear words from every mouth, each saying something different. "We're alive," "Don't kill me," "Go to the cave," and "Save us." Their words were various, but they were all trying to communicate the same message. The corpses wanted her to do two things: save them and go to the cave.

Back when Rainer had been lying in that cavern, not a single corpse had said anything. He couldn't understand why they could suddenly communicate. Had something happened to specialist number nine? Had someone else enabled them to speak?

As Rainer's body chased Rolonia, he considered this question—until he reached an answer. *I can't believe it… How can this…how can this be happening?* Rainer's high hopes plummeted to despair in the blink of an eye.

Why were the Dead Host talking? The only answer he could think of was that the fiend controlling them had ordered it.

Rainer also immediately understood why it had made its corpses talk.

Specialist number nine was trying to lure the armored girl into the cave. As for what it would do there, Rainer could only imagine that it planned to kill her—and she hadn't figured it out yet. At this rate, she was going to die.

Stop, Brave! There's nothing in there!

And that wasn't the only reason for Rainer's despair. Once the armored girl realized it was a trap, what would happen?

The answer was obvious: The Braves of the Six Flowers would believe Rainer's messages to be part of the enemy's plot and assume that Tgurneu had dropped clues of its secret weapon to lure the Six Braves to their death.

What do I do? What do I do?!

The girl in the armor had already gotten farther away. Dodging and weaving, she used her whip to pull herself up into a tree and dashed along the branches deeper into the forest. Then she was gone.

Rolonia had vanished. But even now that Adlet was aware, he couldn't chase after her. They were still fighting to push number nine toward the southern mountain. They were gradually making progress, but the fiend's defenses were as solid as ever.

"Damn it, damn it! What do I do?" Adlet muttered as he lobbed a bomb. Rolonia must have gone off for the sake of the Dead Host. Did she not understand how dangerous her situation was? He didn't understand what her real motives were. Was she actually trying to save them, or was she trying to trick Adlet, as Nashetania had said?

"…What am I thinking?"

A corpse lunged at Adlet from behind in an attempt to pin his arms behind his back, but the boy coolly ducked, caught the impact, and grabbed the corpse by the arms to throw it forward. He slammed it on the ground headfirst and stomped on its neck for good measure.

What was he doing, suspecting Rolonia? She'd just fallen for Tgurneu's and Nashetania's tricks. How could he *not* go to save her? The wheels of Adlet's brain spun as he mulled over what he should do, and what he had no choice but to do.

"Goldof!" he yelled. Goldof, who had been about to charge the center of the enemy's formation, glanced over to him. "Protect Chamo! Don't let Nashetania or Dozzu lay a finger on her!"

"What are you talking about?" Goldof yelled back.

"Just listen! I'm making sure we're ready for Dozzu and Nashetania to betray us! If I find a single scratch on Chamo, you better believe that Nashetania is gonna die!"

If Adlet was going to leave to find Rolonia, the problem would be Chamo. Once he left, she'd be stuck alone surrounded by Dozzu and its allies. Goldof was basically still on their side, so Adlet had no choice but to let him protect her. The young knight was fighting for Nashetania's safety, not her ambition. Adlet didn't know how effective threats would be, but that was all he could manage right now.

"Adlet, what are you talking ab—" Nashetania tried to say, but Adlet ignored her and yelled at Chamo.

"I'm trusting you to handle the rest, Chamo!"

"What do you mean?" Chamo replied, but Adlet wasn't listening. He was already running off after Rolonia.

Adlet couldn't find any Dead Host patrolling the forest. They'd probably joined the pursuit of Rolonia. As Adlet ran, he wondered why she was going so far to protect the Dead Host. *Think. There has to be a reason.* He considered the things that had happened since they'd learned about the Dead Host, as well as their fight in the Phantasmal Barrier, but none of it rang any bells. So he reached further back to two years earlier, when they had met on the mountain where Adlet had been training. He sifted through each and every memory.

That was when one certain incident rose again in his mind. "No way...Rolonia...," he murmured.

It couldn't be that, he thought.

Meanwhile, Rolonia was thinking back on the past, too, recalling the time when she had first met Adlet Mayer.

*   *   *

Rolonia Manchetta believed that life was something you put up with until you died. As one who was unfortunate enough to be born, she was required to endure life until her death. There was nothing that could be done about it. It was inevitable. This was what Rolonia had always believed—until the day she met Adlet Mayer.

She'd been born on the eastern edge of the continent, in Lind, Land of Blue Winds. It was a very small country, and most of the other Braves wouldn't have known where it was. A majority of the people in the Land of Blue Winds made their living by raising cows, and Rolonia's parents were no exception. She grew up watching the cattle leisurely chewing their cud, and the sight never bored her. Rolonia's job was to blow her flute to call her father or the herding dog whenever the occasional cow looked liable to stray from the herd.

Rolonia loved cows. If she were asked what was the most wonderful thing in the world, she would name them as her answer without hesitation. She loved them so much that later, when she would make her personal armor at All Heavens Temple, her design was cow-inspired—though it was so extremely cow-like that the other Saints thought it was awful.

Her father was a taciturn but kind man. Her mother was cheerful and talkative, and she knew how to have a good time. They cultivated within Rolonia a heart full of love for all things and vulnerable to sorrow at the misfortunes of others. If Rolonia had lived a life without incident, she would surely have ended up a simple and kind cattle herder. That life would certainly have been better for her, too.

When Rolonia was seven years old, her home village was attacked by brigands. When they appeared out of the blue, the tiny little village in the tiny little country was powerless to resist. The outlaws pillaged the town as easy as snatching up loose coins in the street. In just one night, Rolonia lost her parents and everything else important to her. After that, Rolonia learned the cold, hard truth that the world was filled with tragedy and pain, and that those without power, knowledge, or charm could do nothing but flee.

Now an orphan, Rolonia was taken in by a wealthy merchant of a neighboring land. People called him a loving and good man for raising children with no family—but that was just the mask he presented to the world. He made the orphans work on his farm. The ones who slacked off were whipped mercilessly, and the ones who worked hard received not even a single copper coin in reward. The children were slaves in all but name.

The children in this harsh environment did not choose to change their lot or rebel against their horrible circumstances. Rarely would any even try to escape. Instead, the children found an outlet for their discontent and despair in the weakest among them. The one who came to serve that role was the stupidest of the group, Rolonia.

Every time Rolonia made some mistake, the other children would hit her and insult her. They never overlooked a single misstep, no matter how small. The children enjoyed seeing who would discover her next blunder. Eventually, they even came to do this openly in front of the adults who monitored them.

Rolonia never fought back. She believed the situation was her fault. Everyone was angry at her because she had screwed up. She was convinced that she was the wrongdoer, and the others were all her victims. She would try to never make another mistake, but even then, she couldn't work to their satisfaction. And even when it wasn't Rolonia's fault, the other children still said it was. Gradually, she learned that she was no good, no matter what she did. Despite her best efforts, there was no point. She was slow, couldn't do anything, and would only ever be a burden on the people around her. Rolonia thought she could avoid being a burden at the very least, but even that effort was in vain.

No matter what the other children did to her, Rolonia never talked back, so they started blaming every bad thing on her. They tormented her, making their own failures and unhappiness with their circumstances all

Rolonia's responsibility. In the end, she stopped even trying to avoid causing trouble. She would just smile her meek smiles and pray they wouldn't
bully her.

Then a theft occurred on the farm. The leaders among the children
had planned it, but the whole deed was pinned on Rolonia. Even then,
Rolonia believed it was her fault.

Cast out from the farm, Rolonia wandered to survive. She would find out
about a position and ask to be hired, but she was refused. This happened
over and over.

Walking through one town, she encountered a girl dressed well but
with dirty shoes. Rolonia resolved to go speak to the girl and was permit-
ted to polish her shoes with her own clothes. And then, with a subservient
smile, Rolonia said to her, "Please let me work. I'll do anything." That
girl was an acolyte who aspired to become a Saint at the Temple of Spilled
Blood. And thus Rolonia got herself a new job.

But just having somewhere new to live and different meals to eat
wasn't going to change her life. She was still as dim-witted as ever, and the
people around her still saw her as nothing more than a scapegoat for their
resentments and discontent. Rolonia didn't question it, nor did she feel the
desire to escape her circumstances. Everything she did ended in failure.
Her only goal in life was to stay as far out of anyone's way as she could, and
her only wish was to avoid angering anyone.

Rolonia came to think of life as something you survived until your
death. Her selection as the Saint of Spilled Blood was another such
occasion.

At first, she thought it was some kind of mistake. Then she prayed, *Please
let it be a mistake.* There was no way someone like her could be fit to be a
Saint. She'd never managed to do anything right her whole life. She could
do nothing but quiver, imagining how people would insult her and call her
the worst of all the Saints.

When it was decided that the members of the temple would perform the ceremony for her to return her Saint's power, Rolonia was momentarily relieved. She figured that being a servant rather than a Saint would mean people would be angry with her less often. But her nightmare had only just begun.

On the recommendation of Mora, the Elder of All Heavens Temple, Rolonia was saddled with special Saint's training. This was part of Mora's scheme, but Rolonia couldn't have known that at the time. When Mora told her she should aspire to be a Brave of the Six Flowers, Rolonia was so scared she had struggled to breathe and passed out. When she opened her eyes, she thought in a moment of relief, *So it was just a dream,* and then she was informed that this was real life. She passed out again.

Just as Mora had anticipated, Rolonia had exceptional potential as a Saint. Mora told her that it surpassed that of the authorities of the temple, such as herself and Leura, Saint of Sun. Mora even told her that she could rival Chamo Rosso, the most powerful Saint alive.

But that knowledge didn't please Rolonia—it only frightened her further. She believed she was destined to be called an incompetent, utterly useless Saint, despite her unrivaled potential. After so many years of soaking in self-condemnation, she was not going to change so easily. Mora even ordered her to study under famous fighters, but Rolonia was incapable of learning anything from these seasoned warriors. It was just a waste of time.

Then Rolonia visited Atreau Spiker, the mysterious fiend-extermination specialist, and met Adlet Mayer.

Rolonia remembered well the first time she encountered Adlet. Her first impression was that of pure fear. Adlet had been naked from the waist up, teeth clenched, eyes bloodshot, wearing his fingers raw throwing needles at a target. The moment Rolonia saw his face, it struck her that he resembled the fiends from the legends of the Braves of the Six Flowers, a creature focused solely on hate and killing. That was her initial image of him.

"Adlet Mayer," he'd said by way of introduction. "Eventually, I'll be the strongest man in the world. But not yet. Don't talk to me."

She wouldn't have wanted to talk to him, even if he had asked. Rolonia bowed her head repeatedly and tried to escape. But an instant later, Adlet roared and lunged toward her. She wrapped her arms around her head and sank to the ground—but Adlet's target was Atreau. Calmly, Atreau threw Adlet to the ground and then kicked him, over and over. Once he couldn't move anymore, Atreau stomped on his face and spat on him.

Rolonia had just been witness to something dreadful. Why had this just happened? Watching the scene, she cursed her fate.

Days passed. Just as Adlet had said, the two of them didn't interact much at all. Atreau lectured Rolonia on the subject of fiends, and she also studied by herself, perusing the books that Atreau had written. Atreau took care of her everyday necessities.

In between the lectures and her study time, Rolonia watched Adlet. His activities looked less like training and more like self-torture. Once every day, he would have a match with Atreau, but to Rolonia, their fights just seemed like one-sided beatings. She wondered what he was doing, but she didn't have the courage to talk to him.

Rolonia didn't even know why she was so curious about Adlet. Perhaps she'd fallen in love with him the moment they met, and she'd never noticed. Perhaps she just found his injuries distressing. Or perhaps seeing him wounded on the ground reminded her of her own experiences being bullied. But one night, Rolonia stepped into the cave where Adlet slept, breaking Atreau's order not to associate with him. She figured that she would heal his wounds while he was asleep and then immediately run away. That way he wouldn't be able to get angry with her.

But the moment Rolonia touched Adlet, he jolted awake. "Why are you in here?!" he yelled.

He was angry with her. Worst case, he might even kill her. Rolonia jumped back into the the corner of the cave and began trembling. "M-M-Master Atreau told me to treat your wounds…" She tried to deceive him with a spur-of-the-moment lie, but she quickly regretted it. Her lies were always exposed eventually. But surprisingly, Adlet made himself available without a fight.

With her inexperienced hands, Rolonia healed him. Her abilities were the only thing anyone aside from her parents had ever praised her for. How long had it been since she had last been useful to someone? Rolonia was so glad, she cracked a tiny smile.

After that, the two of them spoke. When Rolonia told Adlet about herself, he yelled at her, furious, and demanded why she would throw away the power she had. Then he started sobbing, telling her he wanted power himself.

I screwed up again, Rolonia thought, and she tried to make him stop crying, but the attempt caused her to start crying, too. Adlet stopped first and ended up comforting her instead. Had anyone seen them, they would have thought them a real pair of idiots.

As dawn neared in the cave, Adlet apologized to her. "I'm sorry. I shouldn't have said that. You've had it rough, too."

"No, it's okay... I'm fine."

"I can't be like this. I have to get stronger. If I were actually strong, I'd never have made you cry," he said, and then he smiled sadly. Rolonia felt that she'd misjudged him. He was a kind boy, hurt and exhausted.

That was how Adlet first caught her eye. Bit by bit, the reason for her attention began to change.

After that, when Rolonia was free, she would talk to him—though he devoted the majority of his time to training, so they couldn't spend much time together. It was totally against orders, but Atreau was either fed up or indifferent about it, so he didn't say anything.

As if trying to make up for his earlier castigation of her, Adlet approached her with kindness. He listened intently when she shared her problems with him and rambled about the past. He offered her advice, sometimes encouraged her, and other times scolded her. Rolonia, in turn, healed his wounded heart and always encouraged him.

But Adlet was not simply a kind boy. When he deplored his own powerlessness, he would wear a visage more frightening than anything she'd ever seen. But even then, he never took it out on Rolonia again. Adlet was an enigma. One moment, his expression would be filled with hatred, like a fiend, and the next, he'd give her a beaming smile. She wanted to avoid him when he had that frightening look, but when he was gentle, they could chat and get along. He was kind but terrifying, and Rolonia didn't know which face was his real one. He was firmly determined to become a Brave of the Six Flowers, but he hadn't told her why.

Gradually, Rolonia came to realize that she looked forward to their conversations. He was the only person she'd ever been able to talk to without being scared, aside from her late parents, and the one person with whom she could be open about her feelings. Though they had only just met, he'd become a significant presence in her life. It didn't take her long to realize that it was love.

Once, at the end of a lecture, Rolonia tried asking Atreau if Adlet could be one of the Braves of the Six Flowers. Atreau replied coldly that it would never happen, that there was not even a one-in-a-million chance. There was one reason for that: he had no talent. It seemed Adlet himself was aware of that, too.

Rolonia was unbearably curious. Why would he try to tackle this task, knowing it was impossible? If it wasn't going to work out, it was better to just give up. Failing without trying didn't hurt as much as putting in the effort and failing anyway. Rolonia was intimately familiar with the fact.

Once, in the middle of the night, she asked him as she healed him. "Adlet, how can you go on without giving up?" she said.

Adlet replied coldly, "So now I'm getting that from you, too, huh, Rolonia?"

She got scared, thinking she'd made him angry. She trembled, imagining her only friend had come to hate her.

But Adlet quickly smiled. "Everyone tells me I've got no talent: my master, the other apprentices who ran off, the occasional visitors like you—everyone. At first, I figured that was just bullshit, but lately I've come to think that maybe they're right."

"Adlet... Then..."

"So I eventually started thinking maybe I was fine with having no talent."

"...Huh?"

Smiling, he said, "It's way more amazing for someone like me with zero talent at all to become the strongest man in the world rather than some genius who was born with it, right?"

"Y-yeah."

"And I know it'll feel awesome to get there. I bet a genius would never feel anything that amazing."

"..."

"I'm not gonna whine anymore about wanting talent. I'll become the strongest man in the world as the person I am."

Rolonia fell silent. She had believed all this time that she was a failure as a human being. That was why she believed it was futile even to try. But Adlet had found an entirely different way to live. She found him over-whelming. What a difference. He could keep fighting and never give up, even if he had no power at all. But Rolonia had kept running away, though at the very least she had talent as a Saint. Suddenly, Rolonia felt ashamed to be near him.

"Adlet," she said, "if you can never get that power...if no matter how hard you try, it's still no good...what would you do then?"

"...That's a difficult problem," Adlet said softly. "But, well, I don't have to think about it. If you never give up until you die, you won't have to worry about it."

Oh...so I just have to think of it that way, Rolonia mentally replied, smiling.

I can't go on like this, thought Rolonia. The cowardly person she was right now, the girl who always ran away, couldn't be with Adlet. She had to change. She had to become stronger. Adlet would look down on her if she didn't.

Rolonia loved Adlet, but he'd never give her the time of day. Becoming a better warrior was everything to him; he didn't have the time for infatuations. Besides, Rolonia was stupid and ugly. She just wasn't good enough for him.

But still, she wanted to be close to him. She wanted to devote herself to him. She wanted to see his smile. She wanted to be good enough. That was her heart's desire.

Meanwhile, Atreau had assigned Adlet a challenge that began the day Rolonia arrived at the mountain. Adlet had one month to defeat Atreau by whatever means necessary. If he failed to accomplish that, he would be expelled and kicked off the mountain.

Even Rolonia, who was a total beginner when it came to combat, could understand how much stronger Atreau was. Adlet would never reach his level, no matter how much he strategized or how often he tried to catch his master by surprise.

On the final day of the challenge, Atreau walked into the lecture room in his hut as if that day were nothing special. An instant later, Adlet, hiding on a ceiling beam, attacked.

Atreau was not the least bit rattled. He thrust his javelin at Adlet, and the boy repelled it with his sword. Atreau kicked him down and sent him rolling to Rolonia's feet.

"I'm sorry, Master Atreau!" Rolonia yelled a moment later. She touched her hand to the cloth inside her bag. Soaked with Rolonia's blood, the fabric splayed out like a living thing and restrained Atreau.

"You've done it, Rolonia!" Adlet cried as he got up. He dodged a second thrust of Atreau's javelin, seizing the weapon with his left hand while the sword in his right hand touched Atreau's neck. "Using whatever means, right?" he said, smiling. Rolonia shivered, watching. Was this all right?

"You had to rack your brains for such a basic idea?" Atreau replied. He silently tossed his javelin aside, peeled off the cloth tangled around him, and left the lecture room.

It was hard to tell, but that did seem to mean Adlet had more or less passed. He flung aside his sword, leaped in the air, and gave Rolonia a hug. "I was so stupid. I never had to fight alone. Whatever means you use—even if you need help from a friend—if you can win, you're the strongest in the world." Then he retrieved his sword and ran back outside. "Thanks, Rolonia. I can't rest on my laurels now. Training goes on!"

Left behind in the lecture room, Rolonia recalled Adlet's embrace and blushed.

Time passed in the blink of an eye, and the day when Rolonia would leave the mountain drew near. The two had become so close, it made their initial meeting hard to believe. Rolonia stopped being so reserved around him and went from calling him Adlet to Addy.

Three days or so before they parted ways, they were in the rear of the dark cave when, suddenly, Adlet began sharing his past. Rolonia didn't quite understand why he felt like talking about it, but she figured to him it was like a final testament. Training under Atreau meant walking alongside death. The slightest blunder could cost him his life. In his own way, Adlet must have wanted to leave behind some proof that he'd lived.

Little by little, he talked about the fiend that had appeared abruptly in his village, how the villagers had transformed overnight, as if they'd become completely different people, and how his friend and his sister had died protecting him.

"Oh…" Rolonia was speechless.

"Can you not tell anyone about this?" requested Adlet. "I mean, don't even touch the topic."

"Why not?"

"That fiend just waltzed into my village. It knew all about the village and everything. The damn thing has influence in the human realms." Adlet's teeth made a grinding sound. "I don't want it to find out that I'm alive. If it realizes I'm planning revenge, it'll come kill me. Right now…it's frustrating, but I couldn't stand up against it."

"But…" This was surely a serious matter, something she should tell to Mora and Willone.

But Adlet shook his head. "I'm gonna be the one to kill it. I'll take its life and make it regret destroying my village. I have to. So don't tell anyone." It was an irrational perspective—but it wasn't really a problem that could be put to rights with reason.

As she promised, Rolonia told no one of what Adlet had related. She knew it was wrong, but she prioritized his wishes. "Addy," she said, "once you've become a Brave, beat that lizard-fiend, and returned…what will you do then?"

Adlet hemmed and hawed a bit. "I don't know. I'll think about what comes after when the time arrives. I'm gonna be the strongest man in the world. I'll be able to do anything."

"What do you *want* to do?" Rolonia asked, and he mulled over it again. "Do you want to go back to your village and live your old life?"

Adlet shook his head. "The people from my village are long dead. They're in the bellies of fiends." He sounded both sad and angry.

"You don't know that for sure. They might be alive."

"I dunno," he replied listlessly. "What would I even do if I met them? They killed Schetra and Rainer. I might kill them all the moment I saw their faces." The look in his eyes then made her shudder, but it quickly turned sorrowful again. "But I'm sure I'd regret it afterward. I might regret it for the rest of my life." His heart was wavering between nostalgic affection and hatred.

"I really don't think you should kill them," said Rolonia, making Adlet smile a little. "I doubt everything will go back to the way it was. And I think it will take time for you to forgive them. But someday, you'll be able to live together in peace again."

"If that did happen…that would be the best outcome," Adlet said, implying that he doubted it.

"Addy…" To Rolonia, it would be unbearably heartbreaking to devote your whole life to attaining power, fighting and risking your life, only to be left with nothing but regret and sadness. She wanted Adlet to be happy. He *had* to be happy.

"I wonder if they're alive?" he mused. "If they're dead, I'll be lonely. I'd be alone forever."

"Addy…"

"I wanna see them again," Adlet said. He buried his face in his knees and quietly began to cry.

Rolonia had never before even considered fighting the fiends. But now, for the first time, she couldn't let the lizard-fiend's crimes go unanswered.

And then she thought, if perhaps by some fluke, by some mistake, she were chosen as a Brave of the Six Flowers, she would save the people of his village. Her idea quickly turned into a conviction. She would rescue the people of his village. She got the feeling that she could become stronger, if it was for the sake of his happiness.

And so Rolonia left the mountain and returned to All Heavens Temple. Adlet didn't go to see Rolonia off as she was leaving. He just noticed her while he was taking a quick break from practicing sword swings and gave her a big wave. He didn't care for her as much as she did for him. Understanding that made Rolonia feel rather lonely.

Meeting Adlet had changed Rolonia—or at the very least, she thought so. She was still a failure, even after her stint on the mountain. She was still an insecure, slow-to-learn coward. People didn't change overnight. But being a disappointment of a human being was no reason not to try. If she was a failure, then she should just keep forging ahead in her own way. If she got no results, she just had to suck it up and try again. Life was something you put up with until you died, so Rolonia made up her mind that she'd be moving on, facing forward, as she survived. If she were to give up like she always had and spend her whole life running away, she wouldn't be worthy of Adlet's friendship.

Rolonia had met many people and received many lessons since she'd first gained the powers of a Saint: there was her greatest teacher, Mora; and Willone, Saint of Salt; Torleau, Saint of Medicine; Tomaso, the legendary strategist; the old hero, Stradd; and the fiend specialist, Atreau. But far more important to her than what they'd taught her was what she'd learned from Adlet—though he probably hadn't meant to teach her anything.

What she really wanted to do was stay with him forever and continue to support him. She wanted to chat with him more. She wanted to heal his wounds and touch him. But he probably wouldn't be glad for any of that.

She might not ever see him again. But that was okay. He'd done so many important things for her. That alone made her happy enough.

Rolonia hooked her whip over a branch, raised herself up, and jumped, over and over as she advanced through the forest. She wanted to shake off all her pursuers before she reached her destination, the cave. She couldn't figure out how to save the Dead Host while fighting them off. There weren't as many of the corpses chasing her now. A little farther and she could distance herself from the rest. "I wonder if the Dead Host are tired, too," she muttered.

She still didn't know what was in that cave. It could be a trap, just like Adlet had said. But even so, she was willing to gamble on that small chance that it wasn't.

When they'd found out that all the villagers had been made to join the Dead Host and Adlet had shut himself up in the other room of the hut, when he'd gritted his teeth and said with a heartbroken expression that he'd abandon them, when he had asked her to stop making his doubts worse, it had hurt Rolonia's heart and made her tremble with anger.

If they just forsook the Dead Host, Adlet would regret it for the rest of his life. That was the one thing Rolonia could not do. She might not be able to save all of them, but still, she wanted to save even just one person from his village. At the very least, she wanted to let Adlet meet them, if only for a glimpse. She wanted to fight for the happiness of the one who had changed her life, the most important person in the world to her. She knew she was causing trouble for Adlet and the others, but even so, she couldn't discard her feelings.

"Almost there!" She was nearing the forest's edge, but she still couldn't shake off all the Dead Host. "Ack!" She turned around. She had no choice but to fight. She would have liked to disable them without killing them, if possible. But she knew that they would never stop fighting unless she went so far as to snap off both their legs.

A pair of corpses drew near, and Rolonia lashed at them with all her might. The corpses evaded her whip nimbly, raising up their arms to attack. "Ngh!" She took the hit with one pauldron. As the impact sent her flying, her whip snapped, aiming as much as possible for non-fatal wounds on the arms and legs. It hit a corpse's leg, and her next slash landed a direct hit on another's arm. A spray of blood danced from the wound as her whip ripped off the sleeve of its clothes. That was when Rolonia saw its arm.

There were words carved on it. She approached the fallen body and read them. *Search and save. Man with words on right arm. Tgurneu's weapon.*

It was a plea to help the people of the Dead Host. She'd seen one just like it before. *Save him. He knows* had been written on another corpse. "Knows" must have referred to Tgurneu's weapon. Was it the Black Barrenbloom? If it was, then that was all the more reason to save the people of the Dead Host. She might find out about this weapon without even reaching the Temple of Fate.

"Maybe Nashetania knew about this," Rolonia said. Nashetania had tried to stop her from saving the Dead Host. Maybe her goal was to conceal the true nature of Tgurneu's weapon.

If so, then Nashetania was in cahoots with the seventh, and Tgurneu, too. They might be trying to keep her away from the Black Barrenbloom.

Rolonia left the two fallen corpses behind and continued walking forward.

Specialist number nine noticed that Adlet was gone. He had apparently discovered that Rolonia had fallen for its trap, so he'd panicked and run off to save her. Tgurneu had warned that Adlet was the one who it should be most cautious of. But he was no great threat. He and his friends had done nothing more than charge in headlong without a plan, and now Adlet had just failed to figure out the trap and was working himself into a panic.

But still, his pursuing Rolonia was slightly problematic. Specialist number nine ordered the Dead Host wandering about the forest to go stop him.

Right at that moment, some sparks from Dozzu's lightning zapped number nine, slightly disrupting the sounds it used to manipulate the Dead Host. *You pathetic zombies. Protect me better!* number nine mentally shouted as it ran southward.

Rainer was rushing through the forest after the girl in the armor. He felt a weakness in his left arm, meaning he could move it again. *If I could just have moved it a bit earlier,* he thought. If only his arm had come free when the girl was closer, he might have been able to show her he was there.

The first thing Rainer did with his arm was to strike the point of his index finger on a tree. A splinter stuck in the digit, and blood dripped from the tip. Rainer used the blood to write *Don't be fooled* on his clothing. He couldn't move his neck, so he couldn't check what he'd written, but the words should be more or less legible.

But more importantly, he had to stop that armored girl now. He had to warn her it was a trap. If she died, he'd never get to tell the Braves about the secret weapon.

Rainer ripped off the part of his clothing with the warning on it; his tattered clothing ripped easily. He balled up the cloth and hurled it straight up in the air, praying that the wind would catch it and carry it to the girl.

While Rainer had been writing with his left arm, his body continued after the girl in the armor. *Is there…is there anything else I can do?* Rainer wondered. His left arm could still move. He could still do something.

He pulled the sharp stone from his pocket, and then he flung his left arm straight out to the side. His upper arm smacked into the trunk of a tree and Rainer was spun onto his back. He wrapped his left arm around the tree trunk, holding his body down. His legs scrabbled about madly while his right arm tried to peel off the left by grabbing it and digging its nails in.

Struggling against the pain, Rainer stabbed his stone into the bark of the tree, moving it to form words.. *The other Braves might be chasing the girl in the armor,* he thought. *I'll tell them not to be fooled.* It took everything he had to carve the lines, fighting to keep hold of the trunk and the rock with his left arm on the rock.

But it was no use. The numbness coursed through his left arm before he'd even written half of his message. His limb was leaving his control again. The moment his left arm relaxed, his right arm ripped it from the trunk. Rainer was forced to stand and run after the armored girl again.

Rainer's eye caught a little cloth falling toward him. He had prayed that the rag would catch on the wind and fly to that girl, but in reality it had just floated in the air for a bit before falling right back down again. *I'm powerless,* thought Rainer. No matter how many words he wrote, no one would see them. Even if he knew about the trap, he couldn't tell anyone.

Rainer was seized by the notion that he was nothing but a witness to all of this. He'd meant to always keep fighting for the sake of the Six Braves, for the world. But he couldn't actually do anything, could he? All he did was watch.

No, Rainer told himself. He thought about Adlet. Adlet had to be off somewhere, enjoying a peaceful life, praying that the Six Braves would defend the world. *I'll protect his happiness. I'm his friend for life, as he is mine. As long as Adlet is out there, I'll never falter.*

This was how Rainer always encouraged himself at times when he felt ready to give up, when he felt crushed by his own powerlessness. *Your arm will come free again. Think! Think about what you'll do when that time comes.*

As Rainer searched for Rolonia, fiends appeared before him again. A lizard-fiend with four long necks attacked him. Rainer prayed for it to stay out of his way, but his prayers didn't reach the fiend.

As they fought the Dead Host, Adlet had recalled that time two years before, when he had told Rolonia about his past and cried in front of her

about how he wanted to see the other villagers again. She couldn't be...
trying to save the Dead Host for his sake, was she?

"You idiot, Rolonia." She didn't have to be worry about him. There
was no need for her to fight for him. All she should be concerned with was
keeping the world and herself safe. In a way, Adlet was the one responsible
for all this. He couldn't let her die. He had to save her.

Dozens of the Dead Host pursued Adlet, and every time one of the
corpses shrieked, their numbers increased. Obscuring their vision with
a smoke bomb, Adlet kept on running, concealing himself up in the tree
branches.

Adlet witnessed dozens of the corpses separate from the crowd that
had been chasing him and run southward. They were probably heading to
fight Chamo and the others.

Adlet evaded attacks from the Dead Host, clambering up near the
treetops to scan around the area for Rolonia. In the corner of his vision, he
noticed a small cloth dancing in the air. "Is...that it?" Had Rolonia tried
to tell him something? Maybe she was closer than he'd anticipated. Adlet
raced along the branches toward the fallen cloth. But there was no one
there, and no sign that Rolonia had fought there, either.

He'd wasted his time. Adlet was about to run off when some strange
cuts in a tree trunk caught his eye. "Are these words?" They looked like
simple notches. But they could be letters, if you decided they were. They
spelled out *don't be fo*, along with signs that there was an attempt to write
something after it.

Adlet didn't know what this meant, but he didn't have the time to
be think about it. The cluster of Dead Host he'd shaken off once found
him again, screaming. The sound summoned more and more of the Dead
Host. Adlet fled again.

He examined the Crest on his right hand. The petals were all there.
Rolonia was still safe.

While fighting the lizard-fiend, Rainer felt the weakness in his left arm
again. This would make it the fourth time that day his arm had come

free. The first time, he'd felt like he was close to victory. But now, it just deepened his despair. The armored girl had run off without noticing him. None of the other Braves were coming, either.

Don't give up. Rainer forced himself to think positively. Then he ripped up more of his clothing and threw the shreds up in the air one after another. He didn't have the time to write *don't be fooled.* He just had to show the Six Braves that something was happening here, that one of the corpses was different. *Notice me, Braves! I'm right here!*

But the fabric he'd thrown just stirred in the wind before falling back to ground. The rags didn't even reach past the tree canopy, never mind reaching any Braves.

That was when Rainer noticed that more fiend reinforcements had arrived, noticed the looming mouth of the lizard-fiend.

Ah—

To Rainer, its wide-open mouth was the picture of despair, announcing that it had all come to an end.

Rolonia made it out of the forest and hurried toward the Fainting Mountains. She couldn't find the cave she was looking for. She clenched her whip tight, alert as she walked. Adlet was right; this might be a trap. She couldn't let her guard down.

She ran in search of her destination. That was when she recalled what one corpse had said: "Meet the hidden woman in the cave." She might know something.

A call sound from far away. "Are you...a Brave?" The voice was so thin it was hardly audible. Rolonia searched around and found a corpse in the shadow of a rock a short distance away. Reflexively, she raised her whip.

"No! I'm not one of the Dead Host... Please, don't attack..." the woman said. She *wasn't* one of the Dead Host. She was filthy and in rags like them, but there was life in her skin, and she didn't have a control parasite on her. She had to be over sixty. At a glance, Rolonia could tell she wasn't strong enough to fight and had no weapons. Of course, she couldn't be a Saint, either.

"I'm not your enemy, please. Please save the Dead Host... Save my husband."

"I'm sorry! Please stay away!" Rolonia yelled, and the old woman stopped in her tracks. Rolonia snapped her whip, slicing the elderly woman's shoulders and thighs with the tip. She didn't want to do this, but she had no choice.

"Agh! You're mistaken! I'm not one of them..."

"I'm sorry," Rolonia apologized. "I'm not trying to hurt you. It's to check." She suspected the old woman might be a transforming fiend. Just the day before, she'd mistaken a shapeshifter for the real Nashetania. Rolonia carefully licked the blood to analyze it.

The old woman was human, without even the slightest taste of fiend blood. Rolonia approached her. "P-pardon me. I-I've come in search of a way to save the Dead Host..."

Before Rolonia could finish, the old woman clung to her. "You came! You really did! You really did come! What a relief, what a relief!"

Rolonia peeled off the old woman and asked her, "Who are you? Do you know how to save the Dead Host?"

"You've come to save me! I thought I was a goner! I thought they'd abandoned me!"

Rolonia soothed the distressed old woman and asked, "What happened? Why are you here?"

"This isn't the time for talking. Please, come with me. If you have mercy for the Dead Host, please!" The old woman took Rolonia's hand and broke into a run. As they ran, she explained, "Ten years ago, they brought me to the Howling Vilelands. Everything after that was hell. Six months ago, they were done with me, and I figured they would make me join the Dead Host...so my son hid me. I've survived by pretending to be one of them."

"Do you know of a way to save them?"

"I do."

"Why?"

"...My son and his allies have been fighting to free the humans in the Howling Vilelands, and they figured out the secret of the Dead Host.

They were all killed or forced into that horrible army...but they managed to tell me the truth."

Rolonia peered into the old woman's face. Her grief-stricken expression and her exhausted, wounded body didn't seem artificial. Rolonia wasn't confident about her judgment, but she sensed she could trust this woman. "The people of the Dead Host told me about this place."

"Oh yes, I knew it! My son and his friends are still trying to save everyone, even after becoming Dead Host, aren't they?" Tears rose in the old woman's eyes.

"Are you...from Adlet's village?" Rolonia asked.

The old woman's eyes widened, and she shook her head. "Um, I don't know anyone named Adlet..."

Rolonia was a little disappointed. She wanted to have him see the people of his home village. But she quickly changed her mind. This rescue mission wasn't only for Adlet's sake. It was also for the Dead Host's sake, for the innocent people who were about to be killed. "So how do I save— "

"Shh. It's right over there." The old woman stopped behind a highish hill ridge and put a hand over her mouth. Rolonia stepped silently up to the ridge and sneaked a glance over the other side. There, under a sheer cliff, was the open mouth of a cave. A spider-fiend stood at its entrance. With its four front legs, it was holding down one of the Dead Host. About twenty enslaved humans stood at the ready around it.

"Um...have you seen the bug-fiend?" asked the old woman. "That knobbly one in the center of the forest."

"Specialist number nine, right? My friends are fighting it right now."

"Actually, there's another fiend that's a part of number nine. These two fiends combine powers to control the Dead Host," said the old woman, and Rolonia listened closely to what she had to say. The spider-fiend hadn't noticed them yet. "That one kills people's spirits, turning them into living corpses. The bony bug then plants the parasites on the empty shells that remain to control them."

If I could just kill that fiend. Rolonia squeezed her whip. She felt her usual stream of curses threatening to spill from her lips.

But before she could start, the old woman stopped her. "It's not that spider-fiend that's killing the spirits of the Dead Host. That one is just protecting it."

"What do you mean?"

"The fiend that's killing the spirits of the Dead Host...is inside that corpse's body." Rolonia eyed the corpse of the Dead Host the spider-fiend had pinned down. "It's a fiend like a leech, about half a meter long. It hides itself inside the human body and then uses inexplicable powers to destroy the spirit."

In other words, kill the spider, save the person underneath it, and kill the leech inside the body. Then the Dead Host would be saved. Rolonia clenched her whip, but then the old woman went on. "But my son told me that you can't kill the leech-fiend before you kill the bug-fiend. Otherwise, when the Dead Host gain their spirits back, it'll clash with the parasites, and they'll all die."

Rolonia thought, *If I could defeat that leech-fiend, the Dead Host would all die, and we'd be able to head straight to the Temple of Fate.* But she couldn't do that. Besides, one among the Host knew about Tgurneu's secret weapon. She had to search for that person and listen to what they had to say.

The old woman explained, "You have to kill the gnarled insect-fiend first, and then the leech-fiend. If you give it even a brief moment, the leech-fiend will run wild, and the Dead Host won't ever be able to get their spirits back."

"I understand. I-I'll try it." Rolonia swallowed her next sentence: *Though I'm not very confident about it.* "I can do it. After all, I'm a Brave of the Six Flowers." Adlet had said that in order to accomplish something, you first had to believe you could do it. Then you had to say it out loud. Rolonia was trying that out, in her own way. "I will do it," she asserted. "Don't you worry."

Rolonia didn't notice how at first she'd been suspicious that this might be a trap, but now she trusted what her informant said entirely. The elderly matron's humanity, the desperate look on her face, her words, and most of all Rolonia's own desires to save the Dead Host had dulled her capacity for suspicion.

Rolonia thrust her whip into the ground and crouched low. Adlet's party would be chasing down specialist number nine right about now. They'd soon arrive at the mountain where Fremy was waiting. There was no more time.

But Rolonia wanted to check one last thing. Looking at the old woman, she asked, "Is the person who knows about Tgurneu's secret weapon one of your son's friends, too?"

"Huh?" The old woman stared at Rolonia as if the question was completely unexpected.

"The messages on the bodies of the Dead Host. Do you know anything about that?"

The old woman was struck dumb by Rolonia's question. "What could that...what on earth...?" She had no idea. Rolonia was about to ask about that when the spider-fiend cried out. Instantly, Rolonia ran for the cave. She'd think about it later. She had to settle this all in one go, defeat the spider-fiend and the Dead Host all at once.

The fiend spewed thread at her. Rolonia jumped as high as she could while simultaneously lifting her body with her whip's power. Dodging the silky strands, Rolonia hurtled at the spider-fiend. It was just barely five meters between her and the enemy. She'd taken the fiend by surprise, and it couldn't yet move.

"Geerk!" it screeched, and at the same time, ten of the Dead Host charged at Rolonia. Quickly, Rolonia cut open her wrist with her fingernails. The blood sprayed out of her like a fountain, far more than what a single human body contained, and rained down on the spider-fiend and Dead Host. The spider-fiend writhed in agony underneath the shower of Saint's blood, while the blinded Dead Host froze. As one who controlled blood, Rolonia used this move as one of her trump cards.

"I'm sorry!" she yelled, whirling her whip in a circle around herself and mowing down the Dead Host before she cut the spider-fiend into pieces. In moments, the spider-fiend was dead.

The corpse, now freed from the fiend's grasp, lunged at Rolonia. Surprised, she just barely avoided the brunt of the attack, but it still hit her shoulder and sent numbness through her arm. "Ngh!" she gasped in pain. But she couldn't let this person die. With her whip, she bound the person's arms and legs, lifting them up off the ground and biting them in the shoulder. She tasted their blood to look for the fiend nested inside their body. But the blood on her tongue tasted just like the blood of the other corpses. That couldn't be.

Rolonia was about to bite again when the old woman approached her. "What are you doing? The fiend is in its chest! Please, let me help you!" The woman ran up to her and was about to touch her when someone shouted.

"Rolonia! Get away from her!" Adlet called from the forest.

Adlet was pushing through the trees with the Dead Host hot on his heels. He blinded them with smoke bombs, showered them with regular bombs, and cut down any remaining pursuers with his sword. He avoided fighting as much as he could, but he still couldn't catch up to Rolonia. The attacks coming at him were fierce. If he lost focus, he'd end up getting killed himself, never mind protecting her.

That was when he heard the shriek of the Dead Host and the cry of slave-fiends close by. *Yes!* he thought, sprinting off in that direction, with the Dead Host following him.

There was a cluster of five or six slave-fiends in this area of the forest. A lizard, a water snake, a water spider, and others were fighting off the Dead Host that continuously pummeled them.

Adlet passed right by the crowd. He felt bad for Chamo's slave-fiends, but he needed them to pick up his Dead Host hangers-on. As he'd expected, about half of the corpses that had been chasing Adlet were distracted by the slave-fiends and stopped following him.

Now things were a little easier. Adlet climbed up a tree to look around. He must have run a ways. Wasn't he catching up to Rolonia yet?

But all that he could see from above the canopy were the corpses and body parts of the Dead Host that the slave-fiends had chewed up and a single scrap of an old rag caught on a branch. He didn't find any trace of Rolonia. Adlet threw a smoke bomb to stir up the Dead Host and then kept on running.

"Tsk!" More of them poured in from the sides. Adlet had already used up all the smoke bombs in his waist pouches. He had still more in the iron box on his back, but he didn't have the time to pull them out and use them. Adlet chose to stop there to block the Dead Host's attacks with his sword. He waited for all the corpses around to come in closer, and then he flung his chain up in the air to catch onto a tree branch above him. When the Dead Host surged toward him, he yanked on the chain and ran up the tree trunk as he threw a bomb at their feet. In midair, he covered himself as the shock wave burned him, driving fine fragments into his skin as he flipped in the air and landed again. The Dead Host dodged the worst of the explosion, but they were thrown back onto the ground. They tried to keep pursuing Adlet anyway, but their bodies were spent.

Having shaken off the Dead Host, Adlet ran in search of Rolonia. Just as he emerged from the forest and was about to head over the ridge of the hill, he heard Rolonia's voice. "I'm sorry!" she was saying. So she was safe. Adlet headed toward her voice.

There was a large cave at the foot of the mountain. Adlet could see Rolonia, a dead fiend, about ten fallen Dead Host, and one more running for her. Rolonia had restrained another corpse with her whip. *This is bad*, Adlet thought. That whip was her only weapon. If she were attacked now, she'd have no way to fight back.

Adlet also noticed an old woman who looked like one of the Dead Host heading for Rolonia. He didn't see any parasite on her back. For an instant, he wondered if she wasn't the enemy. But some random old woman could never have survived in a place like this.

The upshot was that Rolonia was walking into a trap. He had to take out anything that could harm her. "Rolonia! Get away from her!" Adlet yelled. The old woman was already right beside her, and Adlet could see no sign at all that Rolonia was wary. Adlet threw a paralysis needle at the old woman. Whether she was human or fiend, that should stop her, no problem.

But the next moment, the worst thing imaginable happened.

"Wait, Addy!" Rolonia yelled, shielding the old woman. The numbing dart hit her in the wrist, and she went limp, her whip slipping from her grasp. Adlet had landed a direct hit. Rolonia would be temporarily immobile.

"Now!" the old woman yelled, and a five-headed snake-fiend burst out of the ground.

"...Huh?" Confused, Rolonia yelped dumbly. The snake-fiend didn't even give Adlet enough time to urge her to run and coiled around Rolonia. With a limp hand, the paralyzed Brave reached out for the handle of the whip around the corpse.

But before her fingers could reach it, the old woman snatched her weapon away. "Do it!" she cried, and the once-bound corpse stood, swinging its arms down toward Rolonia's face.

"Not happening!" Adlet yelled. Before the corpse's fists connected, Adlet shot his blade into its head. This was one of his secret weapons, a blade gun.

"Come out! Now! It's our only chance!" The woman yelled about her as she fled the scene. The earth swelled up in lumps below Rolonia, revealing more of the Dead Host, and a mass of enemies emerged from the cave, too. Another wave came running out of the forest—they must have been hiding somewhere.

"Why? Wh-why?!" Body going numb and whip stolen from her grasp, Rolonia was not in the position to be fighting. She scrabbled at the snake wrapped around her, trying to rip it off. But the snake-fiend didn't even flinch.

Adlet had to kill that thing. But that was when he realized his own terrible mistake. The Saint's Spike, his ultimate weapon against fiends, was inside his iron box. He'd assumed he wouldn't need it against the Dead Host and had prioritized smoke bombs and other equipment instead. "Run, Rolonia! Run!" he cried out.

"L-let go!" Rolonia gave a yell as blood spurted from her wrist. The snake fiend screeched in agony as the fluid showered over it, but even then it didn't release her.

Adlet hurled all the bombs he had all at once, but he couldn't take down the Dead Host surging toward him from every direction. "Gah!" One of them was right behind him. Its strike skimmed his back and knocked the wind out of him. The five of the Dead Host that had avoided Adlet's bombs rushed all at once toward the paralyzed Rolonia.

This can't be, thought Adlet. Were they going to lose one of their own in a place like this to a single trivial enemy for the sake of such an obvious trap? Why had he left Rolonia on her own? Why had he failed to trust her? If he'd been with her, she never would have fallen for such a simple trap. "*Roloniaaa!*" Adlet yelled. He could see her eyes were closed in fear.

And then—there was a flash of light around Rolonia, and in an instant, the heads and arms of the corpses descending upon her were dancing in the air. The snake-fiend coiled around Rolonia was sliced into pieces.

"...Huh?" Rolonia made another dull cry.

One of the Dead Host held a sword in each hand. That corpse patted her head and then turned to Adlet. "*Hrmeow.* What're ya doin', Adlet? It's yer job to protect the group."

Rolonia, her face white as a sheet and voice shaky, said, "...Hans?"

Dirty all over and clad in rags, Hans smirked.

It didn't take them long to finish off the ten-odd remaining corpses. Hans was responsible for most of them. Adlet could just help out, and all Rolonia could do was stand there in a daze.

Hans dodged the attacks as if he knew they were coming. With each stroke of his sword, he cut down a corpse with perfect precision. It was almost like watching a well-polished dance. In the just under three hours since this battle had begun, he'd come to perfectly understand the Dead Host's behaviors and habits. Perhaps it was this ability to learn so quickly that was his greatest strength—even more so than his inhuman skills in martial arts and his unique swordsmanship.

The Dead Host defeated, their environs had fallen quiet. It looked as though they'd handled all of the Dead Host stationed there for the trap.

Adlet helped Rolonia up. Fortunately, her wounds weren't serious. He then yanked his sword blade out of the head of the corpse he'd shot and shoved it back into its sheath.

Touching its body, Rolonia said, "There's no leech fiend... It was...a lie..." She hung her head. "Why? She was human."

Adlet discovered a body on the top of the ridge. The old woman who had deceived Rolonia had fallen there. When Adlet approached it to check, he found she was already dead. The Dead Host had killed her.

Adlet didn't know why she'd helped them set a trap for the Six Braves. From what he could see, it didn't seem her family had been taken hostage. Had they told her that her life would be spared even after they destroyed the world? Or had they told her that they could postpone her death with the powers of fiends?

It didn't matter. Adlet turned back to Hans. "I'm impressed you knew Rolonia was here, Hans," he said, staring as he spoke. The costume really was amazing.

His skin and hair were covered in dust. He'd rubbed rotten meat on parts of his body to discolor his skin. He must have gotten the clothes off some corpse. He'd tied a dead parasite onto the back of his neck with string—the string that he'd taken from Adlet's iron box. He'd been planning all along to disguise himself as one of them.

"*Meow-hee-hee,* I had a feelin' somethin' like this might happen."

That's not a reply, thought Adlet.

"Thank...you...Hans," said Rolonia.

Shrugging, Hans said, "They really got you easy. *Meow,* I figgered you was dumb, but you're *really* dumb."

"Erk..."

Adlet looked at her. He just couldn't bring himself to be angry with her. She'd done it out of consideration for him. She'd been unable to watch him suffer.

"Ya think y'all can kill specialist neowmber nine, Adlet?" asked Hans.

"We're chasing it down, but I think it'll take some more time. I'm worried about Chamo. Let's head back," said Adlet, and he took Rolonia and started running.

That was when, suddenly, something felt off to him. What had that cloth fluttering in the air been? "Hans, did you toss up any cloth?" he asked.

"What're ya talkin' ameowt?" Hans replied.

Apparently, Rolonia didn't know anything about that, either. So who had thrown that rag? Had it just happened to rip off and fly up for some reason? Was that even possible? It was such a trivial thing, but somehow it bothered him.

"Addy, Hans." Rolonia, who'd been following behind them, stopped. She seemed to have something on her mind and appealed to them with a grave expression. "I've done nothing but cause trouble…and I'm sorry to bring up something like this…but please listen… There's one more thing."

"What is it?" asked Hans.

"There's something I want you to see." Rolonia went off to search for something. She found a fallen corpse and raised up its left arm.

Adlet and Hans read the message there. *Search and save. Man with words on right arm. Tgurneu's weapon.*

"Some of the Dead Host have these messages on them."

"Uh-huh, Rolonia. So yer sayin' one of the Dead Host is alive, and they kneow about Tgurneu's secret weapon?" Hans smiled, but a hint of anger burned in his eyes. "You got amnesia or what? Didja already ferget about gettin' tricked and nearly dyin'?"

"This is… This is different!"

Adlet stared at the message. He recalled what had happened before—the place where the cloth had been tossed in the air, the scratches in that tree nearby that could have been letters. He got the feeling those letters and the words on this corpse's arm were similar.

"The woman who tricked me didn't know about this," said Rolonia. "She didn't know about the messages on the Dead Host or about Tgurneu's weapon."

"...*Hrmeow?* What do ya mean?"

"They're different. The one who left these messages here and the people who tried to trick me are different. Tgurneu *did* deceive me. But there's someone else who wrote these messages."

"Rolonia...there's no way—" Hans began.

"Someone in the Dead Host is alive, and they know about Tgurneu's secret weapon!" Rolonia insisted.

"Impossible. There's just neow way—" Hans was about to argue, but Adlet stopped him. Hans gave Adlet a surprised look.

"I think she's right. I saw it, too. Rolonia's not lying!" Adlet yelled out as he set off at a run. "One of the Dead Host is alive! A corpse with a message on its right arm!"

But at that time, Rainer was lying on the damp earth of the forest, faceup toward the heavens. He was gazing at the blue sky through the gaps in the tree canopy.

His body would no longer move. The parasite had given up on controlling him.

It's over, he thought. The image of the old woman who had told him about the Black Barrenbloom rose in his mind. *I'm sorry, ma'am. It was no use. I tried as hard as I could, in my own way. But it was no use.*

A few of the strange fiends and dozens of the Dead Host were fighting around him. The howls of the mysterious creatures and the shrieks of his fellows sounded far away to him now. His left arm had come free again, but he didn't even try to move it now.

He recalled Adlet's face. In his mind, he called out to his friend, wherever he was. *I never became a Brave, Adlet. I was just an insignificant man.*

He was now immobile. Both his legs had been torn off, and the only evidence that he was alive, the message on his right arm, was lost.

Rainer's right arm had been ripped off at the shoulder.

Chapter 6

Once Again
with a Friend

"Dummy, dummy, dummy, dummy, dummy!" Chamo yelled on and on as she fought the Dead Host.

Just like Rolonia, thought Goldof.

With each swipe of Chamo's pointer finger, the slave-fiends she had deployed all around moved in a well-coordinated manner. They fought off the Dead Host's attack, destroying their defensive formation with volleys of acid and poison. "What's Adlet thinking?! Chamo's gonna kill that moo-head!" she yelled.

Once again, the three humans and one fiend were charging the Dead Host guarding specialist number nine. They were already very close to the mountain where Fremy and Mora lay in wait. This was no longer a time for planning. They just had to plunge straight ahead.

The status quo wasn't an easy one to work with. Rolonia aside—she'd been basically useless anyway—Adlet's absence had left a large hole. Goldof had to fight that much harder to make up for it, and he charged in headlong, scattering their enemies. He'd analyzed the Dead Host's patterns somewhat, and he predicted their movements as the deft manipulations of his spear brought him close to number nine.

"Doggy! If you come any closer, Chamo's gonna kill you!" Chamo was yelling from behind Goldof. Dozzu, who'd been backing Goldof's charge with lightning strikes, panicked and ran. She really might do it.

As Goldof battled the Dead Host, he paid special attention to everything Nashetania and Dozzu did. As Adlet had said, there was a chance the two of them would use this opportunity to kill Chamo. Goldof was the only one there to protect her. He was doing this for Chamo, but at the same time he was doing this for Nashetania, too.

Nashetania summoned blades from the ground, smiling as if to assuage his fears. "Haah!" She divided the enemy's formation with her blades, and Goldof took advantage of the opportunity to plunge forward again.

As the clash wore on, Goldof wondered if Rolonia was safe. Adlet had just run after her. As long as he was with her, the two of them would probably avoid the worst. But Goldof was also forced to acknowledge the possibility that Adlet was the seventh.

What was Hans doing? Were Fremy and Mora safe? Where was Tgurneu now? Goldof felt like his head would explode. There were too many things to worry about.

"Raaagh!" Whatever the case, they still had to push specialist number nine to the mountain. He'd worry about Rolonia after.

Adlet broke into a sprint, running through ideas of how he could seek out the corpse with a memo on its right arm.

Behind him, Hans said, "*Hrmeow*, you serious, Adlet?"

"Yeah, I'm serious. One of the Dead Host is alive, and they know about Tgurneu's secret weapon."

"*Meow*, I can't believe it," said Hans. And indeed, common sense would lead one to believe it was unlikely.

Adlet explained, "I saw letters carved into a tree trunk. They were messy and barely legible, just like the message on that corpse. Who wrote it? It wasn't one of us. It wasn't a fiend. It had to be written by a Dead Host."

"*Meow*..." Hans seemed skeptical.

"You didn't see it all, so you wouldn't know, but the enemy was fixated on doing one thing: leading Rolonia to that cave. Nothing about a corpse with a message on its arm came up in their story. Don't you think that's weird?"

"Meowbe, but..."

The question was whether Adlet trusted what Rolonia had said or not, and he judged that he could believe her. She'd fallen for a trap that had unquestionably nearly gotten her killed. If Hans hadn't made it in time, she certainly would have died. She couldn't be the seventh. Most importantly, she'd been doing it all for him. How could he not trust her?

"Meowkay, then. I'll go along with yer decision," said Hans.

Adlet looked at Rolonia. "Rolonia, you can save one of the Dead Host, right?"

"I think...I can do it," she replied. "If their heart isn't dead yet, then... No, I *know* I can do it."

They still had some time before Tgurneu's forces would reach the Fainting Mountains. It should still be possible to find the corpse in question before they took down specialist number nine and reached the Temple of Fate.

Adlet was also worried about Chamo after abandoning her amid Dozzu and its allies. But Goldof would protect her. Besides, he doubted she would go down easy, even against both Nashetania and Dozzu. They had to prioritize finding this unique Dead Host.

"All right, let's say yer right." Hans spread his arms. "How do we find this thing?"

They heard the shrieks of the Dead Host ahead, and then three corpses appeared in front of them. Hans pounced on them as if dancing while Adlet and Rolonia readied their weapons.

Suddenly, something strange happened. All three of them flung their heads back in perfect synchronization, as if they'd just been hit by lightning. They wailed, writhing in agony. Meanwhile, screams rose from here and there all around the forest.

"What the heck?" said Hans, glancing around warily. But Adlet immediately understood what had happened.

The others had killed specialist number nine.

"Raaaaaagh!" A charging corpse slammed into Goldof's armor as he attacked. The knight let the impact of the next hit roll through him, using his opponent's strength to launch it backward. The corpse crashed into the other behind it.

Realizing it was in danger, specialist number nine turned tail and ran. Goldof was chuckling on the inside. They'd made it to the mountain where Fremy was. Now they just had to wait for their sniper to make her shot and ensure that specialist number nine never found out about the ambush. Then it would be over.

But Goldof turned around and yelled back, "Highness…please leave this to me…and get back! Chamo, too!"

He was warning them back because he was wary of Fremy's fire. She could be the seventh, targeting any of her inattentive allies after disabling Mora. Goldof was confident he could block a shot from Fremy, and he didn't care if Dozzu died.

"Understood, Goldof," said Nashetania.

"Why're you giving orders?" Chamo grumbled.

The two of them retreated from the front line, as directed. Dozzu gave Goldof a look and nodded. It seemed to understand what Goldof was doing. Now they just had to wait for Fremy to shoot. The success of the operation was hanging on both her skill and her loyalties.

Mora was with Fremy, lying low in the thicket on the slope of the mountain. They could see out over its entire northern foot, and they could hear Chamo, Dozzu, and the others engaged in combat, too.

With her clairvoyance, Mora was aware of every occurance on that small foothill. When Adlet and Rolonia had been helping to fight specialist number nine, no Dead Host had been nearby, but now there were a number of corpses searching the area.

"Mora. Don't move. You'll be seen," cautioned Fremy.

The two of them were seated, huddled together. While waiting for their prey's arrival, they had dug a hole in the ground, covering the area with leaves and tree branches to hide themselves. This sort of camouflage was Fremy's field of specialty. If the two of them were to be discovered now, the entire plan would come to nothing. Keeping her breathing quiet, Mora kept her supernatural eye focused.

Chamo's and Goldof's attacks had driven most of the Dead Host to retreat onto this mountain, but Mora had yet to see any fiend resembling number nine.

"This is odd," Fremy muttered. "Adlet isn't with them, and neither is Rolonia."

Their allies still weren't within Mora's range. Mora peered through the gaps in the trees into the distance. She couldn't see clearly, but the number of combatants did seem low. "Has something occurred? It couldn't be that the seventh…"

"If anything big happened, Adlet would have thrown a flash grenade and smoke bomb to let us know the operation is off. At the very least, he's chosen to continue the battle," said Fremy.

"Then what is it?"

"I don't know. We'll just have to ask the others." They had to complete their mission as soon as possible.

That was when Mora's clairvoyance picked up a gnarled bug-fiend. Mora was certain that was their target. "There it is," she said. Her hands were clenched into sweaty fists.

By contrast, Fremy's face was the picture of calm. "Direction and course?"

"Straight ahead of our position, about twenty degrees to the left. It's proceeding up the mountain in a nearly straight line."

"Its surroundings?" Gun still in hand, Fremy silently closed her eyes. She wasn't taking aim yet.

"Fifteen of the Dead Host are close enough around it that they could link arms, and specialist number nine is at the center. Around fifty more corpses surround them. It's entirely walled-in. The slave-fiends are trying to get close, but the Dead Host is preventing them."

"Where's number nine located within its formation?" Fremy asked.

"Nearly in the center, or just a touch behind that."

"Which direction is it looking?"

Mora focused every ounce of her powers to closely observe number nine and found compound eyes on the part that was most likely its head. She pinpointed where those eyes were facing. "At Goldof. The fiend is wary of our young knight's attacks."

"That's enough," Fremy said, and then she pushed the muzzle of her gun out of the brush.

Mora was surprised. *She intends to take it out in one shot?* The fiend was surrounded by walls of the Dead Host with no unobstructed line of fire.

Fremy plucked a hair from her head and flicked it away, telling Mora quietly that she was checking the wind. "When Goldof charges again, say '*now*,'" she said.

Goldof was still outside Mora's range of observation. She poked her head out of the thicket, checking on their fighting allies. Goldof's black armor was particularly conspicuous. He was yelling, breaking the Dead Host's ranks as he pushed toward number nine.

"Now," said Mora.

A breath later, Fremy fired.

With her clairvoyance, Mora saw number nine's reaction to Goldof's shout, pushing its face just slightly above the walls of Dead Host. In that instant, Fremy shot it through its head.

All of the Dead Host stopped, screaming and writhing in agony. Not a single one was left standing.

"Looks like a success." Fremy loaded a new bullet. "Perfectly assisted. That's what made it so easy."

"Indeed. But let's go now and convene with the others. I'm concerned about Adlet and Rolonia."

Chamo seemed to have recognized that the fight was over, as she was waving in Mora and Fremy's direction. The pair got up and dashed down the mountain slope.

Even with his right arm and both legs torn off, death had yet to visit Rainer. His shoulder had already stopped bleeding. The parasite on the back of his neck apparently had the power to fortify its host's vitality. The Dead Host wouldn't even be granted a peaceful death. As Rainer's consciousness dimmed due to the overwhelming pain, he simply wondered why he'd failed. He'd managed to gain intelligence about the devastating weapon, so how could he have failed to pass it on to the Braves?

What…will happen to the Braves? Was the world coming to an end, then? Or would the Braves conquer even the Black Barrenbloom and reach victory? Either way, it still meant that Rainer's long fight had brought about nothing. *Please, Braves…fight. Protect the world. Protect my friend.*

Rainer wondered where he had gone wrong, what else he could have done. But he couldn't hit upon anything, so he gave up his ruminations. *It's all over. I can relax now.* He hadn't been a Brave. He'd just been an insignificant, ordinary human. Perhaps he'd known that full well all along.

He felt a bolt of agony in the back of his neck. His mouth decided to let out a cry of pain with or without him, and his body began thrashing. On the fringes of his vision, he could see the other Dead Host corpses in torment. He immediately understood what had happened. The Braves of the Six Flowers had killed the fiend controlling them. He understood also that he would die soon. He knew his own body well.

Rainer realized he could move his left arm. Specialist number nine's death must have affected his body. But that didn't matter anymore. Now that he'd lost the writing on his right arm, the Braves of the Six Flowers would never find him.

The forest was filled with the moans of the Dead Host. Adlet, Rolonia, and Hans paused, listening to the sounds. Cold sweat beaded on their foreheads.

"I knew they'd pull it off. But I wish they'd waited a bit longer," Adlet muttered. What bad timing. If what Dozzu had said were true, then in a mere fifteen minutes all of the Dead Host would expire. Would the one who knew about Tgurneu's secret weapon survive after number nine's death? Adlet didn't know, but it seemed unlikely.

"We have to find him fast, or we'll lose our chance to learn what he knows," said Rolonia.

"Though he might've already kicked the bucket a while back neow," said Hans.

Rolonia was about to run off when Adlet called out to stop her. "Wait! Searching at random isn't gonna work!"

"Yeah, mew got any leads?" asked Hans.

Adlet leaped into the tallest nearby tree and clambered up to the top. From there, he looked out over everything he could see. He looked hard to see if the one who knew about Tgurneu's weapon had left any clues. Had he tossed up some cloth like before? Was there anything else? Even the smallest thing would do. Adlet prayed for him to please leave some kind of clue.

But he couldn't find anything.

"What do I do?" Finding just one of the Dead Host among all the corpses scattered throughout this huge forest in only fifteen minutes... was clearly impossible.

Adlet considered sending Chamo's slave-fiends out to search, but they'd run out of time before they even made it to Chamo to explain the situation. "Chamo! Fremy! Mora! Goldof! Can you hear me?!" Adlet yelled. "Look for a corpse with writing on its right arm!" But the forest full of moaning cadavers made quite a din. No matter how he yelled, they would never hear him.

Adlet's brain was whirling. He had to assume that both the cloth and the tree carvings were signs left by this potential informant. That person had been there just a little while ago, and those were the only clues. Could he figure out where they were based on such tenuous clues?

"...No. Don't ask whether you can do it or not." He *could* do it. That was what he would believe. *If I'm the strongest man in the world, then it's possible.*

Up a tree, Adlet frantically racked his brains.

Rainer's body twisted as moans poured continuously from his mouth. Around him, the other fallen corpses writhed in the same manner. But

Rainer's heart was quiet. Incoherent thoughts wandered about his brain. He'd once heard that memories of the past come back like this when someone is about to die.

What he recalled was his home village. His first love, Schetra Mayer. Even now, eight years after her death, he could still remember her vividly—her cheerful smile, the warmth he felt just by being beside her. He remembered the small festival in the village square in the fall when the harvest was over, and the times they'd sung together. They'd performed the same songs every year, never getting tired of them. He hadn't sung once since coming to the Howling Vilelands.

He saw the faces of the villagers Tgurneu had deceived. Not a single one of them had been a wicked person. It was fear that had driven them to kill Schetra and nearly kill him. Tgurneu had manipulated them into that foolish task. Rainer didn't hate them. He was just sad.

Then he recalled Adlet and the childish face he'd had eight years ago. He'd be eighteen now. But Rainer just couldn't picture him as an adult. *I want to see him*, thought Rainer. *I want to see him again.*

"Addy! We have to go look now!" Rolonia was calling to him from the base of the tree. Adlet didn't reply to her. He desperately kept working through the problem.

What he knew for sure was that the one they were looking for could write and throw cloth. Based on that, Adlet hypothesized that the person probably couldn't move on their own. If they could have, they would have come to the Braves the moment the battle began. All this person had been able to do was carve messages and fling cloth.

Another hypothesis presented itself: The informant had been trying to write, *don't be fooled*—in other words, they'd known that Rolonia was walking into a trap. They'd been chasing her. If they had been close, they would have thrown that cloth at her, not up in the air. So that meant they had been pretty far from her.

"Rolonia!" Adlet yelled. "Were there any Dead Host chasing you before you came to the cave?"

"There were! Yes, there were!" she called back.

"What happened to them?"

"I shook off most of them!"

"Did any of the ones you defeated have writing on them?"

"N-no...I don't think so!" Rolonia replied, though she was hesitant.

Adlet followed the logical path further. So what had the informant done after Rolonia had escaped them? He thought back on all the things he'd seen the Dead Host do. One possibility was that they had joined in the fight over where number nine had been. Adlet had seen hordes of them running in that direction. Or they might have chased Adlet. Dozens of corpses had been after him. That was the most likely. The last possibility was that he had been held off by Chamo's slave-fiends.

It had to be one of those three. If the informant had joined in to fight against Goldof, Dozzu, and the others, they would be in the southern area of the forest. If they'd been chasing Adlet, they'd be in this area. And if they had been fighting the slave-fiends, they'd be on the western side of the forest.

"Remember!" Adlet muttered. He scoured his memory for clues. Had any of the Dead Host chasing them had writing on their right arm? Adlet couldn't remember. He felt like maybe, maybe not. He'd been totally focused on saving Rolonia, and hadn't been attentive to the bodies of the Dead Host.

"Addy!" Rolonia was yelling up at him from below. There wasn't much time left. He just had to run and think at the same time. Adlet jumped down from the tree and gestured for the other two to follow him.

He sprinted as fast as he could, gasping for breath. Rolonia couldn't keep up, and he quickly pulled away from her. Hans, running beside him, whispered, "Adlet, be honest, don't ya think this is hopeless?"

Adlet glared at him and said, "You moron. We can't give up on this." He could imagine just how painful a struggle this person must have borne.

Adlet didn't know how the informant had found out about Tgurneu's secret weapon, but they'd fought with all their strength to tell them about it. They'd written those messages on the Dead Host and hurled cloth into the air. They'd probably fought desperately just to manage that much. How could the Braves of the Six Flowers fail to respond to such dedication to communicating with them?

Where in the forest would they search? He couldn't afford to pick the wrong option.

Slowly, Rainer's consciousness dimmed. Bit by bit, his spasming body went limp. Moans were still coming from his mouth, but they were getting gradually quieter.

Sleep now. Forget everything and sleep, he thought, but that moment, he heard a voice, and it brought him back from the brink of oblivion.

"Is anyone alive?"

"Is anyone alive?" Adlet yelled hard enough to make his throat bleed. The site he'd chosen was the western side of the forest, the battlefield with Chamo's slave-fiends. They had less than five minutes left.

It was a most trivial lead: a single scrap of cloth he'd found while chasing Rolonia, a fluttering rag, caught on a branch. When he'd first seen it, he hadn't thought anything of it. It had just appeared in the corner of his vision, and he hadn't spared it a second thought. But now, he understood. The one who could tell them about the weapon had thrown the fabric. They'd thrown it into the sky as a signal to their whereabouts.

It wasn't definitive enough to be called proof. But right now, Adlet had no choice but to bet on it.

"If anyone's alive, give me a sign!" he yelled. "Tell me about Tgurneu's secret weapon!"

Chamo's slave-fiends were gone now, but the scene was the picture of hell. The remains of Dead Host that had been slaughtered by slave-fiends were lying everywhere, and those that were still alive writhed and moaned unceasingly.

Adlet called out to them, checking each of the fallen corpses. He'd lift a right arm, scan for any messages, and then move on to the next one.

"The secret to a locked-room meowstery, a piece o' Tgurneu,

Nashetania, and now a livin' Dead Host, huh?" said Hans as he searched right arms for messages like Adlet. "Ever since we came here, we've been doin' nothin' but look fer stuff," he griped. Adlet ignored him and continued searching the right arms.

That was when Adlet found a piece of cloth caught on a tree branch. It wasn't a natural shape for something ripped off during the fight. *So I wasn't imagining it*, he thought.

Rolonia finally caught up with them. Still panting, she helped search for a body bearing a message. But there were so many on the ground, Chamo's slave-fiends had been fighting over such a wide area, and they didn't have enough time left.

"Are you there? Give us a sign! Is anybody alive?" Adlet yelled.

But no matter how he looked, he couldn't find the one.

They've come; they've finally come. They came looking for me. When Rainer heard that yell, he was temporarily elated. But resignation and despair quickly overtook his heart. They were too late. The only sign they could use to find him, the words on his right arm, were gone. Rainer's body was still moving. His mouth was still making anguished groans. But his consciousness was already vague and hazy.

"Are you there? Give me a sign! Is anyone alive?!" the Brave was yelling.

Rainer weakly raised his left arm and waved his hand. But so many other Dead Host were writhing around him. His gesture was lost among them, and the Brave couldn't find him. The Braves had to search such a large area, they didn't even come close.

"Are you alive? You're alive, right?" The yelling reached Rainer's ears.

But he thought, *It's no use now, Braves of the Six Flowers. You guys are too late.* He was so sleepy. His mind was falling into darkness. He didn't have the energy left to fight it anymore. His left arm fell weakly to the ground.

"*Hrmeow!* Answer us!" That had to be the messy-haired swordsman, the first Brave he'd encountered.

"Is there anyone alive? We've come to save you!" That was the girl in the armor. Their voices didn't reach his heart.

But that was when he heard the other Brave. "Don't give up! If you're alive, don't give up!"

Funny... Rainer thought. When he heard that voice, he felt as though he had to fight. He couldn't give up yet.

"The strongest man in the world is here! And I *will* find you, so don't you give up!"

What a weird guy, thought Rainer. But oddly enough, the voice brought Adlet's face to his mind's eye. *I...won't give up, Adlet.* Rainer remembered that once, he'd sworn he'd become a Brave. He had told his only friend that he was a hero. And what made someone a real hero, a Brave, was that they never, ever gave up.

Think. Think of a way to tell the Braves you're here—a way to show them you're still alive. He couldn't do that with his hand. There was no point in writing anything, either. He'd die before the Braves found the message. He had to call out to them with his voice. But all that would come from his mouth were moans of pain. His left arm was free now, but he couldn't move his tongue, lips, or throat of his own will.

There had to be a way... some way.

"...?" Adlet's hands abruptly stopped in their search for the corpse with a message. He could hear something. He didn't know what. But he had caught the sound of something important.

"What is it, Addy?" asked Rolonia.

Adlet cupped his hands around his ears and focused. Among all the Dead Host's moans, one sounded different.

"...Singing?" Adlet murmured. Now he could definitely hear fragments of a song they'd once sung on the festival days in his now-destroyed village. He couldn't make out any words. But the tune was clearly from his home.

Adlet ran toward it as fast as he could.

*   .*   *

Rainer's hand clenched his throat. Moans poured continuously from his mouth. When he pushed his larynx up, it made a slightly higher moan; when he pushed it down, a slightly lower one. Rainer sang desperately, moving his throat with his left hand. His singing was off-key and barely even recognizable as a song. But still, he kept on singing.

He'd remembered how eight years ago, he had done the same thing with Adlet and Schetra. No matter how much Adlet had practiced, he'd never gotten any better at singing. So Rainer had grabbed his throat and moved it up and down. The kid couldn't carry a tune any other way.

Can the Braves...hear it? He couldn't speak. He couldn't signal them. All he could do now was sing.

With each step forward, it became even clearer to Adlet that this song was definitely from his home village. Behind the wailing chorus of the Dead Host, he could hear a nostalgic melody. For an instant, Adlet nearly forgot his allies, the Evil God, and even the Black Barrenbloom.

"Where is he...?" Adlet muttered. The one who was singing was the informant and from Adlet's home village.

Adlet ran with the singing voice as his guide. Eventually, he found a corpse grabbing its throat. *We'd never have found him, no matter how much we looked*, thought Adlet. The man's right arm was missing. "Is it you?" Adlet approached the man. "It's you, isn't it?" Adlet clung to the man.

The man's body was already growing cold. He was severely wounded. Without immediate treatment, he could die. Slowly, the man's hand dropped from his throat.

"Rolonia! Come here! Hurry, hurry up!" Adlet yelled. Rolonia, who had been searching elsewhere, panicked and rushed over to him.

"Hold on!" cried Adlet. "We'll save you! Stay with us!" It seemed as though the man couldn't hear well anymore. His eyes were empty, staring at nothing. Adlet yelled again, louder.

What filled Adlet's heart was not the desire to know about Tgurneu's secret weapon, it was joy at seeing someone from his village, someone he thought he'd never see again, one last time. As Adlet gazed at the man's face, he wondered who it was. He was young, and close in age to Adlet. But there hadn't been anyone else his age in the village.

"It couldn't be..." he murmured.

Rolonia ran up and pushed Adlet aside to sit beside the man. She closed up the wound where his right arm had been and then touched her hand to the blood that had seeped in the ground, drawing it out into a spherical glob. She returned the blood to his body and immediately bit into the parasite on the back of his neck, paralyzing it before she slowly pulled it free.

Watching, Adlet thought, *I can't believe it. He was alive?* He pushed the man's long, wild hair aside to see the scar on his forehead. He could never forget that scar. Adlet had given it to Rainer when they were little.

"You're...alive...Rainer." Adlet's knees crumpled. All this time, he'd wanted to see his friend, wanted to thank him for saving his life. And to apologize for having escaped without him. "You've got to be kidding... Rainer? Is this even possible?"

That was when Hans approached them from behind. Seeing how rattled Adlet was, he quickly inferred what was going on. "Does it look like this feller from yer village can be saved?" he asked.

Adlet couldn't form words, so Rolonia replied for him. "I can't tell yet. His vitality is almost entirely exhausted..." Silently, she continued removing the parasite. All the feelers and legs were out of his flesh.

"Rainer! You're alive?! It's me! It's Adlet!" Adlet tried to raise him up, but Rolonia quickly put her hands on Rainer's chest and used her techniques. She still wasn't done.

"Adlet, calm down," said Hans. "You'll mess up Rolonia's healin'."

Adlet settled down and waited for Rolonia to finish the treatment. *Please save him,* he prayed fervently. *He's my only friend.*

Rainer's mouth opened. "Tg..." His voice stopped. A wheeze leaked from his throat, but it was so shriveled and dry, he couldn't talk at all.

"Addy, water," said Rolonia. Adlet nodded, pulled out his water flask, and poured some into Rainer's mouth. The flask was quickly emptied.

Now able to speak, Rainer opened his mouth again. "Braves...of the Six Flowers...listen...Tgurneu..."

"Rainer, it's me! Can you recognize me? It's Adlet!" Adlet was clinging to him.

Hans stopped him again. "Listen to him first. Mew can be glad about seein' him after." He was right. Rainer had fought to tell them about Tgurneu's secret weapon. They had to listen to what Rainer had to say first.

"It made...a Temple of Fate. A temple...to steal power...from the Saint...of the Single Flower."

Rolonia was channeling everything she had into her healing techniques. Judging from her expression, Adlet could tell immediately that the prognosis wasn't good. He listened carefully to Rainer.

"It made...a hieroform...that steals power...from the Saint...of the Single Flower. The...Black Barrenbloom." All three of them simultaneously held their breath. Rainer knew about the Black Barrenbloom, the very thing they were after. There was no time to ask why. They hung on every word.

"The Black Barrenbloom...absorbs the power...left behind by...the Saint of the Single Flower. If the Black Barrenbloom...absorbs...all of it... like the power over fate...to defeat the Evil God...and to block its toxin... the Crests will be destroyed..." Blood leaked from Rainer's mouth. He gasped out the rest in one breath. "Kill the Black Barrenbloom before it takes all the power."

"Kill it? What do you mean, Rainer?" Adlet asked him. But he realized that Rainer couldn't hear him anymore.

"The closer...the Braves get...to the Weeping Hearth...the stronger... the weapon...gets. Before you fight the Evil God...kill the Barrenbloom... It will come to the Braves...eventually... It has to be close...or it can't absorb their Crests' power ..."

Adlet could tell that Rainer's body was gradually giving out. Rolonia poured her all into healing him, but he still wouldn't make it. Adlet wanted to yell at him to stop talking, but he understood that he couldn't. Rainer was trying to impart knowledge that would influence the fate of the world. He had risked everything to bring it to them.

"The Black Barrenbloom is..." Rainer's voice was fading. Adlet had to lean his ear toward Rainer's mouth to hear. "The Black...Barrenbloom is..."

The three of them listened to his next words. Adlet immediately blanched. Rolonia's and Hans's eyes widened in shock. They shared a look.

"Rainer, is that true?" asked Adlet. "What the hell do you mean by that?!" His heart was racing, and his teeth wouldn't stop chattering. He couldn't believe what Rainer had just said. Adlet shook him—but then he realized: Rainer had gone entirely limp.

"You can't! You can't die yet, Rainer! Wake up! Open your eyes!"

Rolonia clenched her teeth and frantically struggled to heal him. Adlet could tell she was already using all her power.

He had to ask for more detail about what Rainer had just said. But more importantly, he had to save his friend. He had to take Rainer back home with him to the human realms, to their village. But Rainer's expression was a peaceful one. It said he had left nothing undone.

"Don't you...give me that look, Rainer. Let's go home. Let's go home together, Rainer."

This can't be, he thought. *He was actually alive. I actually got to see him again. And now it's over like this?*

"I'll teach you how to use a sword this time. I've gotten so strong. You'll be shocked. Come on," Adlet said to him.

Rainer's closing eyes opened once more, and he gazed into Adlet's face.

Rainer had managed to tell them about the Black Barrenbloom. He hadn't been able to tell them everything, but that should be enough. Now that he was done, what filled his heart wasn't joy. It was relief, along with the thought *I can sleep now, right?* That was how exhausted and wounded he was.

But before he fell asleep, he called out in his mind. *Hey, it's just like I told you, Adlet. I was a real hero. I saved the Braves of the Six Flowers. I saved them all when their lives were in danger. Now they're sure to defeat the Black Barrenbloom. They'll make it to the Weeping Hearth, defeat the Evil God, and save the world. They couldn't have done any of that without me. Who else could've pulled off something like this? Nobody else in the world, that's who.* His heart was brimming with satisfaction.

As Rainer was falling asleep, someone grabbed him, shook him. The man was saying something. Rainer softly opened his eyes and looked at his face.

Ha-ha… Isn't that funny? Rainer thought, opening his mouth. "Hey… you look like…my friend." And then he slowly closed his eyes.

"Rainer…" Adlet was frozen, holding his friend's motionless body. Rolonia gently removed her hands from his chest. There was nothing more she could do.

Adlet vacantly stared at Rainer's body.

"He was your friend?" asked Rolonia. Adlet gave her a small nod. "I'm sorry, Addy. I couldn't save him," she said quietly.

"And here we were headin' out to find out ameowt the Black Barrenbloom, and we hear a shockin' tidbit like that. If this is true…it's a big deal."

But Rolonia couldn't bring herself to think about that yet. Her heart was filled with frustration for failing to save anyone at all. Tears dripped from her eyes. She'd wanted to save the Dead Host. She'd wanted to give Adlet the chance to see the people of his village again, even just one of them. She hadn't done all that fighting for such a tragic ending.

If she'd only acted faster, if she had just paid more attention and watched the Dead Host more closely, she might have been able to save this Rainer person. She had never regretted her own stupidity more than in that moment. In her head, she apologized over and over to the Dead Host and to Rainer. *I'm sorry I couldn't save you.*

"What am I gonna do if you're crying here?" said Adlet. Flustered, Rolonia wiped away her tears.

"Rolonia, you were right," admitted Adlet. "You were the only one of us who was. We shouldn't have abandoned them. I'm ashamed of myself for failing to understand that."

"Addy…"

"Thank you. I'm really glad you were with us."

She was having a hard time listening to him say this, so she lowered her eyes—because she knew he was holding back tears. Now he was really alone.

Suddenly, Adlet drew his sword and said to Rainer's body, "I'm sorry, Rainer. I couldn't save you. But your dedication won't go to waste. So… fight with me." He cut off a tuft of the other boy's hair, tied it up, and tucked it into one of his belt pouches. "Don't worry, Rolonia. I'm not alone anymore. Rainer is with me from now on." Adlet stood up and faced Rolonia and Hans. "Let's go. We have to meet up with the others."

"Mew can do a little more cryin'," said Hans. "We're lucky. It don't look like the fiends are comin'."

"…If I've got time to cry, I'll use it to fight. I'll defeat the Evil God and save the world—like he would have wanted. 'Cause I'm the strongest man in the world." Adlet turned away from the pair of them and started walking, but then he stopped. "Actually…wait just a bit." He clung to a nearby tree and buried his face in the trunk. Then he quietly began to cry.

Watching him from behind, Rolonia decided to try to be with him as much as she could. She would encourage him and keep supporting him. She'd never be able to do much, and she might be a burden, but still, she swore that she would give him everything she had.

He might have been the strongest man in the world, but he couldn't live his life all alone. *I never want to make him cry again. I will take care of him.*

Meanwhile, Goldof was running through the forest, with Fremy ahead of him. They were headed for the cave Rolonia had gone to earlier.

The others had left the forest and were heading for the Temple of Fate. The original plan was for all of them to meet up on the way there, so it was possible that Adlet and Rolonia had already gone to the temple. But Fremy was worried about Adlet and couldn't wait, so she set off to search for him.

"What is the meaning of this, Goldof?" Fremy glared at him with reproachful eyes. "Why did you let Rolonia go off on her own? Why did you allow Adlet to get into danger like that?"

Goldof worried about how to explain. If he bungled this, Fremy might attack him, or worst-case scenario, she could blow up the bombs on Nashetania's knees. "I'll…explain," he said. "Once we've…met up with… Adlet and Hans." Fremy clicked her tongue and kept up the pace.

Earlier, Goldof had checked the Crest on his shoulder. The petals were all there. Adlet and Rolonia had to be safe. Goldof was relieved—they couldn't be losing allies in this place.

Goldof and Fremy arrived at the cave, but Adlet and Rolonia weren't there, only fallen Dead Host and two dead fiends.

"Where did they go? Seriously." Fremy was irritated.

"We must have…passed each other. Let's…head to the…meeting point…too."

Until now, the defense of the area had been entrusted to specialist number nine. Now that it was dead, though, the fiends in the Fainting Mountains would start to take action. They'd probably swarm this area. Goldof and Fremy had to meet up with Adlet and Rolonia as soon as possible and get out of the forest.

"No. I'm looking a little more." Fremy searched the area, but the missing Braves hadn't left any messages. She had no idea where they could be.

Once Adlet was done crying, the trio left Rainer's body behind. They didn't have the time to dig a grave for him right now. Adlet swore that once they'd defeated the Evil God, he would make a proper one for his friend. He prayed that Rainer wouldn't be eaten by fiends before then.

He slapped his cheeks a few times, to drive grief from his heart. He had to think about what was going to happen next, now that they knew what the Black Barrenbloom really was.

They swiftly walked deeper into the forest. All of the others must already have left the forest and started toward the Temple of Fate. They had to hurry up and catch up with them.

The Fainting Mountains were now in a flurry of activity. Evidently, now that the nearby fiends had realized specialist number nine was dead, they had begun massing to strike back against the Braves of the Six Flowers. The battle with number nine was over, but they wouldn't have the time to catch their breath. The fight was still ongoing.

"...Addy. About Nashetania..." Rolonia suddenly began.

"What?" Adlet replied.

"I wonder why she targeted me?"

Adlet considered. He'd already pulled himself together, and the wheels in his head were beginning to turn.

"Addy, I don't know anything about that fiend flute. I never tried to trick you, either. But what can I do to have everyone believe me?"

"Relax. You've got me." Adlet had doubted her once, but those feelings were gone now. She'd done all this for him. She was the one who'd fallen for a trap.

"I wonder who placed that flute on me? If we can figure that out..." Rolonia was thinking.

Adlet glanced at Hans, who was walking a little behind them. Hans smirked. "The culprit's right over there," said Adlet.

Rolonia turned around with a foolish "...Huh?" Hans smiled and waved.

You bastard. Don't tell me you pulled that stunt? thought Adlet.

"What...do you mean?" asked Rolonia. "It was you, Hans? Um, so are you the seventh? Then why did you save me?" Rolonia was confused. Without even thinking, she clenched her whip and readied herself for a fight.

Not the least bit coy about his actions, Hans said, "As expected of the strongest man in the world. So ya saw right through my perfect plan, huh, Adlet?"

"You can't screw around like that," berated Adlet. "Rolonia nearly died."

Unsure what to do, Rolonia stopped, her whip still ready. "Can you... explain?"

"Sure," said Hans. "First, Adlet, tell me how ya figured it out."

Adlet sighed. "You must have wanted to see how she'd react. You isolated her and put her in a desperate situation to see what she'd do, and you used Nashetania to do it. Isn't that right?"

"Half right, *meow*. I'll give ya seven outta ten." Hans grinned.

"Um...I don't understand. Could you explain from the beginning?" asked Rolonia.

Hans shrugged and started explaining. "...To boil it down, I've always been suspicious of ya, Rolonia. Well, I'm suspicious of everyone but Mora, so it's not like yer gettin' special treatment, though."

"Huh?" said Rolonia.

"Yer close to Adlet and Mora right now, and everyone trusts them meowst. Neither of them are really watchin' ya. Awful convenient position to be in for the seventh." As they walked, Hans continued to talk. "The seventh is scared of gettin' found out. They've had a bunch of chances to kill us, but they haven't done neowthin'. The seventh'd rather do anything than be suspected."

"That's true..."

"Ya saved my life. And then after that, ya did everything Adlet said. Ya made mistakes sometimes but never caused no trouble yerself. It looked to me like you was tryin' to blend in and not raise any hackles."

Rolonia was aghast. Hans went on. "When I heard about the Dead Host, I knew right away what Tgurneu was gonna do. Playing with our emotions to trap us is its specialty. Or meowbe it just likes those tricks." Tgurneu had done exactly that with Mora and with Goldof, too. The commander manipulated its enemies by putting their loved ones in danger. With Mora, it had used her daughter, and with Goldof, it had used Nashetania.

"It's a pretty darn effective way to do things—dependin' on the enemy. Sometimes I do that sort of thing myself, so I really got what it was goin' for." Hans smirked. Adlet was reminded that Hans was an assassin—a villainous sort with no qualms about killing people for money.

"I figgered it was probably Adlet who'd fall for this one, and maybe you'd fall for it, too, Rolonia. Adlet surprised me when he kept his head, but you got totally suckered. Then I got to thinkin', meowbe the trap actually got ya—or meowbe you were just pretendin' as part of some scheme."

"What do you mean?" asked Rolonia.

"For example, ya might step into the trap on purpose and pretend to be in big trouble—then the others would run to save ya. Meanwhile, number nine would get away, and that'd buy time for Tgurneu and the other fiends to make it here. And meowr important, ya might try somethin' a li'l bolder, too—fer instance, temptin' Adlet like, *Let's go save the Dead Host together!* Then ya'd catch the guy in yer trap and kill him. Afterward, you'd be goin' all, *Addy died because of me! I'll apologize with my death!* with yer little crocodile tears. Though I guessed ya'd actually be more clever ameowt it to keep us off the trail."

"When did you come up with all this?" asked Adlet.

"In the hut, *meow.* Back when Rolonia and the princess was havin' a spat."

Hans had read so many moves ahead in such a short interval of time. His acuity was shocking.

"So that's why I decided to make the first meowve," said Hans. "And I decided to get the princess to help. I'd plant the flute on Rolonia so that when she went off ameowt savin' the Dead Host, the princess could pull it out. I'd take all her allies away. If she was the seventh, keepin' her isolated would make it hard for her to do as much, since she wouldn't want us suspectin'."

"That can't..." Rolonia trailed off.

"If you was the impostor, Rolonia, it'd work out. If I found out you wasn't, I'd just have to reveal the trick. Either way, no problem."

"Why did you use Nashetania?" asked Adlet.

"'Cause I didn't think I could get Mora to do it, and any of the others might still be the seventh. Funny enough, at the time, the princess and Dozzu were the ones I could trust meowst."

"...I remember now," said Rolonia. "After we had that quarrel, you and Nashetania were talking about something."

"Mew got it. That was our strategy meetin'." Hans grinned. "After that, the princess told Goldof the plan. I made sure Dozzu understood the princess was gonna trick ya, but I told it, *Don't you do nothin'*. And that's how the princess managed to scare ya out of the group."

"And where did you get that flute?" Rolonia asked.

"Her Highness had it."

I get it. So that's what was going on, thought Adlet. Now that he knew how they pulled it off, it all sounded so absurd.

Hans went on, "I'll be honest: I was watchin' from a distance as ya went off by yerself. I was disguised as one of the Dead Host, of course. I knew right away when ya fell fer our trick and that the princess had done a good job."

"..."

"By that point, I figured the seventh wasn't you, 'cause an impostor would accept that they were under suspicion and not go off alone. But I kept watchin' ya—until mew fell into that trap and got captured and just about died."

"Wh-what for? I really was about to die!" exclaimed Rolonia.

"I was tryin' to make sure that Tgurneu was seriously gonna kill ya. Anyone Tgurneu's made a serious attempt to kill probably ain't the seventh. That also means that if it's deliberately holdin' back with someone, they're more likely to be the seventh."

A chill ran down Adlet's spine. That had been a frighteningly dangerous gamble. If Hans had made one wrong move, he could have killed

Rolonia by mistake. That could have led the rest of them to decide Hans was the seventh on the grounds that he'd let Rolonia die.

"I put off savin' her 'til the very last minute, when I thought it was seriously the end for her, *meow*."

"The same trick you used on me, huh?" said Adlet.

"That's right. When yer about to die, yer face can't lie," Hans said with a smile. It was an expression to make the blood run cold. *"Meow,* Rolonia's face right then was pure *despair.* She realized it was a trap, ya wouldn't make it in time, and she couldn't use her whip. The seventh could never make a look like that if they knew they wouldn't be killed." Recalling that moment, Rolonia went pale.

"I killed a lot of people," Hans went on. "And I seen a lot of people all calm 'cause they think they ain't gonna be the one to die. I've never misread a one. Rolonia don't believe she's the seventh, that's for damn sure." Hans didn't conclude that she wasn't the impostor—he was taking into account the possibility that the seventh wasn't aware themselves. "I was basically playin' the whole thing by ear, but it went pretty good, *meow.* I'm quite a guy, don't ya think, Adlet?" Hans grinned at him.

But Adlet's anger was plain on his face. If Hans hadn't made it in time to save Rolonia, or if Nashetania had betrayed them and killed Rolonia right there, or if the seventh or number nine had done something unexpected, it could've been catastrophic. Hans's plan had been fantastically dangerous.

"...What? Mew mad, Adlet?" Hans's expression suddenly turned serious. "Adlet, yer too soft. Protectin' yer allies is important, too, but we ain't gonna win with just that."

"But Hans—"

"We might never find real proof. Eventually, we might have to kill one of the group whether we want to or not. If ya ask me, we gotta get every scrap of information we can for when the meowment comes."

"Even if that means putting our allies in danger?" asked Adlet.

"Of course. There's no safe road through this fight. There ain't no sure victory. Am I wrong?"

Adlet couldn't argue with that. At the time Hans had enacted his scheme, they wouldn't have imagined they'd find out what the Black Barrenbloom really was. There had been no guarantee that making it to the Temple of Fate would gain them anything. Maybe Hans was right, and gathering information wasn't the wrong choice.

"*Meow*, though I sure didn't expect to find out about the Black Barrenbloom that way," said Hans.

Rainer had told them—he'd divulged the secret of what the Black Barrenbloom really was. Adlet thought back on his unbelievable message.

"So what do we do neow, Adlet?" asked Hans.

Adlet deliberated, and then replied. "Let's go to the Temple of Fate anyway. We don't know for sure about the Black Barrenbloom. I don't want to be suspicious of Rainer, but I can't say for sure that his information was correct."

"Are we gonna tell everyone?"

Adlet went silent again. "...Let's not tell the others yet. When the time comes, I'll tell them." Adlet knew this was a terrible choice. But if he told the others, Chamo and Goldof would kill Fremy, and Adlet couldn't make the decision to let her die.

"*Meow-hee!* Soft on Fremy, as usual. But I can't agree to that. We either kill her or at least tie her up."

"Wait just a little longer," said Adlet. "I want to figure out what she's thinking."

"Let her stay free and see how she reacts? *Meow*, that don't sound like a good idea to me, though." Hans wasn't convinced, and Rolonia seemed hesitant over it, too.

That was when they saw two people running toward them from the side—Fremy and Goldof. "We finally found you," said Fremy. "Where were you?"

"Oh, you came looking for us? Sorry," replied Adlet. He wondered if he was capable of acting calm. *Is there anything awkward about my expression?* he asked himself as he eyed Fremy's face.

"What were you doing?" asked Fremy.

"Rolonia was looking for a way to save the Dead Host, but she didn't find anything," Adlet replied. "She fell for a trap, and Hans saved her." Fremy looked at Adlet, aghast, then turned a resentful glower on Rolonia.

"I-I'm sorry, Fremy," Rolonia stuttered. "Because of me..."

"*Meow-hee-hee!*" Hans cackled. "Yep, it was all her fault. Yer allowed to beat her up, *meow*, Fremy."

Fremy ignored Hans's joke and turned back to Adlet. "Every single time, seriously..." She was angry. Adlet could tell from her expression that she was concerned for his safety. He understood that she really did care for him.

But right now, he couldn't look her in the eye.

At the end of his speech, Rainer had said:

The Black Barrenbloom is a hieroform in the shape of a human. A girl with white hair and a horn on her forehead. A girl with frighteningly cold eyes.

His information was difficult for Adlet to believe. Fremy, who had saved Adlet's life—Fremy, who had fought together with them all this time—was a hieroform created for the sake of killing the Braves of the Six Flowers. But he couldn't think of anyone else who fit that description.

"...What's wrong, Adlet? Do you have something to say?" Fremy asked, noticing Adlet was watching her. So she didn't realize they had doubts about her? Or did she actually know and was choosing to act calmly?

Adlet thought back to every expression of hers he had seen so far. When she'd been lovingly holding that dog. When she'd spoken of her past of being raised by fiends. When she'd shared her pain of abandonment. When she'd lamented that the love for her had been fake. When she'd yelled that being with Adlet made her want to live.

Had all of that been a lie?

But Adlet couldn't bring himself to doubt what Rainer had said. He couldn't ignore the report that his only friend had given his life to deliver to him.

"I've got nothing to say. I'm really sorry," apologized Adlet, then he put his arms around Fremy's shoulders and gently embraced her.

"!" For an instant, she seemed totally confused as to what was going on. She quickly became agitated, peeling Adlet off of her. "What are you doing? Where's this coming from?" Her eyes were wide in shock.

Adlet tilted his head and said, "Did I do something weird?"

"You did. What? What the hell are you trying to pull here?" Fremy's face was red.

"*Meow-hee-hee-hee-hee!*" Hans laughed, saying, "Gettin' a little hot here. Though I'd rather y'all put it off until a little later, if ya can."

"...Hans is right," said Fremy. "Leave that sort of thing until later."

Adlet recalled the sensation of her delicate frame in his arms. He'd embraced her without thinking—he'd gotten the feeling that this was his last chance to do it.

Goldof cut in. "Let's go. Her Highness and the others...are headed... to the Temple of Fate. Hans...you're going to tell me...about that matter."

"*Hrmeow.* I got it," Hans said, and he and Goldof set off running. Adlet, Rolonia, and Fremy followed after them. Fremy was still blushing.

As they ran, Adlet thought, *It's still too early to decide. I'll do that once we're at the Temple of Fate and we know everything about the Black Barrenbloom.*

Had Fremy deceived them? Or was she herself not aware that she was the Black Barrenbloom? Was there another horned girl out there besides Fremy? Or was there something else that Rainer hadn't known? Adlet would get to the bottom of this and then decide. Once he'd come to that decision, he wouldn't let himself hesitate.

No matter how cruel a decision that might be.

"They must be breaking past specialist number nine right about now," Tgurneu said thoughtlessly as it strode along the plains of the Howling Vilelands.

Specialist number two replied, "Surely that happened long ago—if the Bräves and Dozzu aren't too stupid."

"Well, I think number nine has done rather well for a fiend cultivated for recycling purposes. Yes, it deserves a compliment."

The troops here, the concentration of the main forces of Tgurneu's faction, were pushing toward the Fainting Mountains. It would be a few more hours until their arrival.

"Is the Black Barrénbloom safe?" asked number two.

Expression puzzled, Tgurneu replied, "You believe there's a threat?"

"No...thëre isn't."

"Then it'll be fine," Tgurneu said with a smile.

Thus far, their entire battle with the Braves of the Six Flowers had gone just as Tgurneu had expected. But for the first time, the commander's grasp of the situation was slipping, and specialist number two had yet to realize that.

Tgurneu drank in the sun as they proceeded leisurely toward the Fainting Mountains.

Epilogue

A Dream
of Days Past

It was one month before the Evil God's awakening. In a corner of the land known as the Plain of Cropped Ears was a human-built hut. The crude building was no more than walls and a roof, and inside slept a fiend. It resembled an ant, but it was far larger than a human. Its abdomen was swollen to an unnatural size, its limbs were slender, and its chest and head were small. Its stomach probably dragged the ground unavoidably when it walked. Strangely, there was something that resembled human breasts on its stomach.

The fiend was dreaming. Like humans, they could dream. This one dreamed of eighteen years earlier.

The room, a hollowed-out cave, was buried in various articles: a stuffed rabbit, a drum that made a noise when shaken, blankets of various patterns, materials, and colors. In the center of the room was a bed. It was soft and luxurious, unthinkable for a commoner. Sleeping in it was a fiend.

"Good morning, specialist number six. It's a lovely day, isn't it?" said the three-winged lizard-fiend that came into the cave.

The fiend called specialist number six bowed reverently, its large abdomen dragging on the ground. "Good morning, Commander Tgurneu. It's warm today, isn't it?"

"No big news?" asked Tgurneu.

"No. It jüst fell äsleep," said number six.

Tgurneu looked toward the bed. A human-shaped baby slept there. When the commander peered at it, it opened its eyes. "Oh! It woke up." Tgurneu waved one claw, and the baby thrust both arms out toward it, smiling.

"It seems more áttached to you than me, Cómmander."

"Ah-ha-ha, you're just lacking in affection, number six."

One of Tgurneu's subordinates came into the cave, carrying something strange. It was a puppy. Tgurneu showed the tiny dog to the baby. The infant's eyes widened in puzzlement, and then it started bawling as if it were on fire.

"Uh...huh? Huh?" Tgurneu was baffled.

"It's a cowärdly child," said number six. "You can't show it such á thing so suddenly." Specialist number six used its front legs to scoop up the baby and soothe it, and it immediately stopped crying. The puppy, now out of Tgurneu's hands, wandered around in obvious confusion. In number six's arms, the baby stared at the puppy.

"It looks like it doesn't häte the creature," said number six. "They should soon bécome friendly."

Tgurneu breathed a sigh of relief. "Oh yes, I've decided on a name for the child. I'm going with 'Fremy' after all. There were various other options, but the one I hit upon first is the best."

"...Fremy," specialist number six muttered under its breath. It was a horribly human-sounding name. But it wasn't so bad for what it was, number six figured.

"Oh, and I finally found out the name of the father, too. Apparently, it was Noria Speeddraw."

"Which means thïs child is Fremy Speeddraw."

"Good grief. You always go and eat them right after you're done copulating. At least ask his name first before you eat him. You made this more work than it had to be."

"I do apológize for that. I just couldn't résist my hunger..." Specialist number six's head drooped as it coddled the baby—Fremy.

"Well, whatever," said Tgurneu. "Now it has a name. It would be rather pitiful to forever call it the Black Barrenbloom."

"Yes, Cómmander. You've gïven it a very good name. The chïld is glad, too."

"From what I can tell, it doesn't seem to understand much of anything, though," Tgurneu said with a smile.

When specialist number six had first birthed this baby, it had been horrified, thinking it a hideous offspring. It had known that a beautiful fiend couldn't be born with a human father. But still, the child was extremely ugly.

At first, number six had been put off, wondering whether it could love the child or not. Tgurneu's orders had been to raise it with love. Would it be able to attain those emotions of "love" that humans possessed? And even if it did, would it be capable of turning them toward such an ugly baby? It seemed an impossible task for it—no, for any fiend.

"Fremy, Fremy," specialist number six called the baby's name over and over. Each time it called the name, joy welled up from within its stomach. Was this what humans called love? It didn't feel uneasy now. The revolting appearance of the child was no reason not to love it. No one else could, and that fact changed number six's heart.

Specialist number six swore that it would never let go of this child.

In the small hut, specialist number six opened its eyes. There was an old dog lying there in the barren room, head hung low.

"...Oh, it's time for your food, ïsn't it?" number six muttered, and it picked up a nearby bowl. With a small wooden pestle, it crushed a rat that it had caught and then offered it to the dog. The animal began eating.

"Are you lönely?" specialist number six murmured.

The old dog snuffled.

"I see. I'm sure she wänts tó see you, too," it said, petting the old dog's head with the end of its front leg. "You'll get to see hér soon. She'll come bäck once the Evil God returns."

The old dog growled quietly.

"It's äll right. I know Commander Tgurneu will protect Fremy. Don't worry. Jüst wait." The old dog quietly sat down. "Yes…he's sure to prótect her. I know that Commander Tgurneu is actually very kind."

The fiend and the old dog quietly awaited Fremy's return.

AFTERWORD

It's been a long time. This is Ishio Yamagata.

Did you enjoy *Rokka: Braves of the Six Flowers*, Volume 4?

The manga adaptation of *Rokka: Braves of the Six Flowers* by Kei Toru-san is currently being serialized in the online *Super Dash & Go* magazine. I'd love it if you could enjoy that as well.

It's gotten remarkably hotter. I'm all right in hot weather, by nature, so I can basically get through summertime with just a fan. But lately, there's been something giving me trouble.

The apartment building where I live has begun doing major repairs. It's so loud outside during the day that I can't open the window. It's quiet at night, but the time that I sleep is right in the middle of their construction schedule.

With the room all closed up, even my ray of hope, the fan, can't exercise its full power. If I open the window, the construction noise keeps me awake, and if I close it, it gets so hot and humid that I can't sleep. If I turn on the air-conditioning, I'll get headaches and a sore throat for the next day.

I can't blame the people doing the construction work. If I keep the window shut, I can live comfortably enough, so it would be unreasonable to ask them to quiet down even more.

*   *   *

Sometimes, I go to karaoke alone for stress relief. I'll drink a beer or a sour to keep my throat moist and just yell my heart out on and on. It helps me forget the difficulties of work for a while.

I hear some people avoid solo karaoke because it's embarrassing, but I think those people are really missing out. I've heard that lately there are even karaoke parlors that specialize in solo booths, though there isn't one in my area yet. I hope they become more popular.

Anyway, my voice is really low, and I just can't sing at the standard pitch. Of course, this just means you have to sing it in a lower key, but I feel like with all the recent pop songs, anime songs, and vocaloid songs and everything that are popular at karaoke, you really have to sing them high for it to sound good. You can force a key change, but it still never feels quite right, and it doesn't feel good to sing it.

So when I go searching for songs with that feeling, the only ones I can pick are oldies from the Showa era. When I'm singing Dark Ducks' "Yamaotoko no Uta" (Mountain Man Song) and Miyuki Nakajima's "Mabataki mo Sezu" (Without Even Blinking) and "Dare ga Tame ni" (For Someone's Sake) from *Cyborg 009*, sometimes I start to wonder what generation I'm from.

Presently, I'm in search of a more recent song that I'll be able to sing well.

And finally, the acknowledgments. Thank you very much to my illustrator Miyagi-san, my editor T-san, everyone in the editing department, and everyone else involved in the production of this book. I'll be counting on you again in the future.

And to all my readers: I'll see you again in my next book.

Best,

ISHIO YAMAGATA